HALF A WIZARD

A CAVAN OLTBLOOD NOVEL

STEFON MEARS

Thousand Faces Publishing

Also by Stefon Mears

Cavan Oltblood Series
Half a Wizard
The Ice Dagger
Spells of Undeath

Spells for Hire
Devil's Shoestring
Zombie Powder
Spirit Trap
Dragon's Blood (coming December 2019)

The Rise of Magic
Magician's Choice
Sleight of Mind
Lunar Alchemy
Three Fae Monte
The Sphinx Principle

The Telepath Trilogy
Surviving Telepathy
Immoral Telepathy
Targeting Telepathy

Edge of Humanity
Caught Between Monsters
Hunting Monsters

Power City Tales
Not Quite Bulletproof
No Money in Heroism

Devil's Night
Portal-Land, Oregon
Stealing from Pirates
Fade to Gold
With a Broken Sword
Twice Against the Dragon
The House on Cedar Street
Sudden Death
On the Edge of Faerie
Confronting Legends (Spells & Swords Vol. 1)
Uncle Stone Teeth and Other Macabre Poems
The Patreon Collection, Vol. 1-4 (Vol. 5, coming soon)

Published by Thousand Faces Publishing, Portland, Oregon

http://1kfaces.com

ISBN: 978-1-948490-14-6

HALF A WIZARD

A Cavan Oltblood novel

1

———

WHEN ASSASSINS BURST THROUGH THE DOOR, WHAT ANGERED CAVAN most was their timing.

After six weeks on the road, half of them just crossing the Dwarf-marches — which smelled just as bad as everyone said they did — Cavan would have liked to pass at least one pleasant evening without someone trying to kill him.

And this inn, the Bent Spike, should have been perfect. First, because it was on the edge of town, so no one important should have had time to spot Cavan, much less pass along his whereabouts to anyone who wanted them. Riverbend wasn't even much of a town, just a way station for those who shipped their cargo down the Red River.

And second, the Bent Spike bustled with people who should have been too busy with their own business to worry about Cavan's. The inn stood three stories tall, the first of fitted stone and the top two of some local green hardwood. Two main rooms on the first floor, on either side of a central kitchen. One full to bursting with travelers and another featuring privacy for those willing to pay extra for a table to themselves instead of sharing space at long bench tables. Cavan and his fellows had even joined the throng in the more public room rather than draw attention by dining in the more private room.

The inn boasted good enough ale to satisfy Amra, and that alone was an accomplishment unachieved in at least a season (to her constant lament).

And upstairs the Bent Spike featured *private rooms* with private baths on the third floor for those with the coin to pay. Amra and Ehren shared a room on the second floor, but Cavan never skimped when he had coin.

Now he had a corner room all to himself. With six thick beeswax candles in sconces along the greenwood walls, all already lit and filling the room with a pleasant smell and gentle light. Shuttered windows — painted red — that could bar to keep out thieves. A hammered copper bathtub along the wall, already steaming with hot water. Next to the tub a shelf with a copper ewer, a brush, towels, and a yellowish chunk of actual soap.

So much space to call his own. Well, for a night, at least. Six strides across each direction, and Cavan was not a short man. He was long and lean like the warrior he should have been. The warrior he was supposed to be. With swarthy skin and brown hair as soft as his brown eyes could be hard. When he needed them to be.

He had the *look* of a warrior. He still carried the longsword he'd trained with for so long, but he lacked some of the most important instincts. Or at least, that was what Ser Dreng said when he sent Cavan away.

The room's bed was long enough that only his feet dangled off the far end, and wide enough that only his hands dangled when he lay in the middle and stretched his arms to the sides.

That was the first thing he'd done when he finished his dinner — roast duck with barley and carrots — and finally saw just what his coins had bought him for the night.

An actual bed. With pillows instead of a rolled up cloak. And both stuffed with duck feathers. So soft Cavan had almost fallen asleep immediately.

But he'd arranged an assignation with a barmaid named Polli, a slender lass with fiery hair and smiling eyes. And he had no intention of being either asleep or road filthy when she arrived.

So he had hung his undyed roughspun cloak on the hook beside the door, along with his sword belt and pouch. His pack he set beside them on the floor. He stripped off his pale green tunic, brown riding breeches and calf-high leather boots. Those he laid out beside the tub, to see to later.

He might have locked the door. He might have even barred it. But he wasn't sure exactly when the barmaid would arrive and the thought of her entering to find him in the tub was not unpleasant.

But Cavan's life rarely worked out that way.

Thus, he was naked, wet, and soapy when the door burst open.

Two assassins, but not professionals. Members of the False Dawn all wore thin, trim mustaches dyed purple — regardless of their sex — and these two were smart enough not to pretend to be what they weren't.

What they were was free-swords hoping for easy coin.

Shaggy black beards and short, field-hacked black hair. Weather-beaten skin. Gray wool cloaks and leather breastplates over rough-spun. They both had naked steel in their hands, whereas Cavan was only naked. And sitting in a tub full of water.

The assassins laughed.

Cavan shunted power into a double-handful of water, tossed it in the air, and said in a ringing voice, *"Zeha da."*

Thick white mist filled the room. Cavan slipped out of the tub. He touched wet fingers to his eyes — wet from the water he'd thrown, not redunked in the tub — and whispered another word.

Now he could see through his own mist.

True, Cavan had failed to become a warrior. And he hadn't quite managed to become a proper wizard either, before Master Powys sent him away. But Cavan did have his ways.

So did these assassins, unfortunately. They might not have been from the False Dawn, but they weren't stupid. They already had the door closed and stood back to back, half-crouched, swords waving back and forth to ward off any blind approach. Effectively blocking the only civilized exit.

"Doesn't have to be like this," one said. Rough voice, like something tore in his throat and never healed right. "Offer us your room and your money and we'll forget we saw you."

Interesting. Or a trick to get Cavan to give away his location.

Truth was, Cavan would rather have paid them than killed them. But pay men like this once and more would show up. And more after them. Not a sustainable practice, and besides, it would mean he couldn't afford to treat himself to rooms like this one.

The mist wouldn't last much longer. If only Cavan's sword and pouch weren't on the other side of the assassins, he might have been able to dispatch them easily. But as it was...

Cavan picked up the copper ewer, dumped its cold water into the tub.

The assassins heard, began side-stepping that direction, staying back to back with swords still swinging.

Quietly as he could move, Cavan crossed the length of the tub. The swinging swords getting closer and closer to his naked flesh now, goosebumped as it was after getting out of the nice hot bath. Cavan kept his focus and laid the ewer across the ridge of the copper bathtub.

He shunted power through the ewer.

"Zehanis skull!"

The ewer clung to the tub as though it were frozen in place. And the two swinging swords yanked down at it, flats of their blades sticking to the ewer as though tub, ewer and blades had all been forged from a single huge ingot of blended metal.

The assassins stumbled as their swords came down, tried vainly to pull them free.

Cavan tackled the closest assassin, the one with the rough voice. Took him to the floor, slamming the assassin's head against greenwood. Dazed him. Cavan had just enough time for a solid punch to Rough Voice's jaw. Stung like hell, but worse for the assassin. Not out cold, but Rough Voice was dazed and shaky when his partner pulled a dagger and turned.

Unfortunately for Partner, the dagger got caught in the spell and yanked out of his hands to bind against the ewer.

Cavan rolled over and kicked his shin between Partner's legs as hard as he could. A groan of pain, and Partner bent forward.

The mist began receding.

Cavan grabbed Partner and yanked him down. Cavan roared and used one assassin as a weapon to attack the other, smashing Partner's head into Rough Voice's head until they both stopped moving. By then the mist had long since cleared off.

Blood on the greenwood floor now. Apparently both assassins had gotten their noses broken somewhere in there. Their lips cut up too. At least they were still breathing. Out cold, but not dead.

Cavan was naked, sweating and shivering both from the cold and the attempt on his life.

He was sitting in blood beside the two assassins when the door opened.

There stood Polli, slender and pretty in her blue linen dress, with all those red curls.

The spell on the ewer finally broke, and the ewer, swords and dagger clattered to the floor.

Polli screamed. She turned and ran, still screaming.

Cavan shook his head. Poor girl. He couldn't blame her a bit. He'd have to find some way to make apology before he left.

He stood and closed the door. Turned back to the two assassins, taking a better look at them now. He could see why Rough Voice sounded so harsh — deep scar all the way across his throat.

Cavan recognized them now. He'd seen them three times on the trek across the Dwarfmarches, guarding a caravan. They'd stood out among the other caravan guards. Partly because they'd literally set themselves apart, keeping to themselves and riding slightly to one side. Mostly, though, Cavan had noted the way they'd looked at him.

Like they knew who he was.

So much for Cavan's pleasant evening.

OF ALL THE PEOPLE CAVAN HAD MET IN HIS TWENTY YEARS OF LIFE, Ehren was the one he never wanted to travel without. Not just because of the man's humor — he even smiled in his sleep — but he seemed to have endless pockets secreted about his person, and his backpack seemed to contain a never-ending list of wonders.

Magic had to be involved, but Cavan had no idea how.

Most recently, Ehren had produced thirty feet of silk rope. *Silk.* Which they'd used to tie up the two assassins before bringing them back to consciousness. When they were done, the assassins' wrists and ankles were bound, and they sat on their outspread knees. Their swords and daggers were laid out on the other side of the room, where they could see them.

Cavan had yet been naked, and just wondering how he was going to get word to his friends, when they knocked on his door. That was Amra's doing, of course. Let three people run screaming through an inn and Amra could accurately guess why all three of them were screaming.

Or at least, that was how it seemed to Cavan.

Cavan had let them in immediately, despite his nudity. Travel long enough with anyone, and modesty beats a hasty retreat.

Ehren, of course, looked fresh and clean as ever. The man could sleep a full hour in a swamp, and when he stood at the end — smiling, naturally — his fair skin and long blond hair would look fresh and clean, his white linen shirt and breeches spotless, and his low, white doeskin boots wouldn't even smell. And that brown leather pack of his? The contents wouldn't even be damp.

All marks of favor from his sun goddess, Zatafa. Signs of a priest in good standing. Except possibly the pack. Cavan wasn't certain about the pack.

Ehren even had the courtesy to be short. A full head shorter than Cavan, which Cavan considered the only reason any women noticed him when Ehren was around.

Now Amra, Amra was a true warrior. She stood shortest of their three, a head-and-a-half shorter than Ehren, with "more curves than any woman this strong had a right to." Her words, not Cavan's, and she always smiled when she said them. And she *was* strong. Over her shoulder she carried a two-handed sword as tall as she was, forged from some dark metal harder than steel. And in her hands it all but sang when she fought. Her tanned skin, short black curls, and equally black leathers were as clean as Ehren's which meant he'd blessed them since they'd arrived.

Unlike Ehren, Amra arrived without her pack. But then, she was more like to address any problems with her sword than anything else she carried.

The two of them had sighed when they saw the assassins, and Amra got to work tying the two with Ehren's rope while Ehren blessed Cavan and his clothes clean. The latter was especially important, since Cavan couldn't take time to scrub his clothes, but didn't want to don the dirty things when he, at least, had bathed.

Then the two of them made jokes while Cavan dressed.

"You know, Cavan, when you told us you'd arranged an assignation we were assuming something else."

"I want to know what they did with the ewer."

Cavan had ignored them then, singing a small tune to himself to keep from hearing their words.

But now he was dressed, and he'd told them what happened and where he'd seen the two before.

"You're sure they *recognized you,* recognized you?" Amra asked. "We've been through this town before. Maybe one of your past ... dalliances was married."

"That can't be ruled out," Ehren said. He had the grace to sound like he wasn't enjoying that possibility as much as Amra was. "It's not as though it would be a first. I've warned you before that you ought to be more careful."

"I *told* you," Cavan said for the thousandth time, "in Myrapek that's not a big deal. Their marriages are for..." Cavan drew a deep breath. "We need to wake these two up and ask them."

Amra shrugged, grabbed the ewer, and splashed the assassins in the face with Cavan's now-tepid bathwater.

Cavan still had to smack the sides of their faces a few times before they came around, moaning and blinking and squirming against their ropes. Snorting bloody bubbles through their broken noses.

Once they got their bearing, they looked back and forth among their three captors, focusing on Ehren because he just had the look of someone in charge.

"So," Amra said, "are you two just stupid enough to jump people at random in an inn? Or is there a specific reason you went after our friend here?"

Rough Voice did the talking for them, and his words ground so hard they sounded painful.

"We didn't want to kill him. Heard he wanted a bath, and—"

"Yeah, yeah," Cavan said, "you figured you'd rob me instead."

"Nothing doing!" Rough Voice shook his head as though deeply offended. "Paying assassins to go away is a long established tradition. It's not like we're with the Order."

"I'll thank you not to mention the False Dawn in my presence," Ehren said, his baritone voice rumbling with menace. His order took particular offense that an order of assassins associated themselves with the sunrise in any fashion.

"Just saying," Rough Voice said.

"What you're saying is that you came through my door," Cavan said, "swords drawn, intent on assassinating me if I didn't pay you off."

Rough Voice shrugged. Amra snickered, green-and-gold eyes dancing with amusement at the brazen admission.

"So who offered you money to kill me?"

Rough Voice and his partner looked at one another. His partner whispered something, and Rough Voice's eyes grew wide.

"You don't know?" Rough Voice said, with a laugh that sounded so harsh it should have coughed up a lung. "The Duke of Nolarr is offering a hundred crowns for your head, Cavan Oltblood. Two hundred if it's not attached to you at the time."

"The Duke of Nolarr..." Cavan said.

"Ridiculous," Ehren said. "Someone is playing the both of you."

"Then the duke's hunters are chasing a lie," Rough Voice said. "Four of them came along with our caravan, all bearing the duke's sigil on their shoulders. Crossed black spears on a field of yellow. Asking after you. Had your description down to the horse and your laugh. Wasn't even sure it was you until we heard you laughing downstairs."

"The duke's hunters?" Amra said, and Cavan heard the thread of excitement in her voice. She was already looking forward to fighting the best the duke had to offer.

"What was the crime?" Ehren said. His voice came out tight too, but that wasn't excitement Cavan heard. It was worry.

"Didn't say." Rough Voice shrugged. "Don't care. Not for that kind of money. Not when we could try to snag you ourselves."

Rough Voice's partner laughed, then spoke in a voice as smooth as a gentle sea. "Told 'em we saw you boarding a barge down the river. Looking around all furtive-like. Heading for Daeron's Bridge."

Daeron's Bridge was a likely destination to give. Maybe a week downriver, but at least a dozen roads fanned out from there.

Cavan should have been asking questions too. But he was trying to remember the last time he saw the duke. Trying to remember if he'd done something to offend him...

"Tell me you didn't sleep with *his* wife," Amra said, but Ehren must have seen the look in Cavan's eye. He grew quiet.

"Cavan," Ehren said, voice low. "What is the Duke of Nolarr to you?"

"He's..." He looked at the two assassins. But before he could say anything Amra had her sword out. In a single swift motion, she brought the flat of her long blade down against the backs of both assassins' heads.

They went out like candles in a strong breeze.

Ehren winced. "Twice in short order? They'll feel that for some time, you know. The rest of their lives maybe, if they can't afford the healing."

"And they can praise whatever gods will listen that they have those days left to them," Amra said, sliding her sword back into its sheath. "And that I didn't just cut their heads off for trying to kill Cavan."

"The Duke of Nolarr is my uncle," Cavan said. "On my father's side."

"Your father..." — Ehren started, but Amra finished for him — "is King Draven of Oltoss?"

CHAIRS. A ROOM THIS NICE SHOULD HAVE HAD CHAIRS. BUT APPARENTLY the Bent Spike expected that those who wanted to sit would do so where they could have a ready supply of drinks and food, and that anyone who retired to a room — even a private room on the third floor with its own copper bathtub — intended only activities that involved a soft feather bed.

Cavan sighed, and spared a thought for Polli the fiery barmaid, and the evening that almost was. Maybe it was the beeswax of the candles around him, but Cavan imagined she would smell like honey. He forced the thought from his mind with shake of his head, then sank down onto the greenwood floor. Bare feet tucked under him and hands on his knees, Cavan's body reflexively chose one of the focusing poses he'd learned in his attempt to become a wizard.

Ehren sat in what he called the Dawn Pose: knees together, doeskin-booted feet under his rear for support, one hand on each knee and leaning slightly forward. Amra lazed with one leg tucked in close and the other outstretched, her back resting against the green-wood wall near the tub. Eyes half-lidded as though she weren't paying attention to everything around her. Which Cavan knew she was.

A study in contrasts, those two. Her in black leather, him in white linen. Him with the easy smile, her with the twisted humor. But neither was smiling then.

And apparently they were impatient, because they didn't wait for Cavan to start talking.

"So," Ehren said, "this isn't about the price on your head in Dunlap. You *do* accumulate enemies, don't you?"

"He does," Amra said, smiling fondly. "Keeps life interesting, wouldn't you say?"

Ehren gave the unconscious assassins by the door a significant look, and said, "The King of Oltoss has three legitimate heirs, two sons and a daughter. All three have hair like spun gold, same as the King and Queen. So you must be—"

"—a bastard," finished Amra, without a trace of judgment in her voice. "Hence the name Oltblood. I take it he didn't acknowledge you?"

"No." Cavan shook his head. "Not officially. So no matter what happens I'll never wear the crown. Not that I'd want it." Cavan shuddered. "He sent me off to a merchant to raise me. A jeweler who sells mostly to nobles. Kent. My mother was the daughter of ... some count or something—"

"You don't know?" Ehren said, shock plain in his voice and all over his face. "How could you not know?"

"It's not like she kept me." Cavan shrugged. "Or even wanted to see me."

He'd wasted too much of his youth wondering about his mother. Trying to find ways to learn her name, where to find her. Until the day the man who fostered him sat Cavan down and told him plainly: "She knows your name, lad, and she knows where you are. So stop looking for a woman who obviously doesn't want anything to do with you."

The words had hurt, but their pain had faded with time.

"Wait," Ehren said. "You may be a bastard, but you're a bastard of *Oltoss*..."

"*Yeah*," Amra said, leaning forward, eyes opening wider now. "You must be entitled to *something*. What is it?"

"Not much," Cavan said, hands coming up quickly. This was

something he hadn't thought about since he left home years ago. "Really."

"Ah, ah, ah," Ehren said, his smile back full-force. "Oltoss isn't like most kingdoms, where all lands and titles pass to the eldest son—"

"Or daughter," Amra said. "In some places the eldest daughter inherits."

"Or daughter," Ehren said with a nod. "But in Oltoss, the eldest only gets half, regardless of sex. The rest is split among the remaining children."

"So you get a third of half?" Amra said.

"A sixth," specified Ehren. "What does that entail?"

"I don't inherit equally," Cavan said, waving his hands as though trying to stop a stampede by the power of desperation alone. "I'm a bastard, remember. I'll get only *one* of King Draven's titles. The meanest. The least land."

"You may be entitled to something through your mother as well, but let's stick to your father for now. The meanest title of a king is still better than..." Ehren let the thought trail off, and looked at Amra. Her mouth twisted up at the corner, her expression sour. She nodded. Ehren continued, his voice serious now. "What is this title, Cavan?"

"It's a small holding. A barony. Few peasants. Goat herds mostly. Yeah, the rents will bring in enough to—"

"*Mountain* goat herds?"

"Yes, Ehren. *Mountain* goats. You know. Shaggy things. Excellent balance."

Amra spat, shaking her head.

"If you two don't tell me what you're on about—"

"This holding," Ehren said. "Where is it?"

"On a border, I think." Cavan frowned in thought, trying to recall details that had never seemed all that important when he was young. "Between the county of ... Twall ... and..."

Cavan's gut tightened. A chill ran down his spine.

"And the duchy of Nolarr," finished Ehren.

Cavan nodded.

"And now the duke wants you dead."

"I think we'd better go check out your land," Amra said. "Because I get the feeling something other than goats has been discovered."

AFTER THE TRIO MADE THEIR PLANS, EHREN AND AMRA WERE ABOUT TO head back to the room they shared on the second floor, but Ehren stopped before opening the door. He looked down at the bound assassins, then up at Cavan.

"We should hand them over to the town watch before we turn in."

"Town watch won't care," Amra said. She shrugged. "Not here. Travelers trying to kill travelers? Probably happens all the time. Now if they'd tried to kill the *innkeep...*"

"Even a town this size has a mayor, and a mayor can't just let people kill each other," Ehren said. "If nothing else, it's bad for business."

"But no one died," Cavan said. "I think she's right. We'd only have our word against theirs."

"I'm a priest of Zatafa. They'll listen."

"We're not in a city, and they're not farmers." Cavan shook his head. "Zatafa may not mean as much here. Not as much as Ulsina."

Ehren gave a rare frown and thought about that. Ulsina was the Lady of Ways, patroness of travelers and traders. But he rallied.

"Zatafa shines her light on all new ventures, merchants alike. I still think—"

"Besides," Cavan said. "The more noise we make about this, the more attention we draw. And in a place where this many people pass through, there are bound to be others who know about the price on my head. Who heard the hunters talking."

"Prices," corrected Amra. "They might know about Dunlap too."

"We're travelers," Ehren said, determined look in his eye. "Yet we didn't know about the Duke's bounty." He glared at Amra. "And no one around here is likely to care about Dunlap."

Cavan's turn to frown. "You *do* know I don't want to kill these two, right?"

"If this were any other situation," Ehren said, "if they came after you for any other reason. *Then* I would know you wouldn't want to kill. I have never seen you take a life you shouldn't."

"Hells," Amra said, "I've seen you spare lives you should have taken."

Ehren pointed at Amra. "And she's argued with you after every one. For all I know her arguments have taken root."

"I didn't kill them when they were armed and trying to murder me. Now you think I'm going to slit their unconscious throats? How long have you known me?"

The answer was three years, but it was half an answer and all three knew it. Three years traveling together and facing death and worse so many times they should have had a dozen songs each. If any one of them wrote songs. Those three years had bound them tighter than any family Cavan had known.

The challenge brought a flush to Ehren's face. Apparently he hadn't thought of it that way.

"I apologize," he said at once, then gave a long, slow sigh. "It's all this talk of nobles. Whenever nobles get involved, people die at an alarming rate."

"And to be fair," Amra said, "we did just find out you stand to inherit a title. That's a pretty big secret to keep from us. Might be you're holding back other stuff too."

Cavan looked at Ehren, but Ehren didn't contradict her.

"You should have told us."

Cavan's jaw dropped. He blinked at them both, but they were clearly waiting for words, not expressions.

"I'm not holding anything back. I swear. I never mentioned the title because I never think about it. I don't care about it. It's just some nebulous future thing, like worrying about what I'm going to dream tonight."

Ehren's clear blue eyes showed Cavan only patience. Amra's green-and-gold looked unconvinced.

"All right. Here's the whole thing. All of it. Yes, I'm the bastard of King Draven and the daughter of some count. I don't know which count. Might be a countess. I don't know which daughter. Oldest, youngest, fifth of eighteen, I don't know."

"I think," Ehren said, "that if any count had eighteen daughters, we'd know. Every minstrel and bard across the land would have a dozen songs about them by now."

"Don't interrupt," Amra said. "Let him finish."

"I was raised by Kent the Jeweler. But he didn't want to teach me his trade and I didn't want to learn it. So he sent me to be trained as a warrior. When that didn't work, we tried wizardry. But that didn't work either. He was talking to the temple of Ulsina about sending me over as a novitiate and I decided I'd rather take my chances on my own. That's when I met you guys. There's nothing else worth mentioning. Unless you want to hear about my failures as a warrior and a wizard. Or about my love life..."

"You don't have to tell *me* you're a failure as a warrior," Amra said, but she was smiling again.

"The less I have to hear about your love life, the better," added Ehren, humor finally unclouding in his eyes. "And I think we all need to get ready for the morrow. But, Cavan, I will have more questions."

"And I'll answer all of them." Cavan raised his hand in the sun salute position Ehren used for blessings: left hand straight up, all five fingers splayed. "I swear."

"Fine," Ehren said with a chuckle. "I believe you. But what about these two?"

"Depends. You want that rope back?"

Ehren shrugged. The rope didn't matter. The *silk* rope didn't matter. Cavan shook his head.

"I'll take care of them then."

Ehren and Amra needed another assurance or two, but then they were on their way.

Cavan dragged the assassins over to the far corner of his room. He frowned down at them. He knew what he wanted to do. Knew what the most elegant solution was. And if he'd made it as a wizard, he could have done it with the barest effort.

Unfortunately, Cavan needed more than the barest effort. And it might not work. In fact, if they were conscious, it probably wouldn't work. But these were as close to ideal circumstances as he was ever likely to get.

Cavan clapped his hands. This wasn't ritually important. He just liked to do it.

He dug around in his belt pouch for an inner pocket in the lining. He dug out a single pinch of sand.

Cavan breathed power into the sand as he whispered, "*Yylin atatha.*"

He sprinkled the sand over the two assassins. That should make them sleep until someone shook them awake. If Cavan did it right.

So Cavan left them tied up, just in case, and went to bed.

He dreamed that night of Polli of the red hair, but she kept calling him "my lord."

EVEN WITH THE RED SHUTTERS CLOSED AND BOLTED, THE MORNING sunlight found its way into Cavan's room. The greenwood of the walls, floor and ceiling took on a grayish hue, and birds began singing. Worst of all, a series of roosters began crowing. As though once one of them got started, they all had to make their voices heard.

Not that Cavan had planned to sleep late anyway. He hadn't planned any specific time at all. He could have wakened with the dawn if he wished. Before even. He had gained that much and more from his wizardry training. Old Master Powys had emphasized that a wizard always knew when the sun rose or set, when the moon rose or set, and when both were at their zeniths and nadirs. Whether at the peak of a mountaintop, or deep within the bowels of the world, a wizard always knew.

"Time is a tool," he used to say, "and it must serve the wizard or the wizard will serve it."

But Cavan rarely decided when he would awaken, unless he had good cause to do so. His own small protest against being either the slave or master of time. So far as he could tell, wizards were all about mastering this thing or that other thing, but Cavan thought alliances sounded like better relationships.

Master Powys had disagreed in this matter.

So Cavan had been perfectly willing to sleep until the sun neared its zenith, if his body so chose. He, Ehren and Amra had debated getting on the road at first light, but ultimately decided that anyone in a hurry to leave town might be witnessed. Better to wait until later in the day, when the world bustled and three lone riders weren't worth noticing.

Apparently, the roosters had other notions.

Cavan tried to lay abed at first, but then he began to smell breakfast frying down below. Bacon. A rare treat in Riverbend, where fish and fowl were far more plentiful than pigs. And well worth starting the day earlier than planned.

Cavan sat up and glanced across the room at his unwanted guests. The assassins snored, clearly sleeping. Good. Cavan made no attempt at silence as he rose and dressed. Still they slept. He clapped his hands. Twice. Loudly.

No response.

He dropped the copper ewer. It clattered on the floor.

Nothing.

Cavan smiled, certain at last that his spell had taken. He unbound them from the rope — no sense wasting silk after all — and carried them one at a time to the empty copper tub, stacking the sleepers within it.

Next Cavan took the good woolen blanket from the bed, draped it over the tub, and tied the blanket tightly to the tub's copper feet.

"There," he said, dusting his hands when he finished. "That should slow you down a little. And who knows?" He smiled back at the tub full of assassins as he picked up their swords and daggers. "Maybe in there you'll find love together and make a happy ending of all this."

The thought did make him grumble as he left his fancy, expensive room. "Gods know someone should make better use of that feather bed than I did."

Downstairs the inn's main rooms were both half-full already. Caravan guards, travelers and pilgrims dining along the public benches in the one main room. The clattering of their dishes and the hubbub their dozens of conversations echoed lively along the fitted stone of the bottom level of the Bent Spike. The sound carried even into the quieter second main room on the other side of the staircase, where local merchants struck deals and traveling nobles dined in privacy. In both rooms the hearth fires burnt bright, flavoring the morning meal with hints of applewood smoke.

In between lay the kitchen, where a fierce, round woman issued orders like a battlefield commander while younger men and women chopped and skinned and boiled and fried a bunch of raw ingredients into the morning meal. Servers came and went, carrying food and drinks on thin wooden trays that — like the servers themselves — must have been stronger than they looked.

Polli was one of the servers, but when she saw Cavan standing at the foot of the stair — carrying swords slung across his shoulder — she looked away even faster than her feet carried her.

Cavan sighed. He definitely couldn't leave without making some kind of apology. Of all the memories he could leave a woman, terror was the last he would have chosen.

At a round greenwood table in the back of the more private room waited Ehren and Amra. They looked ready to travel. Packs beside them on the floor, Amra's sword jutting out over her shoulder, and Ehren's smooth, goldenwood staff leaning against the back of his chair. Three plates at the table, each already full of bacon, runny yellow cheese and dark, heavy bread.

"What do you plan to do with those?" Amra pointed a thick, crispy slice of bacon that made Cavan's mouth water and his stomach rumble. He almost missed that she was pointing at the swords he carried.

"Mostly I wanted to keep them away from the two upstairs," he said as he dropped his pack beside his chair.

"They're still upstairs?" Ehren said.

Cavan filled them in as he sat and started eating. By the time he was done, Amra was laughing, though Ehren did little more than chuckle.

Until his eyes flicked to Polli, refilling their ceramic mugs with fresh water. Then his smile broadened as the girl scampered off without meeting Cavan's eye.

"Don't say it," Cavan said. "Just ... don't."

Ehren chuckled and bit into a hunk of the cheese. Cavan bit his frustration into his own chunk. Better than he expected. Soft, sharp, and flavored with hints of nutmeg.

"She'll probably be the one who checks your room," Amra said. "Wonder what she thinks you had in mind for last night?"

"Can we please talk about something else?"

"All right," Ehren said, lowering his voice. "I think Amra's likely right. There's no reason for the duke to bother with you, unless the land you stand to inherit is suddenly much more valuable."

"Wouldn't it go to one of the legitimate heirs then? With me inheriting something else instead?"

"Yes." Ehren paused for a swallow of water. "Unless the discovery isn't general knowledge. You're next in line to inherit the land and title, but if you die without children—"

"Despite your many attempts," added Amra with a grin.

"—the title probably passes to the duke, who no doubt wants it back in his branch of the family instead of his brother's."

"That's a lot of speculation," Cavan said. "Besides, it's not like they could keep this information from the king. It's his land..."

A cold feeling washed over Cavan. The hairs on his arms stood at attention.

"What?" Amra said.

"Kent. He's steward of the land in the king's name until I inherit it. A gift for fostering me." Cavan stood. "If the duke is playing with this land, Kent's in trouble.

"I need to get home. Now."

2

THE FIRST CARAVAN LEAVING RIVERBEND BY THE EAST ROAD SET OUT
before dawn. Two dozen wagons full of goods, and a half-dozen more
bearing merchants and their servants. The goods wagons were
covered, but Tohen could tell what they carried by the arrangement
of the caravan.

Four heavy draft horses for each wagon, crates stacked no more
than two high under their tarps. Two score caravan guards, led by
grizzled-looking soldiers who had the instincts to keep looking south
of the road, even though Tohen and his three men could not be seen
in the pre-dawn gloaming.

Iron from the Dragon Spikes, no doubt. The best iron came from
the Dragon Spikes. And likely some of those crates carried gold
as well.

Too rich a caravan to trust to forty guards. Not with orc clans
ruling the grassland between the Dwarfmarches and Oltoss. No
doubt the merchants had a wizard tucked away among their number.
Perhaps even two.

The best kind of caravan for Tohen to see. With so much at stake,
no merchant would hire new guards. Not in a place like Riverbend.

They'd only trust those they knew well. Which meant Cavan and his cronies were not among their number.

Tohen settled into the great goldenrods of the field, to wait. And watch.

He was gambling. He knew it. The only word he'd been able to find of Cavan put him on a barge south, bound for Daeron's Bridge. If that were so, then by now Tohen's chase was all but done. He'd waited too long, and he'd never catch his prey. Cavan would have his choice of a dozen roads out of Daeron's Bridge before Tohen could make up enough ground to make a difference. Not without calling in a big favor, and he wouldn't waste that favor on a guess.

Tohen would have to find a fresh lead to follow, at the cost of precious weeks, while word began to spread of Cavan's new value.

And even if those caravan guards were the liars Tohen pegged them for, Cavan had at least as likely a chance of taking either of the two roads west of Riverbend, off wherever it was he was going. Some adventure, no doubt.

But Tohen had hunted men for twenty of his forty years. His black curls had begun to fleck with snow over the past ten, but he'd served those ten as chief hunter for Duke Falstaff of Nolarr. Tohen was a short man, but his muscles and black eyes were hard, and his tanned skin almost as dark as a forest elf. He was as good with bow as with sword, and he carried a hatchet at his waist to cut free whatever proof of deed his lord required of him. Like all the duke's hunters, he wore boiled leather studded with steel, and he'd long since learned the art of keeping that leather from creaking when he moved.

Tohen had honed his instincts through the years. And his instincts told him those caravan guards were fools enough to try Cavan on their own.

No doubt they'd failed. And if they had, then Cavan knew he was hunted now.

Tohen knew little of Cavan, but what he knew said that Tohen's quarry was not a man to run. Once he learned that the duke had offered gold for his head, Cavan would be bound back for Oltoss at speed.

And so Tohen had set his camp east of the Red River, whose waters rushed past swift and blue, not red. It took its name from the blood that had been spilled into it during the War of Three Kings, hundreds of years ago. He and his men had cut a small clearing among the tall, great goldenrods where they would find it easier seeing than being seen. And where even their horses could bed down out of sight.

Great goldenrods grew higher and thicker than their lesser cousins. Regular goldenrods might grow to a man's waist, but great goldenrods could sometimes tickle his chin. The licorice in their scent came stronger, and their stalks more wheat golden than green. But their flowers were the same yellow.

Here the great goldenrods grew high enough that a pack of goblins could disappear into them, should a pack ever grow brazen enough to raid Riverbend.

And here in that camp, Tohen and his men waited. Three experienced hunters in their own rights, with the scars to prove their worth. Even if two of the three lacked patience. Rudyar, the big man whose scar cleaved the left half of his bushy, sandy blond beard. Lutik the Lucky, who'd lost his right eye to an arrow that had somehow missed his brain. Lutik was skinny enough to hide behind a stalk of even common goldenrod, and bald as the day he was born. Qalas, with the ebon skin of the distant south, which made his dark blue eyes all the more compelling.

Rudyar was a good man with an axe, and a better man with a bow. Lutik couldn't shoot since he lost an eye, but somehow he'd gotten even better with that beast of a two-handed sword he carried. And he swore he could hear it when people tried to sneak up on his blind side. Qalas was near as good a shot with his great double-curved bow as Tohen was with his longbow. And while Qalas eschewed the sword, he had a master's hand with his halberd, equally ready to stab with its spike, cut with its axe, or crush with its steel-wrapped base.

Last night all three had questioned Tohen's decision. Rudyar had wanted to find Cavan in the town. Take him there. As though the duke's arm reached this far, and could pluck them out of a mayor's dungeon if they were caught murdering a paying customer in an inn.

Lutik would have had them sailing south for Daeron's Bridge.

Fools.

Qalas, at least, had a reasonable suggestion. He'd wanted to set up west of town, where they could watch two roads and the river. Maximize their chances of spotting Cavan on the move. And if Cavan did go west, Tohen would reward Qalas with a handful of silver.

The other two he rewarded last night. With bruises.

This morning all three'd been quick enough to rise when he woke them, and quick enough to break camp and ready the horses while Tohen handed out watered wine and salt beef to break their fast.

The smell of the great goldenrod all around them flavored the air with licorice. An odd mix with the weak tartness of their drinks, but it eased the boredom of yet more salted beef. Tohen considered breaking out the green apples, but those would wait until they were on the move. Until their quarry had been sighted.

But for now, Tohen waited in the predawn chill. Imagining goblin raids and puzzling through the best ways to set Riverbend's defenses against such small, quick foes.

Finally the sun rose above the Dwarfmarches, that broad stretch of grassland beaten down by twice-yearly migrations between the Dragon Spike Mountains in the north and the great Black Shield Mountains in the south.

The sun's warm kiss felt good, and as it rose it showed the sky to be clear and pale above.

Good hunting weather today, Tohen noted. Good for hawking, had he brought a hawk.

By the light of the rising sun, Tohen watched two more caravans pass on the east road. The first only six wagons long, but moving swiftly. Spices, to be sure. The second, trunks of greenwood from Croma's Forest. Fifteen cartloads worth, most likely that merchant's biggest shipment of the year. Tohen almost lost time wondering where the merchant would sell so much. The greenwood was a good enough hardwood, but not popular in Oltoss.

Most important, Tohen knew that Cavan was not among the guards. Easy enough to tell, for the guards were all wood elves, tall, proud and dusky in their leafy armor. Their long hair in greens and browns and reds. Perhaps the greenwood was bound for the Wailing Woods then?

"We've lost him," Rudyar said. "We should split up. Two head for Daeron's Bridge, two for—"

"We haven't lost him," Tohen said, not turning his eyes from Riverbend's eastern gate. "But if you're so confident, by all means, head south. But ride fast, Rudyar, because after I finish with Cavan, I'll be coming for you."

That was enough to quiet the big man, who went back to checking the horses, the packs, the supplies — anything he could check that would give him space from Tohen. Perhaps Rudyar was finally learning a thing or two.

The sun was no more than halfway up the sky when Tohen saw what he'd been waiting for. Three horses. Hobbies, light and swift. A blue roan, a bay, and a blond chestnut. Riding the chestnut was a smiling man, blonder than his horse and twice as pale, all in white. Ehren, he was called, priest of Zatafa. On the bay, a woman all in black leathers, with too much sword sticking up over her shoulder. Tohen wondered if Amra was as good with that sword as her reputation said, or if she counted on her looks to distract opponents.

And on the blue roan, a lean, swarthy man in green and brown with soft brown hair and the same chin and nose Tohen saw stamped on the gold crowns of Oltoss.

Cavan.

"You were right," Rudyar said, grudging respect in his tone, and showing enough wisdom not to apologize.

"What are we waiting for?" asked Lutik, who already had his sword half-drawn as though he meant to ride them down by the town gates.

"Those are hobbies," Qalas said, shaking his head. "And they're fresh. They'll leave our rounceys behind, and then they'll be ready for us."

"Very good, Qalas," Tohen said. "And we know where they're heading. We'll have plenty of time to catch them on the road."

Tohen watched as the trio set a decent pace. Good for traveling, and not enough to tire out their horses quickly. An easy pace to match. An easy pace to exceed by just the right amount.

Yes. Tohen would have all the time he needed to catch them on the road.

3

THE EAST ROAD OUT OF RIVERBEND WAS WIDE ENOUGH FOR AN ARMY TO march down without trampling any of the great goldenrod growing in fields on either side of it. The dirt packed down so tight it was almost like brick, but springy, it was so easy to walk or ride. Dust didn't even rise under their horses. Some remnant of old sorcery from before the War of Three Kings. At any other time, Cavan might have speculated about the spells, how the road was built.

But right now, Cavan thought about Oltoss. About Kent, with his short, silvery hair and his long silver beard. The laugh that always echoed in his brown eyes even after the sound faded away. The quick, clever hands that could carve a rough stone into a masterpiece. The broad belly that he always claimed proved his success.

The only father Cavan had ever known.

And Kent might be dead right now. Or languishing in the duke's dungeon. Or any of a hundred other possibilities that Cavan didn't want to think about. But he couldn't seem to think about anything else.

He hadn't been back in so long. So very long. Reed and Alec must have gotten married by now. That was always Kent's plan for them. Let his sons help build the business enough that the second or third daughters of prominent families would let their bride prices outweigh their lack of titles.

Cavan hadn't even met Rena, Kent's new wife. Cavan knew she was the widow of a count whose titles had passed to his children — perfect for an old widower like Kent. Younger, though if Cavan knew Kent, Rena's relative youth meant nothing compared to any business sense or connections she brought to their union.

Was she in danger too? Were Reed and Alec?

He hadn't dared ask around for news before they left Riverbend, in case the news included the price on his head. No point calling attention to himself.

So Cavan had even resisted asking about news when he traded the pair of assassins' swords for a double-armful of red and yellow roses delivered to Polli the fiery barmaid along with his note of apology — with enough left over for extra fodder for their horses.

And now, this traveling pace. Faster than when they'd ridden with the caravan, but still too slow. He wanted to dig in his heels and let his blue roan hobby, Dzink, outrace the breeze.

But Oltoss lay clear across the Dwarfmarches and long leagues of orc country on both sides. Too far to ride in a day or a week. A turn of the moon, perhaps. So Cavan attempted patience...

Above him, the morning sun mocked his mood by shining down warm and cheery from a pale blue sky. Even the air was sweet with the scent of great goldenrods. The sky should have been gray with clouds, to suit his mood. And cold. Perhaps an unseasonable cold snap.

But the sun refused to cooperate. Perhaps because Ehren sang it verses praising Zatafa, as he did whenever the road before them was long and the sun shone bright to start the day. The habit was one of Ehren's few faults — especially as he had no gift for melody, despite his good natural tone.

Cavan had heard this one so many times he could have recited the chorus in his sleep.

O'er the world men seek their gold
by digging in the ground.

They must look up, these men so bold,
where truest gold is found.
Zatafa fair, Zatafa bright,
Zatafa light the way.
For into even darkest night
will shine the light of day.

Ehren would probably sing until the time came to rest the horses. Cavan half-expected that any minute a flight of swallows would show up to accompany him like something out of a bard's tale.

No songbirds as yet, though. Few birds in the sky at all so far. Mainly the odd crows or jays on a long flight. And a pair of red tail hawks circled over something south of the road, a fair distance away. Something about the hawks niggled at Cavan's memory, but his thoughts paid it no mind.

"Here," Amra said, tossing Cavan a golden apple. "If you don't chew on something you'll grind your teeth to powder."

"Oltoss is so far—"

"Eat," she said, one eyebrow coming up. "And listen."

Cavan glared at her, but Amra only smirked back. Her bay mare seemed to smirk too. A horse not nearly sweet enough to merit the name Caramel — in Cavan's opinion — but it always seemed gentle with her.

Cavan bit into the crisp apple. Sweet, juicy, and ... almost warm.

"Where did you get this?" he asked around a mouthful of apple.

Amra nodded her head at Ehren. Of course. One more wonder from that pack of his.

"Do you know the difference between a live warrior and a dead one?" she asked.

"Skill," he said, brow furrowed as he wondered where she was going with this.

Ignoring them both, Ehren continued to sing, and Cavan and Amra let their horses fall back a few paces for their conversation.

"Patience," she said.

"Please," he said, wiping juice from his chin with the back of his hand. "The moment those assassins mentioned the duke's hunters you were ready to draw your sword."

"Exactly," she said, snapping her fingers. "I was *ready*. I still am. If one of them sprang out from a tall patch of goldenrod, I'd have his head off before he knew I'd drawn my sword."

"So how does—"

"If you were capable of waiting long enough for me to draw breath, you'd already know."

Cavan made a show of taking another bite from the apple, but had difficulty maintaining his irritated expression against the sweetness of the fruit. The apple tasted almost as though someone had laced it with honey.

"Ready to act isn't acting. Ready to fight isn't fighting."

"And ready to piss isn't pissing. What's your point?"

Amra chuckled through a sigh, but then her face grew serious. "We have a long ride ahead of us. No speed we could get from our horses would make a difference."

Horses, thought Cavan, *and hawks...*

But Amra was still talking. "We may not be able to save—"

"You're right!" Cavan said, sitting straighter in the saddle. But he was smiling. "Horses aren't the answer. But I know what is."

THE SUN WAS STILL SHORT OF MID-DAY WHEN LUTIK CAME RIDING BACK, rushed. Not good. Never good when the point man came back in a hurry. Especially since it was usually a mistake.

Tohen sighed and spurred his rouncey to go meet him. To his right Qalas was already muttering as he matched pace, and to his left Rudyar fingered his axe as he did the same. A wicked thing, that axe, with a curved blade on one side and a spike on the other.

The four hunters gathered in the middle of the wide, hard road. The sun was too warm on Tohen's steel-studded leathers, but that was just the feel of the hunt to him. If anything, feeling too warm was like telling his sword arm to be ready, the time is near. His stomach rumbled agreement, hungering as much for the fight as for salted beef to gnaw on.

And from the look in Lutik's eye, the time to fight might be near indeed.

"They've left the road," Lutik said, panting as though he'd run back from his point position instead of riding. "South."

"South?" Tohen said. The only side road within two days' ride went northeast, not south, and they were nowhere near it. "Why would they go south? This road is the most direct—"

"Hawks," Qalas said, shading his eyes and looking skyward. "Am I wrong, or have those two red-tail hawks been circling the same spot since we set out from camp?"

"So they're hunting," Rudyar started, but Tohen stilled him with a hand. Tohen looked up at the hawks, then back at Qalas. He'd noted the hawks as well, but until now he'd assumed what Rudyar assumed.

"They have, so far as I can tell. What about them?"

"Rumors," Qalas said. "An orc clan. Some say the Firespears have a priest who uses red-tail hawks as his eyes and ears."

"Cavan can't be foolish enough to ride *toward* orcs," Rudyar said. But Lutik only shrugged and added, "those hawks *are* circling to the south."

"Cavan must know something we don't," Tohen said. "We'll have to cut them off."

"If we pick a fight in the Firespears' territory," Qalas said, "we're inviting them to sweep down on us."

"Are you afraid of orcs?" Tohen taunted.

"I have no problem killing an orc. I have no problem killing ten orcs. But when a hundred orcs surround me, I don't expect to live to collect a bounty."

Tohen tried to stare down Qalas, but the dark-skinned hunter stared him right back.

"If the Firespears kill Cavan, we lose the prize," Tohen said, still meeting those dark blue eyes. "If this priest helps Cavan, we probably lose the prize. Now are you hunter enough to risk the *chance* of fighting orcs? Or would you rather go chase rabbits?"

Tohen didn't wait for an answer. He dug in his spurs and sped off the road and into the fields of great goldenrod.

Qalas, Rudyar, and Lutik were right behind him.

All around Tohen, the great goldenrod grew high enough to brush his horse's shoulders. His hooves kicked up dust now, as well as filling the air with the licorice scent.

Tricky riding, this. And dangerous. Fields so tall could hide rocks, snakes, holes. But at least Cavan and his companions faced the same problem. And the hawks were further south than Tohen's men had been behind Cavan.

Cutting them off was just a matter of riding close to the same speed, and finding the right angle...

———

THE GAME TRAIL WAS NOWHERE NEAR AS WIDE AS THE ROAD, BUT IT WAS wide enough for Cavan, Ehren and Amra to ride single-file between the stalks of great goldenrod all around them. Not swiftly, but swiftly enough. It would do.

Riding with a goal, a purpose that could be met that very day, that was enough to give Cavan patience. The bright sun seemed cheerier as it passed its zenith, the pale sky bluer, even the smell of the goldenrod sweeter.

If Ehren had still been singing, Cavan might have joined in for a verse.

But Ehren wasn't singing.

"Many orcs worship a god of darkness," he called out to Cavan. "Randech."

"They won't attack you on sight," Cavan said, over his shoulder. "I'm sure they'll wait until they hear you sing."

Ehren ignored the jibe.

"Randech favors the sacrifice of enemies during the darkest hour of night. And a priest of Zatafa..."

"We aren't going as enemies."

"But do *they* know that?"

"Trust me." Cavan smiled back at Ehren as he led his blue roan, Dzink, through a series of curves and cuts along the trail. The great goldenrod grew higher in patches near here. Some would be as high as Cavan's chin, were he standing. Mounted, they reached only his thighs, and gave him a decent view of the fields around him.

But there wasn't much to see. A little roll to the land, here and there, too low to call hills. A few odd trees here and there, covered by dark green leaves on their many, snaky gray branches. Whatever they were, they looked stunted among the height of the goldenrod.

"I do trust you," continued Ehren, "but—"

Amra cut him off with a whistle. A three-note trill that called all three horses to a halt.

Cavan twisted in his saddle to look back as Ehren and Amra bunched in closer.

"I would remind you two," she said, just loud enough for Cavan to hear her, "we are riding into hostile territory." She raised a hand before Cavan could object. "*Potentially* hostile territory at least. And these damned weeds grow tall enough to hide a double-fist of orcish ambush."

Amra smiled. "So please, for me, try to keep your focus on where you're going before arrows start flying."

An arrow whistled past her head.

"*Down!*" Amra yelled, but Cavan and Ehren were already off their horses, and Ehren barked the command word to make the horses lie down.

More arrows fell, but their targets were moving now and those shafts vanished into the goldenrod.

With a roar, two men came running at the trio. From the game trail behind them came a skinny, one-eyed man with a great sword even longer than Amra's. From ahead came a bear of a man, scarred and bearded, wielding an axe and shield. Both wore leathers studded with steel.

And both wore the insignia of Duke Falstaff on their left shoulders: crossed black spears on a field of yellow.

"Damn it," swore Amra. "I knew I should have ordered the charge instead of the halt." Her dark sword was in her hands and she slipped forward to meet the one-eyed man.

Ehren thumped his staff and cried out to Zatafa in the language of old lost Penthix, the first kingdom to revere the sun goddess. Light flared brighter than a shaft of sunlight in a storm, all focused on the direction the arrows flew from.

Cavan pulled his longsword and a handful of goldenrod blossoms and moved to meet the axe man.

The axe came down at his head. Cavan sidestepped closer, cutting at the axe man's exposed right side, but still the axe man got his shield in the way. Cavan blew power across the goldenrod blossoms. A sharp breath, to send them into the axe man's face.

The blossom's clung to his face, but missed the axe man's eyes.

From the corner of his vision, Cavan could see the others. One-eye was quick with his sword, but Amra was quicker. She pressed him hard and already had split his leathers across his chest in a cut that must have been shallow since he was still fighting.

Ehren was out somewhere among the goldenrod with his staff. Hunting blinded archers.

But one of the archers wasn't blind. Came out of the goldernrod, and Cavan was glad he'd forced the axe man to turn to his right. Both opponents were before Cavan now, instead of flanking him. The archer to his right and the axe man straight in front of him.

The archer had dropped his bow and gained a longsword in his left hand and a dagger in his right. A short man, tanned nearly as dark as a forest elf, with graying black curls and evil-looking black eyes. And he wasn't just an archer. He had a purple stripe across the upper right corner of his duke's sigil, marking him as the duke's chief huntsman.

The axe man came in high. Cavan came across low.

Cavan stepped left again and cut the axe man's thigh, just behind the knee. Blood watered the trampled goldenrods of the game trail.

The axe man bellowed. Tried to twist and swing at the same time. Went down in a heap, between Cavan and the chief huntsman.

Cavan grabbed another fistful of goldenrod in his left hand.

"Stop or die!" bellowed a deep voice in Ruktuk, the guttural tongue of orcs. And with that command, orcs came out of the fields from every direction at once.

BIG ORCS. SMALL ORCS. ORCS WITH PALE GREEN SKIN AND ORCS WHOSE green skin was so dark they might have had ogre or troll blood. Orcs with wild black hair dreaded out and orcs with long brown or orange hair, greased and knotted into braids, each with a tiny blade at the end. Orcs shaved bald. Orcs with short tusks, orcs with broken tusks, and orcs with yellowed tusks so long their lips drooled nonstop.

Every orc was armed with an axe, a spear or a broadsword. Most of the orcs had three or four battle scars, and those were just what Cavan could see. All of them were armored, most in hides or leather but some in patchworks of chainmail.

The air filled with the scent of blood and dirt and foul sweat. The smell of orcs.

Cavan knew immediately who was in charge. Not the tallest or the broadest orc, but the one all in a single set of chainmail, not patchwork. Coif, hauberk and greaves, none showing even a spot of rust. The one who had a great sword on her back, but hadn't drawn a weapon. She had one small tusk on the left side of her mouth, and a broken tusk on the right that was thick enough it must once have been much, much longer. Her skin was dark, and her long brown hair braided with blades.

None of the humans threw down their weapons, which was good. Cavan had already warned Amra and Ehren that orcs would take it as a sign of weakness. Among orcs, throwing down weapons was not merely surrender, it was tantamount to begging for one's life by offering to become a slave.

That the hunters didn't throw down their weapons meant they

must have dealt with orcs before, and not just fought them. Interesting.

"Who dares spill blood on Firespear ground?" asked the orc leader in Ruktuk, her yellow eyes narrowed in suspicion.

Cavan and the chief huntsman spoke at once. The chief huntsman in common Rentissi, the tongue of old Rentiss, a kingdom which had once spread from sea to sea, and whose language had long outlived it. It seemed that all across the land, the various peoples all still spoke and read and wrote Rentissi.

Cavan, though, spoke Ruktuk right now.

"These renegades are wanted," the chief huntsman started.

"We know the glory of the Firespear," Cavan started.

"Stop!" the orc leader bellowed, in Rentissi. She glared at the chief huntsman. Narrowed her eyes. "Ears."

The chief huntsman scoffed, but moved his graying black curls away from the tips of his ears to show that his ears were round as any human's.

The orc leader held her glare for a moment, body language saying she still had her doubts that the chief huntsman was not at least part elf. No doubt due to the deep tan of his skin, so close to the hue of wood elves that he might have had some elf blood, even if it didn't show in his ears.

She turned to Cavan and flared her nostrils, which for an orc was a gesture of consideration. Probably appreciating either that Cavan was more obviously human, or that he'd spoken her own language. In Ruktuk she said, *"You first."*

"My riders and I know the glory of the Firespear. We come not to raid. We seek no spoils. No captives. We come to talk with Iresk the Hawks- peaker, if he will honor us by listening."

"He ... speaks," the chief huntsman said in what sounded like Ruktuk attempted by a goblin, *"lies. No trust."*

The orc leader spat at the feet of the chief huntsman, and Cavan had to fight not to smile. An orc would not smile at the dismissal, would add to the insult by not even acknowledging it. And Cavan knew the orc leader was watching for a mistake. Finally she nodded at Cavan, and said, in Ruktuk, *"Why?"*

"You lead, and are worthy of respect," Cavan said with a slow nod. *"But those words are for Iresk the Hawkspeaker. I am Cavan, called Oltblood in the human way. May I know who commands so many?"*

The orc leader laughed at a traditional orc greeting from the lips of a human, but gave the traditional response.

"Commanding so few gives me little honor, but I am Grench, called Trollkiller in the orc *way."*

Trollkiller? If this orc made a habit of killing trolls, she was not someone Cavan wanted to square off against. Possibly not even someone Amra would...

Never mind that. Amra would do it. But as she was pointing out earlier, only if she felt it necessary.

Grench turned to the chief huntsman and spoke Rentissi. "Why are you here? By what right do you ambush on Firespear land?"

The chief huntsman pursed his lips for a moment, as though trying to remember the right orcish words, but then gave up and spoke Rentissi.

"I am Tohen, called Great Hunter." Grench spat, but didn't interrupt as Tohen continued, "I have tracked this man and his ... riders across the Dwarfmarches for my lord. My chief." Tohen pointed at Cavan. "He wants this one's head, and I must let no one stop me from bringing it."

A weak start, in Cavan's opinion, but a good finish.

"He is no splinter," Cavan said. *"His chief rates him little better than a foundling."*

Several of the orcs around Cavan chuckled at that, since it was less a direct insult that could lead to a challenge, and more general mockery. "Splinters" were the orcs most valued and trusted by their chiefs. "Foundlings" were wandering orcs from broken or beaten clans, usually the weakest because the strongest would be welcomed into a new clan. Sometimes foundlings were taken into new clans, but when that happened they were considered expendable until they proved themselves.

Grench flared her nostrils. "*What do you know of splinters?*"

"*I know if I were a chief, my two riders would be my splinters. We eat, we fight, we kill together. I trust them at my back. I trust them when I sleep. I trust them with my blood, my life, my offspring, and my captives. We walk as three. We fight as one.*"

Grench nodded, looking Cavan up and down again. She nodded at Tohen.

"*Why does this one want you?*"

"*His master wants lands that should be mine in the human way. He sends dogs to worry my head from my neck.*"

"*I AM NO DOG,*" yelled one of the huntsmen in good Ruktuk. This was one Cavan hadn't seen before. Must have been the other archer. He had the ebon skin of the deep south and short-shorn black curls.

Grench looked from this huntsman to Cavan without moving her head.

Cavan tapped his knuckles together, the orcish equivalent of a shrug.

"*I do not know them. I know their master. Their master I would meet with sword or axe. These ... are merely between me and their master.*"

Grench smiled at that.

"No!" Tohen said. "I'll fight you single combat for—"

"You have not earned single combat," Grench said. She spat at Tohen's feet again, emphasizing her point. To her people she spoke in Ruktuk.

"*Cavan called Oltblood, his horses, and his riders come with us to see the Hawkspeaker.*" She took in a dozen of her people with a gesture. "*Give these others a breath to bind their wounds, if they can. Then escort this self-named Great Hunter and his humans to the road. If they cannot walk, kill them. If they object, kill them.*"

Grench looked at Tohen. "You understand?"

Tohen was gritting his teeth so hard Cavan wondered if he'd cracked any. But Tohen nodded.

Grench then turned back to Cavan. "*As we walk, you must tell me who named you orc-friend. For only an orc-friend could know of splinters.*"

And they began to walk.

4

FOUR YEARS AGO...

The Wailing Woods didn't wail, at least not that Cavan had heard. And he'd been riding south through them for three days now.

The trees were giants. They grew so tall and thick in this part of the woods, they had to be as old as the elves said to make this forest their home. Cavan hadn't seen any elves, but he'd seen a great many trees.

They grew in two main types. The ones with the grayish brown trunks grew thinner, which meant that if a lance were driven through one, the tip and the handle would probably be visible. That wasn't true of the trees with the reddish trunks. They grew so thick a stout tower could be carved through their innards and still leave walls thick enough to withstand a short siege. All around them grew thick underbrush that must have hidden colonies of animals, to judge from the rustling and cracking alone.

The branches of both tree types started at least a hundred feet up, and the lowest looked thick enough to bear four fully armored knights riding abreast. The grayish brown had thin, pale green leaves with six fingers, whereas the reds had needle leaves of dark green. All those branches wove into a canopy that kept the summer sun at bay, and the air below as cool as a gentle spring. And as fragrant. The reddish trees smelled warm, like hickory smoke. The grayish brown ones smelled darker, almost peaty.

No doubt each type of tree had its name and its uses. Master Powys would have known both, and their histories, and any magical applications they could be put to. Perhaps if Cavan had known any of those things, he might still be at Master Powys' tower in the center of the forest, studying magic.

Instead he was riding home to Oltoss on a blue roan colt, a parting gift from Master Powys. Riding home along a slender ribbon of black dirt road.

Riding home to tell Kent of another failure.

Cavan knew he should have accepted an escort back to Oltoss, but he was too ashamed. A failure as a warrior, despite the longsword at his side. A failure as a wizard, despite the pouch of spells dangling from his belt. If he met his death on the road, well, at least his string of failures would end.

Even growing a beard was proving too great a task for Cavan, so he kept his olive skin shaved smooth. Not that his cheeks required much shaving.

As he rode, he snacked on nuts from his pack. Cashews and walnuts, with raisins for sweetness. Three more days and he would be through the woods and onto the wider road that would lead to the capital. He looked forward to seeing blue sky above him once again. Despite their height, the trees had begun to feel constricting. In fact, he might want to—

A stone thumped Cavan's head. Pain spiked from the right side of his skull, just above the ear.

The world spun about him. Cavan slumped in his saddle, shaking his throbbing head. Knowing he should do something. His body didn't know what.

Rough hands grabbed him. Yanked him down. Slammed him to the black dirt. Cavan tucked his head just in time to save a second daze. But his ribs took the impact. Kicked the air out of his lungs.

Cavan tried to breathe. Only got enough air to pick up the smell of blood and dirt and rank sweat.

Cavan knew something about that smell from his warrior training. Something that came together when he saw the green hands and arms of his assailant.

Orc.

An orc on top of him. Thin, but with ropy muscles. Thick animal hides armoring the torso. Small tusks. A trio of warts on the left cheek. Short black hair puffing out in dreadlocks.

The orc went for Cavan's sword.

Cavan found his dagger first.

Pressed the tip past the hides and against the green belly above him.

The orc's hand stopped moving.

The orc met his eyes. The orc's were yellow. The pupils big.

Cavan wheezed. Air still eluding him. The orc glanced down at Cavan's still-sheathed sword. Cavan pressed the tip of his dagger a little harder.

The orc raised his hands.

Cavan jerked his head to the side. The orc got off him. Cavan followed, keeping his dagger against the orc's belly. Air finally started easing its way into Cavan's lungs, but it wasn't much of an improvement. Every breath ached from his shoulders to his waist, and his head still throbbed in time to his rapid heartbeat.

The orc growled something that might have been words.

"Rentissi?" panted Cavan.

"Some," the orc said. His voice was higher than Cavan expected. Chin and jaw narrower too. And shoulders...

Was this orc female?

"You're alone?" Cavan said.

The orc nodded. Then spat. "But I not surrender. I not slave. I—"

"Stop." Cavan raised his empty hand, in case the meaning wasn't clear. "Why did you attack me?"

"Alone," the orc said, pointing to herself. Then she waved an arm to indicate the woods around them. "Elves." She pointed to the horse. "Escape."

Cavan pulled back his dagger and made a show of putting it away. The orc narrowed her eyes, then flared her nostrils.

"I want to escape too," Cavan said. "I have a horse, and I have food. You can ride with me if you can promise not to attack."

The orc nodded.

"I am called Cavan. What should I call you?"

"Uulsk." She hesitated then, and later Cavan would wonder what kenning she almost gave herself, but she said nothing else.

Cavan held out his hand.

Uulsk looked at the hand. "You have not promised not to attack me."

"I, Cavan, promise I will not attack you if you do not attack me first."

"Then I, Uulsk, promise the same."

Uulsk clasped forearms with him.

5

____

"WHAT DID I TELL YOU?" QALAS SAID, THE MOMENT THE LAST ORC vanished back into the field of great goldenrod south of the road to Oltoss. Anger stormed in those dark blue eyes, but he kept his tone to merely harsh. "Not one orc or a dozen. I counted at least forty."

"Enough!" bellowed Tohen.

He was in no mood for complaints. For a day with such ideal hunting conditions, it had all shot to hell rapidly. Cavan and his cronies had given them the slip. Worse, Cavan spoke that orc tongue like a native, and none of Tohen's digging about the bastard had indicated any friendship with orcs. What else did Tohen not know?

That didn't matter. Not at the moment. What mattered was that Cavan was gone, and that countless orcs lay between him and Tohen. And Tohen's men were in no shape to pursue.

At least Lutik proved his luck once more, surviving two blows across the chest, either of which might have felled him. The worse of the pair was a slash from Amra that should have opened his guts, but instead caught his ribs just right.

Still, two of his ribs had been cut opened by that sword of hers, along with his armor — including two of the steel studs — and more than a little muscle in two places.

Incredible, the man's luck. How her sword could have carved steel but gotten deflected by a rib was a puzzle Tohen didn't understand. Not that he had time to wonder about it.

As it was, Lutik needed healers. He was pale, shaky, sweating and probably still bleeding after that orc-escorted hike, for all the bandaging Tohen had done himself. Lutik needed more than field patching, or it might be that his luck had finally run out.

Rudyar wasn't much better off. Oh, he'd survive that cut to his leg, but it was deep. The leg wouldn't support him, and he couldn't even ride properly with it. He might be able to ride sidesaddle, but not swiftly, and if not, he'd end up trussed and slung over the saddle like a dead buck.

At least they still had their horses. Tohen had half-expected the orcs to keep them, but they'd handed over the reins with a simple warning not to trespass on Firespear territory again, on pain of death.

As though the Tohen had had any doubt about that.

Then there was Qalas.

Qalas, the newest hunter of the duke's, and apparently the least certain of the pecking order. Qalas, who hefted his halberd as though he were seeking a place to sink its axe. A place like Tohen's neck, perhaps?

"You don't even speak Ruktuk?" Qalas said, his tone implying that half the known world spoke the orcs' grunting excuse for a language. "You could have mentioned that before you made us look like idiots in front of the whole—"

"Did you know Cavan had connections among the orcs?" Tohen said.

"I'm not the chief huntsman."

"But you think you should be." Tohen turned to face Qalas squarely now. Fingers playing by the hilt of his sword while Qalas took his halberd in a ready grip.

"I would have done better with the orcs."

Tohen laughed. He met those angry eyes and laughed. A harsh, cold sound that never came near his own eyes.

"Cavan knew exactly where he was going," Tohen said, "and

exactly how to deal with those orcs. Knowing a few more words of orcish wouldn't have made a difference." Tohen smiled. "But do you know what would have? *Landing your first arrow.*"

Qalas took a step forward. Tohen didn't draw.

"Do you want another fight? Is that it?"

Tohen looked at his sword, then back at Qalas. Tohen drew his hand away from the pommel. He shook his head.

"If you think this is the time to fight, then you're not ready to be chief hunter. I have two wounded men to deal with, and a lot of ground to make up. Because whatever Cavan wants with those orcs, it's going to get him back to Oltoss faster than horses."

"He's gone," Qalas said. "And if you and I will have any chance at catching him, we need to abandon these two and go now."

"A chief huntsman doesn't abandon his wounded," Tohen said. "And a chief huntsman knows the fastest way back to Oltoss. Faster than anything those orcs could do for Cavan."

For the first time in what felt like hours, Qalas said nothing.

"Save your weapon for our enemies," Tohen said. "And help me get these two back to Riverbend at speed or we're going to lose our prize."

6

———

In some places orcs held keeps of their own. Formed towns. Even traded. But among the plains around the Dwarfmarches, the orc clans stayed on the move. They lived by raiding and hunting, fighting as much among themselves as with the humans, dwarves and elves who lived closest to them.

Cavan knew these things. But he had been long enough away from orcs that he had forgotten just how organized their clans could be.

The hike to the Firespear main camp took most of the afternoon, and Cavan spotted at least three sentry lines along the way. And those didn't include the places where Grench interrupted Cavan's story to get quick reports from outrunners.

Clearly Grench was well-respected among the Firespears. Probably a splinter to their chief, or on the verge of being named one. And just as clearly, Cavan could tell that he may have impressed Grench enough to rate an escort — even enough to allow Amra and Ehren to walk close behind Cavan and Grench instead of farther back and ringed by guards — but not enough to hear those reports. Each time an outrunner came up, the procession stopped and armed orcs kept an eye on Cavan, Amra and Ehren while Grench stepped aside to hear, in low voices, what the outrunners had to say.

If Grench was troubled by any of their news, Cavan couldn't tell. Not that he expected to.

Fortunately, Cavan's story was long. After he had met Uulsk in the Wailing Woods they had traveled together for several months before Cavan accepted that he had to return home and face his failure. Cavan was still talking as they left the great goldenrod behind and trekked among low foothills of waist-high green and yellow grasses that carried a nutty smell. Away from the narrow trail grew copses of jacaranda trees, their lavender blossoms shifting in the gentle breeze.

He continued as the afternoon wore on, while above them the sky deepened its blue, though the day never got as hot as it had threatened during the morning. The red-tail hawks continued their circling above Cavan's interim destination. Sometimes wider circles, sometimes narrower, but always circling.

Finally, his story was coming to a close as they neared the perimeter of the Firespear main encampment.

For some time Cavan had been able to see the smoke of campfires. Dozens or scores of them. Something like that. Cavan had been too busy talking to worry about the details. Amra probably counted them, though. Could have estimated the numbers of the Firespear clan before getting even this close.

Just as well Cavan hadn't tried. Any estimate he attempted would have fallen well short.

Thousands. There had to have been more than two thousand orcs spread across more than a league of campsite. They looked to have been broken into smaller units of a hundred or so each, each forming a ring inside the greater circle of the whole encampment, with a large central cooking fire. Everywhere the animal hide lean-to tents the orcs used from spring through summer. Would use until the rains of fall came and they built larger shelters.

Each grouping was practically a clan unto itself, with patrols, tanners, cooks and so forth. The offspring of each grouping gathered in one place as they learned the ways of their people and did such work as they could. Their elderly gathered near the fire, but what they were up to Cavan couldn't guess. Uulsk had never spoken of what it meant to be "old" among the orcs.

One great ring in the center of the campsite. Twice as large as the outer rings, and with at least twice as many orcs. That was where the standard of the Firespears burned. Literally. It looked to be a great spear carved from a single tall, thick tree trunk.

The sharpened tip of that great spear burned bright, even in the afternoon sunlight. But the black wood within the flames still held its oval shape, as though the fire could do no more than harden it.

"I hope you know what you're doing," muttered Ehren, as he had every time the procession paused. Probably still worried about being sacrificed to their god of darkness.

Louder, Amra said, "That would make one hell of a battering ram."

Grench smiled, but said nothing in response. Cavan started to ask if it had ever been *used* as a battering ram, but she clapped him on the shoulder to cut him off.

She turned to the orcs of the procession. Those, Cavan had been able to count. Forty-eight, not including Grench, but including the ones who had escorted Tohen's group to the road, and returned along the way. She barked orders at the group, and thirty-six of them split off and looked to be returning to one outer ring or another.

The final dozen surrounded Cavan, Amra, and Ehren. Grench spoke in quiet tones.

"*Uulsk was right to name you orc-friend,*" she said in Ruktuk. "*I will even say she was right to teach you our ways, as you taught her human ways. But do not talk of her to Chief Ozzik or Iresk the Hawkspeaker.*"

Cavan did his best to give Grench an orcish glare. "*I call Uulsk a friend and will not deny her.*"

"*You speak like an orc,*" she said, shaking her head, "*but you still know little. Uulsk was a rider.*" Grench spat, but it looked more like reflex than a statement, so Cavan tried to ignore it as she continued talking. "*An orc who needs a mount is no fit orc. Great Tilnak gave us legs for a reason. Horses have many uses, but riding is not one of them.*"

"But the elves—"

Grench snorted, and Cavan remembered the first lesson Uulsk taught him: reasons do not matter. Only actions.

Cavan nodded. *"So, where do we find—"*

"You stay here," Grench said in Rentissi, speaking as much to Amra and Ehren as to Cavan for the first time. "You are not enemies, but you are not welcome in our camp either."

"But," Ehren said, "how will we—"

A red-tail hawk landed three strides away. It screeched, a cry so loud Cavan had to fight not to squeeze his eyes shut.

"I think," Cavan said, when he could hear again, "Iresk knows we want to speak to him."

CAVAN HAD HEARD STORIES ABOUT IRESK THE HAWKSPEAKER OVER THE years. Some said the orc stood tall as a troll, with skin their same peat color. Some said he had a third eye in the center of his forehead and a third ear growing out of the back of his neck.

Everyone seemed to agree that gods and demons alike listened when the Hawkspeaker spoke, and the most vicious tangleweeds would part for him at a word.

Cavan had known a wizard or three in his travels, and none he had met ever compared to Master Powys. But the moment he first laid eyes on Iresk the Hawkspeaker, Cavan wondered if he had finally met his old master's match for power.

To begin, Iresk looked too young to have been alive during all the events that the Hawkspeaker was said to witnessed or caused. If the orc had seen thirty-five summers, Cavan would have been surprised. While that might have meant that the name and title were handed down from master to apprentice, Cavan didn't think so. For one, solid reason.

Power.

Cavan could see the orc's power, like a nimbus of faint, violet light spreading out from his dark green skin. He wore no armor, not even the hides that some orcs used. Instead he wore a half-kilt of what looked to be pale green goblin skin that hung to just below his knees, bound at the waist by a lion-hide belt. A pattern of scars crisscrossed his chest, too deliberate to have come during battle.

But he had seen battle, and bore those scars as well. Several on his shoulders and arms, and one that cost him his right ear. And perhaps his tusks. He once had two thick tusks growing from the bottom of his mouth, but both had been broken off, and what remained of them had been carved with runes Cavan didn't recognize. He did recognize the large, curving sword that hung from that lion-skin belt. Vicious-looking steel, it could probably take a head from its shoulders in a single cut.

Scratched along the blade were more runes Cavan didn't know. The letters weren't Rentissi, nor the bastardized form of Rentissi that orcs used for their written Ruktuk. And they weren't any language Cavan had learned with Master Powys.

The Hawkspeaker's long black dreads hung down past his waist, tied in three places along the way with what looked like sinew.

But he did not have the typical orc smell of blood and dirt and foul sweat. Instead a thick, heavy smell wore about him. Like decayed flowers and charred fat.

His eyes were yellow, matching those of the large red-tail hawk on his shoulder, and they looked straight through Cavan the same way Master Powys had, when Cavan was first apprenticed.

And the Hawkspeaker did not come alone.

Apart from the hawk on his shoulder, two others circled high in the air above.

Following the Hawkspeaker were three big, brutish orcs with bald heads, dark green skin, and wicked, double-headed axes. Their chainmail had not been made from single sets, as Grench's had, but it looked sturdy enough, and covered them neck to wrist to thigh. Their thick tusks grew long and unbroken, stained brown with blood. And they smelled more of old blood than anything except perhaps foul sweat.

Almost an afterthought, a young orc trailed behind them. Skittish. Unarmed except for a dagger that might still have been too big for him. Or her. Cavan couldn't tell which, though the little thing wore only a half-kilt like the Hawkspeaker's, apart from a pack on his — Cavan decided that a topless orc was probably a male orc — back.

"These three do not speak Rentissi," the Hawkspeaker said, his voice strong and smooth and deep. "And this one" — he gestured to what had to be his apprentice — "must learn. So let us use your tongue today. When we meet again, we will use mine."

Cavan wasn't sure what to say. That wasn't any kind of orcish greeting he'd ever heard. But before he could say *something* at least, Ehren spoke.

"And on that day we will share a meal. And you shall give thanks to my gods, and I to yours."

The Hawkspeaker smiled. "Very good. I wondered if a Zatafista would have the courage to match my offer."

Now Ehren looked relaxed. More relaxed that Cavan had seen him all day. So much relief in those clear blue eyes.

"Let me guess," Amra said, one eyebrow high, "you're not going to be sacrificed?"

The Hawkspeaker laughed, which wiped the smile off Ehren's face. His words came out an irritated kind of comfortable, as though he'd known the Hawkspeaker for some time and heard the same joke too often.

"Tell me your people have never sacrificed a priest of Zatafa to Randech. Then laugh."

"Why should I begin our conversation with lies?" The Hawkspeaker sank down to sit cross-legged among the tramped down yellowish grass at the edge of the great Firespear encampment. "Perhaps it wasn't for *our* safety that you were not allowed into our camp."

His three bodyguards spread out around Cavan, Amra and Ehren, taking up positions by their horses. That made Cavan nod in approval. Not at anything specifically orcish about the action, but about the implied threat to their mounts instead of their persons. The Firespears had thousands of orcs nearby. And as Grench had pointed out, these orcs were used to swift travel on foot. If Cavan and his friends caused trouble, the bodyguards didn't have to kill them immediately. Killing their mounts would ensure they couldn't get away.

Ehren sat, mirroring the Hawkspeaker, though slightly to one side so Cavan could sit opposite him. Cavan did, sitting the same style.

Amra broke the pattern. She sat with one boot under her and the other leg outstretched. It looked casual, but Cavan knew she could spin up and into action from that pose faster than Cavan could from his.

"Don't your hawks ever eat?" Cavan said, glancing at the two ever circling up above. "They've been up there all day."

"Have they?" the Hawkspeaker asked, with the same maddening little smile that Master Powys used when Cavan asked a question his master considered obvious or unworthy. "How many hawks do you see?"

Cavan looked up. Two red-tail hawks, flying lazy-looking circles. He was about to say so, but stopped himself. Something wasn't quite right.

Cavan muttered soft words. *"Neela asa."*

The sky above darkened to his eyes, then lightened. Lightened. Grew almost gray-white from its natural rich, deep afternoon blue.

And now Cavan could see more than two hawks. Many more than two. Red-tail hawks, elephant hawks, vole hawks, goshawks and black hawks. All circling, but not all in this world at the same time.

"Eighteen," he said aloud, counting as much by the aura of life that surrounded each bird against the between-sky as by their shapes. "I see eighteen hawks. Do you need me to name the breeds?"

"No, Cavan Oltblood. Cavan Orc-friend. Cavan Kingsblood. You have proven yourself for the moment. I will hear your words, and I will consider them."

The Hawkspeaker clapped his hands together once, and the sound rang out like thunder.

"But first," he said, "we will eat."

Food sounded wonderful. Cavan's wasn't the only belly rumbling for the past hour. He was sure he'd at least heard Amra's too.

He only hoped the offered food was something humans could eat.

MORE ORCS BROUGHT THE FOOD. ROAST BOAR AND STEWED ROOT vegetables. Already prepared, fortunately. Cavan was willing to wait through a meal, but if they had to start a new cook fire here at the edge of the great Firespear encampment, and start the process from raw meat, he might not have had the patience.

Carrying the food were foundlings, by Cavan's guess. Their skin was so pale green it was almost blue, which didn't match any of the other Firespear orcs Cavan could see. They were thin through the shoulders, arms, and legs — so they weren't likely great warriors — and they smelled far more of dirt and foul sweat than of blood.

Fortunately the smell of the boar overrode their odor. Uulsk had done her share of the cooking while Cavan and she had ridden together, and Cavan understood something of orcish spicing. Cavan thought he could smell the sweetness of goat blood over the rich smell of slow-roasted boar, but there was something more he could not place. Not the root vegetables stewing from the bronze pot carried by one of the foundlings, but something else. A heavier smell.

"Is that..." Amra said, sniffing the air, "is that roc blood I smell?"

"Very good," the Hawkspeaker said. He did not budge to assist the foundlings as they spooned wild carrots and turnips into bowls made from large skulls — likely cattle or buffalo — then carved slices of boar to lay across the tops. "Most humans do not recognize roc."

"But it's too early in the year for the Feast of Tilnak," Ehren said, confusion all over his face. "That's not until midsummer, I think?"

"Very good indeed." The Hawkspeaker laughed as he spoke, an easy, comfortable sound. "You surround yourself with worthy companions, Cavan Orc-friend." To Ehren he said, "The roc was a gift from great Randech, and the reason we have remained here for so long. Three nights past it descended in the moonlight. Wounded. Wings burning, likely from dragonfire. We lost only six hunters bringing it down."

Amra snickered. "Only three nights? You're still butchering it, aren't you?"

"All will eat well of this bounty. But only orcs shall enjoy the flesh."

"The blood is honor enough," Cavan said, hoping the blood seasoning wouldn't make the boar inedible. "You have our thanks."

The foundlings served. Not only the food, but horns of bloodale, a brew that began by the same steps used to brew regular ale, but at three stages along the lines was thickened with the blood of the vanquished.

During Cavan's travels with Uulsk, she had moaned at length of how she missed the bloodale. How bloodale was the secret of orcish strength, and how traveling without it diminished her.

The bloodale served by the Hawkspeaker had to have been made with roc blood. Cannibalism was a major point of contention between the humans and orcs. Well, not just humans on the one side of the argument, and not just orcs on the other, but the point stood.

Even without considering the source of the blood, in Cavan's opinion the brew was too bitter. He could taste the hops, at least, but the tang of the blood remained in his mouth after he swallowed. Not that it lasted, because even that tang was overridden by the boar. Its dense, muscled flesh served as little more than a delivery vehicle for the pungent, clattering taste of roc blood. So much stronger than its smell, and so much thicker in the boar seasoning than in the ale.

Cavan found himself using the root vegetables to distract his tongue while he ate. Giving himself some relief, at least, from all this blood without insulting his host.

Only halfway through the meal, he could tell that his stomach would not thank him later. Worse, he could not stop eating because he could tell the Hawkspeaker was watching to see how he handled the boar. Cavan was certain of that, even though he could have pointed to no particular cast to the Hawkspeaker's features, nor any furtive glances.

There was just something about the Hawkspeaker's aspect while they ate. Something that reminded Cavan of the way Master Powys could watch him without watching him.

The four of them — Cavan, Ehran, Amra, and the Hawkspeaker — ate in silence, the orcish way. For orcs, food was almost a ritual. Not through any words or gestures or timing, but through focus. Orcs ate every meal as though it might be their last, and so they gave food their whole attention.

The three orcs guarding the horses did not eat at this time, nor did the apprentice do anything more than order about the foundlings to make sure that everyone had their fill.

Cavan and Ehren finished their meals. Amra had seconds.

When the food was eaten and the bloodale drunk, and the horns and skulls taken away by foundlings, only then did the Hawkspeaker nod in approval and speak again. By then the sun had begun to set over Croma's Forest to the west, purpling the sky above them and turning much of the western sky to shades of red and orange.

"So, Cavan Oltblood, what need could cause you to risk Firespear wrath to exchange words with me?"

"Much have I heard of the magic of Iresk the Hawkspeaker. Tales of your feats have—"

"And will continue to, I do not doubt." The Hawkspeaker raised a thick, black eyebrow. "Do not mistake me for a chief or a splinter, who must be praised for five times as long as it takes to ask a favor. Need has brought you here, and I don't think you were simply fleeing from those ... dogs, I believe you called them?"

"Are you familiar with the human ways of ruling and inheriting land?".

The Hawkspeaker did not so much as twitch a muscle. He kept his yellow eyes fixed on Cavan. An orcish way of saying that the question was so obvious that it bordered on insult.

"You called me Cavan Kingsblood earlier." Cavan nodded. "That's true. I am a king's bastard, and my uncle, a duke, sent his dogs after me to rob me of land I stand to inherit."

"Asking the Firespear to help you press your claim might prove interesting," the Hawkspeaker said. He gestured and the hawk on his shoulder took to the air. Another red-tail hawk alighted the same shoulder, differentiated only by having darker wings. But under the slowly darkening sky, Cavan couldn't be sure.

"But," continued the Hawkspeaker, "if that were your goal, you would have asked to speak to the chief."

The Hawkspeaker smiled, and the smile was vicious. That smile did more than the scars on his shoulders or his missing ear to remind Cavan that the Hawkspeaker was also a warrior.

"Watching you prove yourself for *that* would have been interesting. But you came to me. I presume you seek a faster means to Oltoss than the road provides?"

Cavan nodded.

"I cannot promise you *safe* passage. Only passage."

Cavan's turn to stare unblinking at the Hawkspeaker.

The Hawkspeaker laughed. "A pity you were born a human. Very well. I will grant you passage, for the price of a favor."

Cavan nodded. Always risky to promise a future favor, but he was starting to like the Hawkspeaker. And he needed to get to Oltoss quickly.

The Hawkspeaker looked at Amra. "You are the mightiest warrior of the three, and you managed a warrior's portion of food. Promise that you will aid Cavan in that future favor and I'll grant you passage as well."

Amra glanced at Cavan, then nodded.

"Which brings us to you." The Hawkspeaker turned to face Ehren, who looked troubled by the attention. "You are no orc-friend. You are no great warrior. And you revere Zatafa, of all gods. Why should I grant you passage?"

Cavan wanted to answer. Had an answer all ready. But speaking for Ehren now would have belittled his friend in the Hawkspeaker's eyes, which was the last thing Cavan wanted to do.

"It's not enough that I only seek passage to aid an orc-friend?"

The Hawkspeaker shook his head. "And I need no blessings from the sun."

"No," Ehren said slowly, his smile building once more, "but your roc does."

"Our cooks can butcher a roc."

"But can they save all the meat? Three days since your hunters brought it down, and still they work just to butcher it. How much meat will they lose before they finish? How much will go foul?"

"No more than we would feed to the foundlings."

"But a blessing from Zatafa can preserve it. Keep the meat whole and unspoiled until your cooks can finish with it. How many more orcs would eat well?"

"Even your foundlings might grow strong enough to join the clan," Cavan said, caught up in the moment.

The Hawkspeaker laughed, and this time his laugh rang out into the growing twilight. The red-tail hawk on his shoulder took to the air, and Cavan thought he saw a flock of birds flee the nearby underbrush.

"Very well, Zatafista." The Hawkspeaker came to his feet in a single, smooth movement as his legs unfolded beneath him. "My guards shall escort you to the roc where you shall grant your profane blessing while your companions wait here and I prepare the way. Our own priests will have to sanctify the meat before it is worthy again to be eaten by orcs, but you are right. There will be more food to go around."

The guards stepped forward from guarding the mounts to surround Ehren as he, Cavan, and Amra came to their feet.

Amra looked worried about letting Ehren go off with the orcs, especially after all his worrying about blood sacrifices, but Cavan shook his head. This was no trick. He would stake — well, it seemed he would stake Ehren's life on it. But he staked his own as well, because if anything happened to Ehren...

But Ehren smiled his confident smile, either certain of their intentions or certain that his god would save him if anything bad happened. Or maybe he was just smiling to unnerve the orcs. Cavan was never quite sure. But his white linen clothes were unstained by either their meal or sitting on the tramped-down wild grass, and his step was light as he joined his guards.

"Zatafista," the Hawkspeaker said, just before the guards led Ehren away. When Ehren turned back, the Hawkspeaker finished, "I shall still expect you to aid Cavan when he grants me my favor." The Hawkspeaker smiled. "But now I won't expect you to violate your own faith to do so."

"Then perhaps followers of Randech know something of wisdom after all."

Cavan held his breath, but the Hawkspeaker only laughed and waved for the guards to proceed.

THE QUARTER MOON WAS HALF-RISEN BY THE TIME IRESK THE Hawkspeaker finished his preparations. Ehren was well back by then, and Cavan could tell Amra itched to ask about the layout of the Firespears' central camp. How many guards within the perimeter, how they were armed, the numbers they traveled with. All those sorts of things. Cavan could see those questions and others burning in her green-and-gold eyes.

But she knew better than to voice those questions here. And Cavan hoped she forgot them entirely, rather than risk asking them as they traveled through the passage the Hawkspeaker was preparing.

A passage along the borderlands between worlds. A place where gods and monsters walked. A place where space and time did not move as they did here. Cavan did not understand the details, not in the depth he might have had he succeeded as Master Powys' apprentice, but he understood at least some little bit about it.

If they left tonight. They might arrive by morning. Or noon. Possibly the following morning. The arrival time was a detail that depended on factors Cavan had trouble reconciling in his head. Of one thing he *was* certain — this route would shave weeks off their travel. At the least. If they survived.

But first, the Hawkspeaker had to open the way.

He had not made his preparations where they ate, but back near the edge of the Firespears' encampment. Shortly after Ehren had gone to bless the dead roc, the Hawkspeaker had called forth more attendants — more blue-green-skinned foundlings, by the look of them — who carried scythes and wood and woven baskets that smelled strange. Almost musty.

Cavan didn't particularly think about smells though, any more than he wanted to think about food. That roc-blood-roasted boar did not sit right in his stomach. It hung in his mid-section like a tight ball of angry, and he could feel how it slowed his movements as his body attempted to beat it into submission.

The battle was a loud one.

Amra, despite her short-stature, seemed to have no similar problems that Cavan could hear. And her movements were as light and quick as ever, even if she'd had nothing to do but wait. Cavan would have sworn sometimes that the woman had the all-digesting belly of a dwarf. She certainly had the drinking capacity of a dwarf.

The foundlings led the procession a good distance from the encampment. Then, following the Hawkspeaker's orders, they cut down the green and yellow wild grass in a wide diamond formation, some thirty strides across side to side. But the angles weren't at the cardinal points the way Cavan would have expected. They must have signified something different.

Then the foundlings gathered up the stalks and carried them away while the Hawkspeaker's apprentice took a maul that looked entirely too big for him and broke up any small rises or irregularities in the ground until the diamond of dirt was level.

Around the time the apprentice finished that step, Ehren returned. And if he had any problems digesting the orcish cooking, Cavan couldn't tell. Ehren practically shone in the darkness, as though their meal had already processed for him and fueled his inner fire. Zatafa probably burned the meat away for him or something.

Next the Hawkspeaker took what Cavan had assumed was firewood, and laid the split logs end-to-end in the center of the clearing, forming part of the diagonal between two points. Chanting something in a harsh, guttural tongue, the Hawkspeaker then poured first water, then two kinds of oils over the logs.

The twelve logs. Cavan wondered what factor the number represented.

Ehren might have known something, from the way he nodded.

"What?" Cavan whispered.

"The twelve types of darkness." Ehren never took his eyes from the work of the Hawkspeaker. "And water to quench. I'm not sure about the oils though."

"Would you boys like to ask?" Amra said, apparently bored with the speculation.

Cavan and Ehren both shook their heads. Watching.

Amra sighed.

With the wood watered and oiled, the Hawkspeaker walked around one end of the wooden line to the far side. He carved marks in the dirt with his curved sword. Then he walked around the other end and carved different marks on the near side.

"Come forward," the Hawkspeaker said.

Cavan led the way, Amra on his left and Ehren on his right, each a step behind. All three leading their horses.

The darkness was rising all about them now. Cavan could not see much beyond the diamond of dirt. The foundling assistants seemed to be gone, and the apprentice was somewhere in the background.

In front of them stood Iresk the Hawkspeaker. His skin seemed to darken with the night, deepening its shade of green even further. But his eyes. His yellow eyes seemed to glow even brighter than Ehren.

The Hawkspeaker reached into a pouch inside his lion skin belt and when he took his hand back out his fingers trailed rusty red…

Blood. It had to be yet more blood.

It had been too long. Cavan had forgotten just how into blood orcs were. That was one reason he didn't spend more time with them, even the ones he liked. That, and the cannibalism.

And yes, what was on the Hawkspeaker's fingers smelled like blood, which made Cavan's stomach gurgle and twist unhappily. But he could also smell something wild and floral, and underneath that something earthy. Apparently a number of herbs — and mushrooms if Cavan was not mistaken — had been blended into this bloody mixture.

The Hawkspeaker anointed Cavan beneath each ear, then beneath each eye. Beneath the nose came next, then beneath the lips, then finally the inner skin of Cavan's wrists. The Hawkspeaker anointed Amra the same way, then Ehren. Then, to Cavan's surprise, the Hawkspeaker anointed the horses as well, using the breastbone instead of the wrists they lacked.

To Cavan's even greater surprise, the horses didn't seem to mind the bloody paste.

More harsh, guttural syllables from the Hawkspeaker now, but this time Cavan could feel the breath of power within them. Every place he had been anointed felt cooler, almost icy, and a tingling began to spread throughout his body.

The night darkened around them. Even the bright moon above looked dull, tarnished. Its glow unable to shine upon Cavan.

"Mount," the Hawkspeaker said. Cavan and his friends swung up into their saddles.

The Hawkspeaker spread the paste along his curved sword now, and when he whispered more power across it, the runes darkened to a blackness that seemed to suck light from the world around them. The darkness smoked, trailed as the Hawkspeaker raised his sword in both hands.

He stepped to the edge of the line of split logs.

With a roar the Hawkspeaker slashed down through the air, splitting the log he struck.

And with that, rending space itself.

Above the logs now was no longer visible the fields of wild grass, but a dark, pebbled trail within rocks the color of obsidian. Above the trail a midnight, starless sky.

"*Follow the trail,*" the Hawkspeaker said in Ruktuk. "*Narrow or broad, do not leave it before the end. Go!*"

Cavan urged his blue roan through the rent in space.

7

The black pebbled path ran narrow along the edge of the obsidian cliff. And the cliff looked like literal obsidian. Shiny and brittle, with tiny chips of it broken up to form the trail. The trail was all there was of the cliff on this mountain of obsidian, so narrow that Cavan and his friends had to ride down single-file.

Cavan in front on his blue roan, the Amra on her bay, then Ehren on his blond chestnut. Amra had argued with the Hawkspeaker about the riding order. She wanted to be the first to meet any hazards between them and their destination, as always. But the Hawkspeaker insisted — this was Cavan's need and Cavan's path. He had to lead or they might wind up somewhere else.

The air was still, but cold as a lichyard at the hour of the wolf. Cavan could smell only the blood anointing his upper lip, as it anointed seven other places on his person.

No moon in the sky above them. No stars. Only a blackness deeper than the obsidian of the mountain. Even the Hawkspeaker's hawks did not follow them here.

The world seemed reduced to Cavan and his companions, their path, and their horses. Their horses, whose hooves did not echo, only crunched with every cantering stride.

Sweat gelled quickly on Cavan's forehead. At the back of his neck. Formed and gelled without so much as a drop rolling its way down his back. Just one more thing that was not right in this place where nothing was quite right.

Cavan's stomach twisted with more than the remnants of his bloody meal. This was not his world, and the wrongness of it echoed within him. He thighs ached to kick. To urge the horses faster. Bring them to a gallop.

But their speed didn't matter. The Hawkspeaker said so. They could have walked the horses and arrived at the same time, if they wished. Movement, more than speed, was what mattered.

But Cavan could not simply walk.

If the Hawkspeaker's magic was anything like what Cavan had learned in his time with Master Powys, will and focus made a difference. And Cavan focused better on travel when he rode. Walking was a time for letting his mind wander.

"No song?" Cavan called back to Ehren.

"Not in this place," Ehren said. "We don't need the attention."

The question had only been meant in teasing, but Cavan was shocked to realize that he actually would have welcomed a song. The familiarity of it. Even the confidence of its meaning.

Something had truly gone wrong in Cavan's life. His inheritance looked to be valuable enough to kill for. His foster family was in danger. And he would have welcomed the sound of Ehren singing.

Truly, this was a time as dark as its place.

A glance up and down the cliff side showed Cavan that they'd begun their journey somewhere in the middle of the towering mountain, hundreds of feet up. Below them the valley gave his thirsty eyes their first break from the relentless blackness.

Gray. Gray boulders, copses of gray trees (that had the look of evergreens, which, Cavan supposed, made them evergrays), and darker gray dirt.

And gray bodies. Sixteen of them. Hanging from the lower branches of the nearest tree to where their path looked to pass.

"Are those humans or orcs?" Cavan called out before the curve of the mountain hid the bodies from sight for a time.

"Can't tell from here," Amra said. "But we'll find out soon enough. They aren't going anywhere."

"Don't be too sure," Ehren said.

He had a point. In a place like this, the dead might rise and move about without even so much as the twitch of a finger from a necromancer.

And if those corpses started moving, they would have an agenda of their own. An agenda that might not include letting Cavan and his friends pass.

Just what Cavan wanted to think about as he rode the trail down the mountainside. He'd been lucky enough not to fight the dead so far in his life, and he'd hoped that would never change.

Soon enough the bodies were out of sight, gone until the next circuit on the route down. And now Cavan could see thick, deeper forest. Shades of gray as far as he could see. And splitting the forest in twain looked to be a path.

Cavan had a sneaking suspicion he knew what path that was...

When the curve took him away from the forest, it showed him more obsidian mountains, including his first look at actual color. Three peaks away, a red-orange flame burned atop some kind of spike...

...or spear.

It cast no light beyond itself. The orange-red light of the flames unreflected in the obsidian of the peak beneath the spear. Cavan pointed to the flame as they rode, but neither Amra nor Ehren felt the need to comment.

Round and round they went. Each curve around the mountain was progress. A few more dozen feet down. The trail never broadened, but neither horses nor riders were worried about that. Cavan, Ehran and Amra had ridden their share of mountain passes before.

And each pass brought them closer to the sixteen hanging corpses.

On the third pass down, Amra called, "Orcs. At least half of them are orcs."

On the fifth pass down, she amended, "Half of them are orcs, six are humans, and two elves."

"Are you sure?" Ehren said. "The skin."

"Want me to put a dagger in the pointed tip of one of their ears?"

"No!" Cavan said and Ehren at the same time.

Amra only chuckled.

But finally the trail reached the foot of the mountain and led them among the dark gray of the cracked, rocky ground.

The cold air still did not move down here, but Cavan was getting used to the smell of the bloody paste smeared at various spots on his body. Here the trail was no longer the black pebble of crushed obsidian, but instead the paler gray of the boulders around it. The smallest of these boulders reached about the height of his blue roan's shoulders, but the largest looked like enough raw material for a sculptor to carve out a small keep.

Cavan could only see the trees past such boulders because the trees grew taller still. Tall enough that they might have been welcome among the shorter trees in the Wailing Woods.

Or perhaps they were the same kind of trees. Only younger. Grayed out as they were, and in the absence of their smell, Cavan couldn't begin to guess.

The trail twisted its way between the boulders, wider now. Barely enough for the three of them to ride side by side, which Cavan only realized because Amra pulled up next to him on his right and Ehren did likewise on his left.

Thus, they were riding side by side when they rounded the last boulder and saw the trail lead into the thick forest ahead of them.

And standing between them and that forest, sixteen dead men, and orcs, and elves. Each trailing a noose from his throat. And each with a reddish gleam in his eyes.

THE CORPSES WORE RAGS. NOT TATTERED BY AGE, BUT MORE AS THOUGH they'd been stripped of whatever they'd been wearing in life before they were hanged. That they were sent to the gallows in whatever detritus could be found so that passersby would not have to look upon their naked shame.

Cheap wools and roughspun, some kind of bark-beaten cloth for the elves.

The head of each corpse had been shaved clean. Ritually. Hair, eyebrows, whatever whiskers they might have had. Their lips were sewn shut with what looked like sinew.

No brown skin nor fair skin for the elves, no green for the orcs, no pale skin for the northern humans nor inky skin for the one who looked to have been from the deep south. All sixteen corpses had the same skin tone in this place: uniform slate gray. Not quite the pale gray of the boulders and the trail, but not quite the darker gray of the dirt around them.

They smelled of turned dirt. As though they'd dug themselves out of their graves, but that made no sense to Cavan at all. And not just because they all looked to have been hanged and left to rot. Cavan knew that orcs ate some of their dead, and left the rest where they fell, to rot or be eaten by whatever animals would have them.

And though Cavan had never seen it himself, he had heard it stated as fact that elves dissolved their dead. Whether through some potion or spell — or perhaps just the nature of elves — Cavan didn't know.

But all the corpses looked to have been hanged. And they all smelled like grave dirt.

Amra reached for her sword, but Cavan whistled the horses to a halt.

He raised one hand in greeting.

"Hail, you who have fallen. We seek no quarrel with you. We have important business that takes us down this path. Please. Stand aside. Let us pass in peace."

A human in the center took one step forward. He had old battle scars that must have healed without magic. Cavan could see their ugly, jagged edges peek out around the man's roughspun rags.

A voice came out of the dead man. His sewn-shut lips never twitched, nor his cheeks. His lungs never moved with air, and the apple of his throat never bobbed. But a voice came out of him anyway. A hollow, sad sound that seemed to echo with longing and loss.

"Go back, living man. This world is not yours."

Something about that voice. Cavan remembered the day Kent told him to stop seeking his mother. Cavan felt that same sink to his belly and shoulders once again. That same bitterness on his tongue. And underneath those feelings, a sense of hopelessness. Of the unwanted.

Those feelings pulled at Cavan...

But Cavan knew the pull of magic, and how to press his will past it. He inhaled deeply and focused on his task. Kent was at the other end of this path, and Kent was in trouble.

"I don't claim this world," he said. "But I must follow this path before I return to my own world."

"Go back, living man. This path is not yours."

Cavan was ready for a memory this time, but it still hit him hard.

Cavan remembered standing in the stables of Master Powys' tower, mounting his blue roan Dzink for the first time. The smell of straw and horses. But most of all, the feeling of failure, like a hole in his gut that tried to drain away everything he wanted or cared about in life.

A failure. Again. Not focused enough to be a warrior. Not patient enough to be a wizard. He was good for nothing at all. A waste of time, and air, and food, with no reason at all to go on living.

Cavan had to slap himself across the face to yank himself back to the present. To the place between, where sixteen corpses stood between himself and the family that raised him. To his right, Amra was shaky and pale. Her teeth were gritted and her grip on her sword, white-knuckled. But she had not yet drawn.

On Cavan's left, Ehren's brow looked untroubled. His lips moved constantly in silent prayer.

All three horses shifted uneasily, but did not so much as nicker. As though afraid of drawing attention to themselves.

"I must ride this path through to its end," Cavan said. "Those who need me are waiting."

"They are lost, living man. All are lost. Go back, or we shall string a noose for you."

No memory this time. Just pure despair, welling up from deep within Cavan. Overwhelming him. Of course all was lost. Of course Kent was dead. And his new wife, Rena. And Reed and Alec. And their wives too. And whatever children they had.

All gone. All lost. All because of Cavan's failures.

Better to lay down his sword. He wasn't fit to carry it anyway. Better to let them fit him for a noose. End his suffering. End his...

No.

Cavan had failed at everything he had ever tried to become. A warrior. A wizard. He'd even failed in his desperate flirtation with thievery.

But Cavan had never stopped trying before. And he would not stop trying now.

Low sounds came from all the corpses. Almost a kind of chanting, in some lost, forgotten language. The tongue of the dead, perhaps.

Cavan tried to kick Dzint forward, but his legs wouldn't move. He tried to whistle the charge, but his lips were frozen still.

So he focused on his arm. His sword arm. Poured all of his considerable willpower into making his arm move.

The corpses came together then, their arms outstretched and hands weaving. A sickly orange light grew among them and Cavan could see a twist of rope forming in the hands of their leader.

No. Not this day. Not with so much at stake. Not with Ehren and Amra ready to fall at his side. He would not doom them. He would not doom himself.

Today was not the day Cavan would die.

He would not fail Kent this time.

His arm came free as though a chain had snapped. He ripped his sword free of his scabbard and gave a cry of defiance.

Then Amra had her sword drawn too. Her cry echoed his own.

Ehren lifted his smooth, goldenwood staff high overhead and sang a paean to Zatafa, in Penthix. *"Ia anay Zatafa, meen nares esh ata na!"*

Golden light flared out from him. Drowning out the orange of the corpses' magic. Banishing from the hands of their leader the noose they forged.

All sixteen pairs of red eyes came up in shock.

Cavan whistled the charge, and all three steeds leapt forward as one.

Cavan leaned forward. Sword ready to slash.

But the corpses were gone. Back, hanging from their tree branch. Without a sign of life or movement from any of them.

Cavan sheathed his sword and urged Dzint to even greater speeds.

Pace might not influence how fast Cavan reached Oltoss, but his will to get there all the sooner blazed even brighter in light of those recent feelings of despair.

And if that meant he put more distance between himself and these corpses, so much the better.

Cavan, Amra, and Ehren charged forward into the deep, gray woods.

The forest was as cold as the mountain had been. And the path in this place between shouldn't have felt cramped. But it did.

The path itself was plenty wide. Wide enough for all three horses to ride abreast, and still leave room for Cavan and Amra to swing their swords without interfering with each other. Even Ehren had room to swing that staff of his. If it came to a fight.

Cavan hoped it didn't come to a fight.

The path here was not dirt or stone, but seemed to be made of thousands and thousands of dark gray needles from the great trees around them. Soft enough that the hooves of their hobbies made no more than a hushing sound as they trotted along. Slower, now that Cavan felt comfortably past those hanging corpses who spoke and chanted through sewn-shut lips.

Or at least as "comfortably past" them as he would feel in this place. And he could not get his mind away from them completely, because the smell of rot clung to the still air. Not the smell of corpse rot, but of wood rot. Tree rot. Decomposing needles and bark, wet and fermented.

More death. And if hanged corpses could rise and interfere, why not trees that smelled of decay?

And it was those trees that made this forest feel cramped.

They didn't look rotted. Despite their odor they looked like healthy pines, with pale gray bark and dark gray needle leaves. But they were far too big to be pines. The smallest of them was as wide as Cavan's sword was long. And the broadest could have been transplanted to the Wailing Woods and fit right in. Easily wide enough that all three of their horses could have stood inside it — nose to tail — and fit.

The canopy of all those trees blotted out what passed for the sky in this place. And yet the trio did not ride in darkness. Not in this place of perpetual twilight. Cavan could pick out no place that glowed. Nothing that provided them relief from the pitch blackness he would have expected under so thick a canopy. Still, all about him was a shadowless world in shades of gray.

The branches of those trees came low enough, even stretched out over the path, that every hundred strides or so, Cavan could have swung his sword over his head and nipped the bark of a low branch.

And the branches felt even lower than that. Cavan felt the urge to duck his head as he rode. To his left he could see Ehren feeling the same urge. Instead of riding tall in the saddle as he usually did, he kept his chin tucked down. Even Amra, to Cavan's right, had her brow furrowed and her neck tucked in.

Must have been the first time in her life she felt too tall.

"I keep expecting to see faces," Amra said. "In the trees, I mean. Eyes watching us. Mouths chanting or gibbering."

"The trees aren't the power here," Ehren said. "I'm not sure what is, but it's above us. Not around us."

"Terrific," Amra said, glancing up. "Well, if it's up there it hides well."

"Shouldn't we be hungry?" Cavan said, desperate to change the subject. "Even if we haven't been riding for hours, it *feels* like we have."

"We don't eat here," Ehren said, shaking his head and keeping his eyes on the high branches. "Nor drink. Same way we haven't sweated away the places Hawkspeaker anointed us. I'm not even sure we're breathing. Not really."

Amra flared her nostrils in a deep, loud inhalation.

"That's not what I mean," Ehren said. "There's more to breathing than air. Deep breaths should relax us. But they don't here. The air is missing something."

"Life," Cavan said. "Nothing in this place is alive. Nothing but us."

"Exactly," Ehren said. "Even our own aliveness is ... suspended here." He shook his head. "But I'm not sure anything is really *dead* here either."

A scuttling noise above them cut off whatever Amra started to say.

"Anyone see it?" Ehren said.

Cavan shook his head.

"No," Amra said. "It was too quick. Sounded big though. Bigger than our horses."

Cavan whistled the horses to a stop.

"What are you doing?" Ehren said, exasperation plain on his face and in his voice. "We need to keep moving. Maybe it won't—"

"It will," Cavan said, voice calm and certain despite the jangling along his nerves. "The corpses wouldn't let us ride past, and neither will this. Better to face it now than waste time trying to elude it."

Amra smiled and drew her sword. Cavan nodded and drew his. Ehren sighed and took his staff in hand.

"You might as well come down," Cavan called. "We know you're there. We don't want trouble, but we're ready to defend ourselves. So whatever it is you want, let's get this over with."

What jumped down from the trees was too big to properly call a "spider." Cavan had seen spiders over the years. Countless spiders. Most of them no bigger than his toenails. Maybe a dozen or two as big as the last joint on his thumb. Perhaps a half-dozen as big as his palm or his whole hand.

The thing that landed quietly in the middle of the road was a spider the same way the gigantic trees mixed in among the forest around them were pine trees — similar in look, but different by orders of magnitude.

It was bigger than their horses. Bigger than all three of their horses. So big that the tips of its eight legs straddled the path ahead of Cavan.

Its whole hairy body was shades of gray. Cavan might have noted a pattern, except two things drew his attention. The first were its dozens of eyes, blacker than the night sky. Black as the mountain behind them had been, but without any glimmer or reflected shine to them. The second were its fangs, each as long as Amra's sword and dripping a pungent, pale gray venom that curled Cavan's nose.

His stomach tightened up in primal fear. All along his spine, nerves shouted that this thing shouldn't exist. And Ehren might have had a point about breathing, because Cavan felt like he might never breathe again.

But training at both wizardry and war had taught him to operate even when frozen in terror. That was why Cavan noticed that his horse didn't rear. Didn't buck. Didn't bolt. Didn't seem to react at all to a sight and smell that should have sent even a fully trained warhorse into a frenzy of self-preservation.

But he noted that only in the back of his head. The cool, collected part of him knew it had a job to do. So his voice sounded surprisingly calm when Cavan said, "Thank you. Please understand that we do not wish trouble with you, but we will defend ourselves if we must. Great need requires us to ride this path to its end. So, please, stand aside and let us pass."

Like the corpses, the spider spoke in a hollow voice, with nothing moving on its body. Not even its venomous fangs.

"Mmmmmmeat," it said.

"We have some rations," said Ehren who, damn him, looked as completely composed and unafraid as Cavan had ever seen him. "We would be happy to share."

"Frrrrresh mmmmmmeat."

"We don't carry fresh meat," Amra said. She, at least, had the grace to look pale. "We'd have to hunt. And I doubt we'd find much here."

"Chooooose."

"You can't have our horses," Cavan said, raising his sword, "and you certainly can't have us. So ask for something else."

"Chooooose."

"Fine. We choose you. Eat yourself."

"Chooooose."

Amra got as far as "Your—" before Ehren cut her off, visibly speaking to Cavan and Amra and not the spider. "No jokes. It's asked three times. Ritual. What if we—"

"We're not giving it anything," Cavan said, refusing to take his eyes off the spider. His stomach settled now as the readiness to fight flowed through his veins. "No sacrifices. No offerings. No parts of ourselves left behind here. And I won't consign our horses to that fate either." Cavan shook his head. "Besides, I refuse to be robbed by a spider."

The spider lowered itself, either to block the path more completely or readying itself to spring. Cavan stood in his stirrups and pointed his sword at the great monster.

"I called and you answered. I thank you for that. I asked what you wanted, and you answered. I thank you for that as well. But you seem to have mistaken curiosity for weakness. We are not your food. We are not your prey. So if all you want is meat, seek it elsewhere. We are travelers." Cavan lent steel to his tone as he said, "And you are in our way."

The spider sprang.

It should have cast a shadow. So gigantic a spider, leaping into the air. Forelegs raised. Fangs wide and dripping. But in this lightless, darkless place between, everything *was* shadows, and nothing *cast* shadows.

A flicker of thought through Cavan's mind. No more. It got as little attention as the foul, pungent smell of the thing's dripping fangs. Because Cavan had been waiting for the telltale twitches that told him the spider was about to spring. Like a tiny ripple of movement through the joints. Something he'd seen countless times in the miniscule things he was used to thinking of as spiders, especially in the tower of Master Powys.

And the moment he saw that same ripple go through the limbs of the gigantic thing in the shape of a spider, Cavan whistled the charge.

The horses bolted forward. As they'd been trained. Cavan held his sword high, ready to block any kicking leg or stabbing fang from the airborne creature. Ehren held his staff two-handed, likewise ready.

Amra chose to attack.

She swung her sword toward the sharp black tip of the nearest spider leg. Her dark blade sheared right through it. Black ichor gushed forth, smelling of rot. Amra tried to twist the blade and reach for the belly of the beast, but it was too high, too close to the apex where horse and spider crossed.

Cavan jammed his sword back into his scabbard. He leaned forward, egging Dzint for more speed while digging through his pouch of spells. Beside him he could hear Ehren's voice weaving prayers out of syllables of Penthix.

"Landed," Amra said, watching the rear as the horses galloped. "Turning. *Running.*"

Cavan held a spell between his fingers. Or at least, the physical part — if physical was the right word in this place. He held a spell he didn't want to cast. A spell he'd always had trouble controlling. And a forest was the worst place to cast it.

But this wasn't really a forest, he told himself. Any more than that was really a giant spider chasing them. Any more than actual corpses had gotten up and tried to hang him.

Weak words. They might not have been enough to make him raise the charcoal seeds where he could see them. Where he could breathe power across them.

But those fangs. Those humongous dripping fangs. One bite and any one of them were done for.

So Cavan did raise those charcoal seeds, and he did breathe power across them.

And he flung them hard over his shoulder as he yelled out, *"Ze axa nah!"*

Boom.

The spell called forth pure fire. Primal fire. Fire that sprang not from wood or lightning or friction, but from its essential nature. Spirit given form. When Master Powys taught Cavan that spell, the great wizard had emphasized the importance of control. Of burning out an obstacle or — in emergencies — a foe. But never letting it get out of hand.

Had Cavan called that spell in a town, or a keep, or a dirt road, he could have controlled it. In a nice, *wet* forest, he could have kept the damage to a minimum.

But this was not a wet forest in the world Cavan knew. This was the place between, where spirit took form readily.

And fire did what it does best.

Consume.

The explosion lent color to the gray world. A great orange light, and a hot wind that blew Cavan's hair and roughspun cloak forward. Amra, who had been looking back, threw her arm over her face, cringing away.

The world was not a cold place now. It was hot as a dry summer day in the desert.

And in the heat behind him, something screamed.

Cavan risked a glance over his shoulder.

The great spider lay crumpled, twitching and burning with

orange flame, legs up. And it did not burn alone. The needles that formed the path behind them burned just as bright. And the trees nearby took flame like seasoned wood.

Cavan whistled the charge again, urging the horses to greater speed.

"A bit excessive," Ehren said, "don't you think?"

Cavan didn't bother responding. But he did glance back to make sure the great monster was dead.

It was. All signs of movement gone from it now, and the flames surrounding it fading to gray. In fact, all the flames were gray now, as though they'd never been orange at all. But orange or gray, the fire spread.

It burned its way out into the forest. It burned its way along the path toward them. It burned its way up among the branches, heading for the canopy.

"More spiders incoming," Amra said, looking up into the now-blazing canopy. She'd sheathed her sword, both hands on the reins.

"Don't throw that spell at them," Ehren said.

"I'm not trying to kill us," Cavan said.

"Could have fooled me," Ehren said.

"Did you *want* to feel those fangs?"

"Focus!" Amra yelled. "Ride hard."

Cavan leaned forward in the saddle, urging Dzint to the best speed his blue roan could manage. Which was impressive, even for a hobby. From the corners of his eyes, he could see Ehren and Amra doing the same on their blonde chestnut and bay.

Cavan's guts felt tight as his shoulders. His hands stayed light on the reins out of habit, but he had to keep working his jaw to keep it loose. So much fire. So many spiders.

So many ways this could go so very wrong.

Fortunately, it seemed the other giant spiders had figured out the riders were the *source* of the fire. They fled from the flames, but showed no signs of interest in Cavan and his friends as they sped past.

The same could not be said of the fire. It spread faster than it should have. Faster than it could have in a normal forest. Perhaps because these trees burned easier. Perhaps because of the nature of the fire in this place. Or perhaps, in this place between, the fire sought a home in the one who summoned it.

Cavan didn't know and he didn't want to find out.

So as the fire spread around them he pressed for more speed. All three horses should have been frothing by now. Fast as they were riding. But no froth came, any more than sweat formed on Cavan's brow under all this heat.

"Oltoss!" Ehren yelled. "Oltoss!"

Oltoss? Did Ehren see it or...

Cavan would have smacked his forehead if he could have risked taking a hand off the reins. Of course. *Oltoss.* Their destination. Focus mattered more here than speed.

But the fire crept ever closer. Cavan was sure he could feel flames licking at his boots.

He refused to look. Instead he focused on Oltoss. Not Oltoss proper, the capitol city where the king made his home, but on Tradeton, the town where Cavan grew up, perhaps a half-day's ride from the capitol. The town that *was* Oltoss, for Cavan...

Cobblestone streets in reds, grays and browns. The stones pulled from the nearby twin rivers. Oaks, ashes and elms everywhere. In the springtime, bluebirds and robins sang their battles for supremacy. And all through the town Cavan would have sworn he could smell bread baking. Homes, inns, even taverns, all baking those dark rye loaves. With a nutty edge that bordered on cinnamon, found only found in Oltoss bread.

Loaves so rich and thick one loaf could sustain a man for two days of hard work. The last bite every bit as good as the first.

Cavan had grown up eating that dark rye bread, and it was Oltoss every bit as much as those cobblestone streets and the two-story stone-and-wood house where Kent had made Cavan welcome. He could remember one summer day — perhaps his sixth summer — tearing hard to split a small loaf between himself and Jamse, his best friend.

Jamse! How long had it been since Cavan had seen his freckled face? His carrot-colored hair? He could almost picture Jamse, the way he was that day. Dirt on his sweaty face. Eagerness in those blue eyes, eagerness for his share of the bread they'd earned by—

"Cavan!" Amra yelled, and he realized she was tugging on his cloak.

Cavan blinked.

They were out of the forest.

ROLLING HILLS OF PALE GRAY ALL AROUND CAVAN, ALONG RIVERS SO dark they were almost black. Starless, cloudless night sky above them again, and the world was once more a place of shivery cold. Cavan, Ehren and Amra sat atop their horses in the middle of a narrow path that looked like slate gray dirt.

Well, Cavan and Dzint were in the middle of the path. To Cavan's left, under Ehren, Highsun's hooves dented pale gray grass. Much as Caramel's hooves did under Amra, to Cavan's right. The path was only truly wide enough for them to ride single file. Why were they risking letting their horses' hooves off the path?

Wait, why were they sweating? Horses and riders. Only Cavan and Dzint seemed as dry as...

Realization like a low gut punch. Doubled Cavan forward in his saddle. One moment he'd been six years old again. The smell of fresh baked Oltoss rye in his nostrils. Dirt and sweat on his forehead, and on Jamse's. But that wasn't right. He'd been here, in this place between. Riding through the fiery woods. Woods burning with flame from his own spell. A spell to burn away that monstrous spider.

"Breathe," Ehren said, one soothing hand on the back of Cavan's neck.

"I thought you said we don't really breathe in this place," Amra said.

"We don't," Ehren said. "And I'm sorry, Cavan, but deep breaths won't be enough to calm you here. Still, you have the habit of calming. You have the practiced techniques of gathering yourself under stress. Draw on those habits now. Those techniques. They will still serve you here because they are part of who you are."

Cavan closed his eyes and pulled into himself. Found his center. Who he was.

I am a bastard, he thought. *The man between families. The man between professions. I am no one thing. But I am.*

It was an old line of thought. Something he developed at first when the well-born looked down on him. Refined through the self-honesty of warrior training, and honed through the self-knowledge of magical training. And so he continued that line of thought. Honest statements about himself, said without judgment.

By the time he opened his eyes again, Cavan was again in control of himself.

"I sweated on the mountain," he said. "I can remember it gelling on my forehead. But not in the forest. And not here. But you sweat here. Why?"

"I have guesses," Ehren said. "Not answers. There's a metaphysical school of thought—"

"It's an arrow flight," Amra said with a shrug.

Cavan and Ehren looked at each other, then at her, eyebrows raised.

"You don't shoot at a distant target by pointing your arrowhead at the target. You have to arc the shot. That forest was probably the middle of the arrow's flight of our arc through this place. Furthest from ..." — she waved her hand — "our world. So the least like it."

Amra shrugged and went back to surveying the area around them, eyes sharp for the next threat.

Cavan looked over at Ehren. Ehren shrugged. "That's as good an explanation as any I have."

"Try not to sound so surprised," Amra said.

Cavan was on the verge of asking why *they* were sweating here, but not him, but stopped the question before it could escape his lips. They'd been sitting still long enough.

Wait. Why were they sitting still?

"Why did we stop?" he said. "We were making good time, weren't we?"

"Too good," Ehren said. "You were pulling away from us. What were you focusing on?"

Cavan thought of Jamse and the rye bread. He shook his head.

"Old memory. Doesn't matter."

"Well, try to include us in the next memory," Amra said.

Cavan and Ehren looked at each other, eyebrows raised again. Amra was always the one of their three who never wanted to hear how Cavan's magic or Ehren's prayers worked.

Could so-very-practical Amra be thinking — finally — about more esoteric matters?

"If you two don't stop giving each other such shocked looks, I'll be more than happy to pound serious expressions onto your faces."

Amra tapped her fist into her palm and fluttered her eyelashes at them.

"Right," Cavan said. "Do your horses need a break?"

"No," Ehren said. "Not here. Not as long as you don't try to leave us behind again."

"You're sure of that?" Amra said, sounding more like the Amra Cavan knew.

"Positive," Ehren said with a nod.

Cavan clucked his tongue and started Dzint forward. Ehren fell into line behind him, and Amra brought up the rear, all three horses now on the slate gray dirt path.

The path wove between pale gray hillsides, while the near-black rivers rushed silently past.

"Two rivers here," Cavan said aloud. "And there are two rivers near Oltoss. Does that mean we're close?"

"I think that lightning bolt of speed you put on earlier means we're close," Amra said. Ehren nodded.

"How will we know when we..." Cavan let his words trail off, because he could see the answer ahead of him now. Just barely visible around a bend in the road, between two hills.

There, on a broad, arched stone bridge that was the gray of a forming storm cloud and nearly as tall as the hills they rode among. A tear in the space above the bridge. Paler than the sky, at this angle, but that was all he could tell. Still. Cavan suspected it was just like the tear they rode through from the Hawkspeaker's ritual site to get to this place between.

At last. At long last, Cavan could see the door back into the real world.

Unfortunately, he could also see a guardian perched in front of it.

At first glance, Cavan had mistaken the guardian for a decoration. It was the same storm cloud gray as the bridge, and it was shaped like a gargoyle. But this gargoyle had bat wings that flexed above the bulging muscles of its humanoid body. And when its head turned to gaze at Cavan, its eyes burned the same vivid orange as the fires of Cavan's spell.

"Guys," Cavan said, but didn't bother saying more because Ehren was already nodding and Amra said, "I see it."

The gargoyle hopped from the ledge of the bridge to stand in front of the rift in space. It spread its wings and completely covered the rift.

And Cavan would have sworn it was smiling.

GOING AROUND THE GARGOYLE DIDN'T LOOK LIKE AN OPTION, THOUGH Cavan did feel some gnawing curiosity about what would have happened if he tried to ride through the rift from the other side of the bridge. Would it even have been there? Would it have taken them home? Or would it have taken them to some third world, even more distant from the world Cavan knew as home?

He couldn't risk finding out.

But thinking about that gave him something to focus on as the trio followed the dark gray path around the curve of the slate-gray hillside to the matching bridge. Slate gray hills. Slate gray bridge. Slate gray gargoyle, except for the burning orange eyes.

Cavan couldn't wait to get home and see greens and browns again. Maybe even a blue sky, if he was lucky.

But first, he had to get past that gargoyle.

The bridge looked broad and stable as Cavan, Ehren and Amra rode closer. It looked like the sort of stonework done by the old Rentissi — lots of decorative carvings and filigree along the rails and the outside of the bridge. And most of the bridges built by the Rentissi remained, as strong and solid as ever. Much like their roads, and more than a few of their castles.

Odd to see their design work here though. Was that a reflection of how close Cavan was to his own world? Amra's arrow-flight theory? Or did it imply that the Rentissi had been here too? Or even were they here even now, continuing to exist, if not really living, here in this place between?

Was the gargoyle an independent creature? Or something carved by the hands of a Rentissi artisan, given life by need and nature in this place between?

Cavan had no time for these questions though. He forced himself to focus on what he knew. What he could tell about this place.

The path before him stopped at the rift. He could see as he approached that, past the rift, the bridge was uniform in its coloring and the dark path did not continue on the other side. The road there was the same slate gray as so many other things around it.

And through the rift, Cavan thought he could see hints of blue sky, but it was so close to gray that might have been a trick of perception.

He could smell magic from the gargoyle. Not in any usual way he detected magical forces, but in a more visceral way. Something about the gargoyle smelled of philters and herbs, the same as every magical laboratory Cavan had encountered or built. Normally the smell relaxed him these days, but here and now it made the hairs on the back of his neck stand up.

The air felt moist, as well as cold here. Cavan considered that a good sign. An indication of how close he was to his own world. Because he did not remember that initial mountain as dusty, or the forest as woodsy. But the water in the air here added to the ambient chill, the way it had so often when Cavan rode over rivers among hills back home.

The gargoyle watched the riders approach, and Cavan noticed that it continued to smile. He decided that this was the expression given to the gargoyle by the artist who carved it, not any sign of malevolent glee.

At least, Cavan devoutly hoped that wasn't an expression of malevolent glee.

He stopped at the foot of the bridge, maybe forty feet from its apex, where the gargoyle — and the rift to home — waited.

"We don't want to fight," Cavan said, though the words came out more perfunctory than hopeful this time. He didn't believe for a moment that the gargoyle would simply let them pass. "So we hope you will step aside and let us pass in peace. This path" — Cavan pointed to the dark gray path that stopped at the rift — "is the path we must follow. We must pass through that rift to return to our world. To save people who are in danger. My family."

Cavan drew himself as straight as he could in the saddle. "So, please, let us pass in peace."

The gargoyle spoke in the same hollow voice as the spider, and the corpses before it. And like them, it spoke without any sign of movement. The gargoyle's frozen smile did not budge as its words came.

"This is your world now. You may not leave."

"No," Cavan said slowly. "This is the world we must pass through to *get back* to our world."

"This is your world now. You have changed it. Burnt its forest. Killed its creatures. You may not leave."

Cavan could feel Ehren's glare, but refused to look away from the guardian as he spoke.

"We defended ourselves when attacked. As we said we would. Any damage beyond that was ... accidental."

Cavan hated that he cringed as he said that last word, but he couldn't help it. He knew well that he might have been able to control the flames. If he'd become a full wizard.

"This is your world now. Forged by your own hand through its challenges. Fed by your memories. You may not leave."

"What *is it* with you people and threes?" Cavan said, throwing up his hands. "Fine. You're not going to answer me now, but I'm telling you straight. My friends and I — and our horses and possessions — are going through that door. Rift. Whatever. I've asked nicely for you to stand aside. But I'm not asking anymore."

Cavan drew his sword in one hand and dug through his spell pouch with the other. To his right Amra drew her sword, and to his left Ehren hefted his staff, a golden glow already limning its length.

Cavan pointed his sword at the gargoyle. "Stand. Aside."

The gargoyle did stand aside, and Cavan felt so surprised he almost lowered his sword.

But then the gargoyle took to the air and spread its arms wide, words coming out of it in a language Cavan didn't recognize.

The rift rippled, and began to close.

SOME FORTY FEET AHEAD OF THEM ON THAT SLATE GRAY BRIDGE, THE rift began to shrink. Already its torn bottom edge was off the path and nearly a foot off the ground.

Cavan dropped his sword and slid from his saddle, his focus entirely on the rift. Searching his mind for what he could remember of the Hawkspeaker's ritual. If he could connect himself to the magic that opened the way, maybe he could stop the gargoyle from closing it.

Beside him he could hear Ehren chanting. See the golden glow of his goddess' magic begin to ebb out from the tall, blonde man.

An arrow from Amra's bow snapped uselessly against the gargoyle's neck.

And the rift shrank another foot.

"Go!" Cavan yelled. "I'll try to hold it open."

"Forget it," scoffed Amra, launching another arrow into the joints of the gargoyle's right wing. It proved no more effective than her previous shot.

"We're not leaving you," Ehren said.

"Take Dzint's reins and get through that rift," Cavan said. "Now. If I don't make it, I need you guys to save Kent."

Those words should have done it. Should have given them more than enough reason to get through that rift before it closed. But Cavan had no more attention to spare for his friends. He could only hope they listened. If he failed, he needed to know that they would be there to save Kent and the others.

And Cavan didn't like his chances. He spoke Ruktuk as well as any non-orc, but he hadn't understood a syllable of the Hawkspeaker's chanting. The symbolism, though. That he'd been able to understand. The chopped wood for the physical link to the rift. The water and the oils he did not have. The spelled blood to tie them to their purpose and to their own world as they passed ... through ... this one...

The spelled blood. That had to be the key. Or at least as close as Cavan could get to it here and now.

Cavan licked his fingertips, and touched them to the mixture of blood on his wrists, then knelt spread some of the residue along his sword blade. He breathed power along the blood, adding some of his own magic to the Hawkspeaker's, in hope that the combination would serve him here and now.

Cavan stood, raised his sword, and charged up the bridge, screaming a battle cry.

The gargoyle swept down to meet him. Or at least to block his way. Hands still wide and lipless chanting still working at closing that rift.

Cavan slid across the smooth bridge stonework on the knees of his leather riding breeches. He flung his sword past the landing gargoyle and at the rift.

"*Zendexi hawnasa ela!*" he yelled at the flying sword.

The breath of his power blended with the magic of the Hawkspeaker. The blade burned with fire the deep green of the Hawkspeaker's skin.

The blade struck the edge of the rift...

...and stuck.

It wedged there in mid-air, like a spike in a door. And the rift, only eight feet wide and tall now — suspended six feet off the ground — shrank no further. And through it, Cavan was sure now that he could see a blue sky peeking out behind the gray.

"Ha!" roared Cavan, pointing at the gargoyle. "My magic is of my world not yours. And my world wants me to come home."

"That may be," the gargoyle said, folding its wings behind it. "But I will kill you first."

Cavan instinctively reached for his sword, but it was busy elsewhere at the moment.

He hopped to his feet, drawing a dagger in each hand. He opened his mouth to give a challenge, but Amra tapped him on the shoulder.

"Allow me," she said, stepping in front of him, that dark metal two-handed sword of hers held high and ready.

"Honestly," Ehren said, stepping forward, his goldenwood staff limned with sunlight, "as though we'd abandon you now."

The gargoyle spread its wings to take to the air, but Ehren cried out in the tongue of old Penthix and a golden dome spread over the four of them. A dome with a ceiling no more than eight feet high.

Amra leapt forward and swung her sword through a series of attacks too fast for Cavan's eyes to follow. The gargoyle blocked each one — at first — with each blow raining chips of stone from its arms and wings without appearing to damage that amazing sword of hers.

Amra pressed her attack, each blow coming faster than the last. The gargoyle backing away steadily until its wings were pressed tight up against the dome. Chips started falling from its torso and head. Its wings began to sizzle where they touched the golden dome.

"Mercy!" it cried. "Mercy!"

Amra stilled her blade, but held it ready to strike straight for the gargoyle's neck. She did not look away from the creature, but Cavan knew she was letting him make the call.

"We should grant mercy," Ehren whispered. "Don't let this place change you."

Cavan gave Ehren a disgusted look and muttered, "As though I'd kill a surrendering foe. What's wrong with you?"

Louder he said, "We will grant you mercy, but you must undo what you did to the rift and you must fly away and let us leave in peace."

"I will stand aside and let you leave in peace, Cavan Oltblood, but I cannot leave the bridge, and I cannot undo what I did to the rift."

"You're lying," Cavan said, stepping closer.

"No," it said, and while Cavan couldn't be certain he heard sincerity in the creature's hollow voice, he definitely heard fear. It continued, "My nature is guardian. I protect. Deny. Withhold. I have no power to open or admit."

"That does make sense," Amra said, not that she lowered her sword.

"All right then," Cavan said, "swear to do nothing to impede us or further reduce the gate. Swear you will move aside and let us pass in peace, doing nothing to attract other guardians or bring any harm to us. Swear these things and we will spare you."

"I swear them by the Rock at the heart of your world, and the Sea at the heart of mine."

Amra glanced back, and Cavan nodded. Ehren dismissed the golden dome.

"Where was that dome when we were facing a spider?" Cavan said.

"Do you really want to talk about how we handled the spider? Here and now?"

"Later for that, boys," Amra said. "Let's go."

She strolled back casually and swung herself up into Caramel's saddle.

"How?" Cavan said.

Amra looked expectantly at Ehren. He shrugged.

Amra scoffed.

"Honestly," she said. "As long as you two have been riding."

She rode Caramel back to the foot of the bridge and turned around. She waved her hands to get Cavan and Ehren to move their horses out of the way. Cavan looked at her. Looked back at the rift. Surely she didn't mean...

"Cavan," she said, "you should come last. Just in case the rift closes when you pass through."

Then she galloped Caramel up the bridge and cleared the lip of the rift in a single bound, vanishing from sight.

Cavan looked at Ehren. "Are you feeling as stupid as I am right now?"

"Let's just not talk about this," Ehren said, riding Highsun back to the foot of the bridge and charging up to the rift before clearing the lip in a single deft leap.

Cavan looked over the gargoyle, now perched on the side of the bridge, where Cavan had first seen it. "If I pulled my sword out..."

"I wouldn't risk it, were I you," the gargoyle said. "That might start the rift closing again."

Cavan sighed and mounted Dzint. He rode back to the front edge of the bridge, then galloped toward the rift. Closer and closer he rode, trying to remember exactly where he should make his leap.

"Up, boy," he yelled at what he hoped was the right spot.

Dzint leapt high into the air, and straight through the rift.

8

———————

THERE WERE A FEW STORM CLOUDS IN THE SKY, BUT CAVAN DIDN'T care. For one thing, they weren't uniformly gray. They were shades of black and dark gray. Even better, they were few, and they were off to the north.

Through the first half of the year, the winds in Oltoss blew from the south. No northern storm would touch them. A southern storm, sure. An eastern or western storm, once in a while. But a northern storm? Never before the peak of summer.

The rest of the sky was gloriously blue. Wonderfully blue. The blue he remembered from childhood, so rich it could have iced a berry cake. Cavan drank the color in with his eyes. Just sat there atop Dzint, grinning at the sky like a madman, and maybe he was. Just a little.

He didn't care. Just seeing colors in the world again was worth a few minutes of madness.

Those dark storm clouds were rolling away, even as he watched. Cavan could feel a touch of the southern wind that carried them, softer down here than up there, but still enough to muss his brown hair and make him laugh. It smelled of rivers and trees and green grass.

Grass!

Cavan slipped down off of Dzint's back and buried his hands in the thick, strong, *green* grasses that grew atop the hill they'd landed on. He knew these hills, maybe an hour's ride south of Tradeton, where he'd grown up. But in the moment, that didn't matter. What mattered was that this grass smelled delightful. Another reason to laugh, and this time he heard Ehren and Amra laughing along with him. They were off their horses too, but still standing. Ehren, through his laughter, was singing some paean to Zatafa.

Their horses only cared about the grass as the meal they no doubt felt was long overdue.

Or did they? True, they were nibbling at the blades, but Cavan knew he had felt no hunger in the other world. Had the horses?

Cavan laughed and rolled onto his back, abandoning the question for the scholars in their high towers. Here the sun was warm and bright and yellow. The sky was blue, and the grass was green. After that deadly, gray world, these things were all that mattered.

Cavan hadn't realized how much he'd missed green grass. After that long trek through the Dwarfmarches, then into the great goldenrod, all of them shades of yellow. But here they grew the green of childhood, complete with tiny yellow-and-white flowers that might have been weeds but he never thought of them as such.

And Cavan was alive, and not trapped in that other world. Alive and alongside Ehren and Amra, the truest friends he'd ever known. Closer than friends. Family.

Family!

Kent!

Cavan was on his feet in an instant, hand checking automatically for his absent sword.

"We have to get moving," he said. "We—"

"We need to sit," Ehren said. "And eat."

"Are you sure?" Amra said, inspecting Caramel. "I would have sworn Caramel would need a rubdown after all that riding, but the signs aren't there. No sweat, no effort in the muscles, even her breathing is relaxed and even."

"The horses don't," Ehren said, "but we do. For our minds and our souls, as much as for our bodies. The horses were spared the worst of the trials by their nature. We're not so lucky."

Ehren dug through that strange bag of his and pulled out strips of jerked beef, hardboiled eggs, and somehow fresh golden cherries and apples. He looked at Amra, who was still stroking Caramel's mane, and at Cavan, who he knew had his agitated let's-get-moving expression, and said, "Sit. Eat."

And Ehren sat.

Amra turned to Cavan and said, "You know what he's like. Better to do it now and spare the lecture."

"I don't lecture," Ehren said as Amra sat. But then he looked at Cavan, eyebrows high. "But if you doubt me, I could *explain* why this is necessary. At length."

Cavan shook his head and sank down to sit cross-legged next to his ... *hobbled* horse?

"When did..." he started, but Amra said, without looking, "While you were busy cloud-gazing. *One* of us has to be responsible, after all."

"Speaking of responsibility," Ehren said, as Cavan tore off a chunk of jerked beef, "let us discuss the giant spider."

"Must we?" Amra said, around a mouthful of hardboiled egg. She swallowed. "We're alive. It's dead. What else matters?"

"More than that spider died, but only that spider threatened us."

Cavan stopped chewing the salty beef and swallowed a hunk. "One of us had to do something. I didn't see you trapping it in any golden domes."

"That's not how they work," he said. "We would have had to be inside the dome."

"Not a bad defensive option, but I'm pretty sure we couldn't have outwaited a spider."

"Or outrun one," Amra said. "Even down a foot that thing practically flew."

"I repeat," Cavan said, meeting Ehren's clear blue eyes, "one of us had to do something."

"And that was all you could think of?" Ehren said. "Burning down the forest? The gargoyle might have let us pass if you hadn't done that."

"We might not have been alive to pass if I hadn't done that."

"Stop," Amra said, and her tone reminded Cavan that — unlike himself — she had commanded men in battle before. She waited until both Ehren and Cavan were looking at her before she continued. "I know you're not a warrior, Ehren, and I don't expect you to be. Cavan's not either, really, but he's had enough training to know a basic rule of battle: action is better than inaction."

Cavan nodded. "I learned it as 'better to do the wrong thing than nothing at all.'"

"That explains so much," Ehren said with a sigh. "If this is what all warriors are taught, no wonder our battles degenerate into—"

"Watch that," Amra said. "You've never fought in a battle. Not anything bigger than the three of us on one side, anyway. So don't talk about what you don't understand." She smiled. "Unless you want me to start espousing opinions about gods and temples."

"Please don't," Ehren said, and Cavan would have sworn the golden priest shuddered at the thought. "But it's a bad comparison. This wasn't some battle between armies. This was us against a single foe. A skirmish."

"A foe that could have killed any of us in a single bite of those huge, poisoned fangs. Why are we even..." Cavan shook his head. "No. I get the problem. Ehren, look. You want me to say I did the wrong thing? I'm not sure I can. Maybe I could have waited longer first. Tried to get out of the forest. But I had no idea how much forest was left to go."

"And it *was* gaining quickly," added Amra, and Cavan felt grateful for her support as he continued.

"Far as I knew, I only had time for one spell, and it had to be big enough to take that thing out." Cavan shrugged. "Too big? Maybe. But it did work."

Ehren drew breath to speak, but Cavan didn't give him the chance.

"That said, you know what I'd do differently if that forest and the giant spider had been here in our world?" Cavan blew out a breath. "I don't know. Maybe stopped to keep the fire from spreading. But if I thought more of those humungous things were coming…"

"Enough," Ehren said, raising a hand. "I had no idea you could cast such a spell. And I'll be honest, the thought of that much destructive power in your half-trained hands makes me wonder a bit about Master Powys' sense of responsibility."

Cavan shrugged. He'd wondered the same thing himself, on more than one occasion.

"But," he said, making a calming gesture at Amra, who apparently had some kind of remark ready, "as long as I know you'll be careful with it in the future, that's really all I can ask."

Cavan considered pointing out that since Ehren had never seen the spell before, obviously Cavan was careful and when and where he cast it. However, he decided to quit while he was ahead.

"Wait," Cavan said, holding up an egg like the physical support of a spell. "You do realize I'm going to keep learning more. In bits and pieces, yes, but I already know more than I learned from Master Powys."

"And I'll expect you to exercise caution with those new spells as well. In fact," — a slow smile spread across Ehren's face, like the sun rising over a tall mountain peak — "I'd be happy to discuss how and when each spell might—"

"Forget it," Cavan said, tossed the whole hardboiled egg in his mouth.

"Worth a shot," Ehren said, and the three of them went back to finishing their meal.

Then, after entirely too long in Cavan's opinion, they were heading into Oltoss.

9

———————

"THEY'RE NOT COMING," QALAS SAID FOR THE FIFTH TIME SINCE DAWN. And for the fifth time since dawn, Tohen considered gutting the man just to still his tongue. Since the sun was only now near its apex, that meant one of the two of them might be dead by day's end. "Either that, or they've come and gone before we got here."

Tohen closed his eyes and sighed. Satisfying as it would be, gutting Qalas was not the answer. The southerner was still a good man with his halberd, even if not as good with that double-curved bow as Tohen had thought. And when Cavan and his cronies did show up, Tohen might need that halberd fighting beside him.

"Sit," Tohen said, pointing to the other chair with one hand and slapping one of those evil little flies with the other. The chairs were weak, and rickety, but then the room was cheap. Creaky, raw floorboards still showed patches of someone's dried blood. A low, slanting roof kept all four of them crouching unless they stood along one wall. The room smelled of must and mildew, though some of that might have been coming from the wooden pitcher full of "fresh" water.

Tohen had demanded a copper pitcher of fresh water from the innkeeper — hand on his sword to emphasize the importance of his request — and gotten it. But the serving man never bothered to take away the wooden pitcher, or even change the dank water. The wooden pitcher sat next to its copper cousin on that small table with uneven legs, next to four wooden cups that were, at least, marginally better than the wooden pitcher.

One of the worst rooms Tohen had stayed in since becoming the chief huntsman to Duke Falstaff. The worst he'd stayed in since he was a wandering mercenary more given to spend his coin on drinks and women than on accommodations.

But he had chosen this room for a reason.

This was a room where no one would ask questions about who stayed here, or why. Where Tohen and his men could come and go by a back stair that regular inn patrons didn't use. And most of all, a room whose single window could provide a view of both the front and rear entrances of the house where Cavan was raised.

The house Cavan had to be heading for as his first stop in Oltoss.

A good plan. As good as any could be. But this was their sixth day in this room. Watching. Waiting. It was only natural for impatience to set in. Tempers to flare. Tohen knew this. Knew he shouldn't give into it.

But he knew he shouldn't take smart talk from the men in his command, either.

Nor should he take the kind of hard look Qalas was giving him, from where he stood near the one, small window. One hand near the dagger on his belt. Smart. Smarter than trying to fight with a halberd in this tiny space.

But intolerable.

"I said sit," Tohen said, one hand casually resting near his sword pommel and the other near a dagger. Just in case. "Don't make me say it again."

Qalas stepped from the window to the chair and perched on the edge, one hand resting on his dagger hilt now. If the flies bothered Qalas, Tohen couldn't tell.

Tohen, by reflex, checked on his other two men. Both sleeping. Lutik stretched out on top of the blankets of the small bed that was miraculously free of fleas and lice. More of Lutik's luck, no doubt.

Luck he'd proven once again by surviving the ride to the healer, despite those awful wounds.

Rudyar slept on the floor, his back against the tall wall, with his huge axe across his lap. One word and he'd be on his feet and ready.

Tohen looked back at the angry Qalas.

"I get it," Tohen said, pulling his hands away from his weapons and folding them across his stomach. "You don't believe we got here faster."

"We," Qalas started in an angry tone, but to his credit he cut himself short with a glance at the sleepers. He flared his wide nose in a deep breath, and continued in a harsh whisper. "We wasted two days in Riverbend getting those two healed. Yes, you got us a teleport. And yes, I'm impressed that you knew that wizard was even there, much less that she'd be willing to help us. But how do you know Cavan didn't get a teleport from the orcs?"

"I'm chief huntsman to Duke Falstaff of Nolarr. That's how."

Tohen allowed himself an evil smile as Qalas started to ask the obvious question, but stopped and settled for glaring as he waited.

"I may not speak that grunting excuse for a language that you're so fond of," Tohen said, "but that doesn't mean I'm entirely ignorant of orcs."

He glanced out the window to get the feel of the street. If Cavan were near, people would recognize him. There would be signs. Enough to get everyone in position before Cavan himself came into view.

Nothing yet, so Tohen looked back at Qalas as he continued.

"What do you know about the Firespear?"

"Biggest clan west of the Dwarfmarches," Qalas said in a tone as suspicious as his expression. "Could probably fight two or three of the other big clans at the same time. Might even win."

"That's not news." Tohen smiled, enjoying reminding Qalas who was in charge and why. "You can't do better than that?"

"Cavan was after the Hawkspeaker. Sounds like a shaman of some sort."

"But you don't *know*."

Qalas sighed and sat back in his chair, despite its creak of protest.

"No orc has ever mastered teleportation," Tohen said with a shake of his head. "Not that I've ever heard, and believe me, if orcs started popping up unexpectedly, word would get out. So Iresk the Hawkspeaker must have provided the next best thing: passage between worlds. Faster than riding, but dangerous and unreliable."

"Fine," Qalas said. "But how do you know they're coming to Tradeton? Maybe they're heading straight for the duke. Sounds like something a hothead like Cavan would do. Or maybe they're heading straight for—"

"They're coming," Tohen said, certainty all through his voice. "He'll want to check for himself. Figure out how bad things are before he acts."

"You're sure about this," Qalas said. "Because if you're wrong…"

"If I'm wrong it's my head on the block, not yours."

"No," Qalas said, and there was anger in his tone again. He wasn't whispering now, but he kept his volume low all the same. "If you go down, you take us with you. And you know it."

"Never said it was an easy job," Tohen said, shrugging as he stood. "But let me tell you three things." He held up a finger. "One. We beat Cavan here." He held up a second finger. "Two. He *is* coming here, and when he gets here we'll be ready. My gut says it's soon."

He leaned forward and held up a third finger. "Three. Wake Rudyar and get some sleep. If I don't get a break from your nattering I'll add your blood to the stains on these floorboards."

Qalas reached for his dagger, then stopped himself. Eased his hand back away. He stood tall, breathing through his nose, likely because he'd clamped his jaw shut. He turned to wake up Rudyar.

Tohen smiled and went back to the window.

Soon.

10

———

Even Dzint's hooves on the cobblestones of Tradeton sounded like home to Cavan. And not just because of the near-soundless gray world they'd ridden through to get here — though Cavan knew deep inside he'd be seeing, hearing, and smelling that place and its disturbing inhabitants in the quiet hours of the night for some time to come.

But each clop of the blue roan's hooves might as well have been saying "home." How long had it been since he last rode through these streets? Five years? More? Had to be more, since he'd been riding with Ehren and Amra longer than that, and he'd never been here with them. Never been closer than the outskirts of the countryside, not with them.

Certainly not on such a fine day, the mid-afternoon sun almost gentle after the relative heat near Riverbend.

Still, worry gnawed at Cavan's gut. Worry about Kent and his family. Made the jerked beef, eggs and cherries Ehren had forced on him gurgle uneasily in his stomach. He might have sped the horses the rest of the way, except that he knew better. Fast riders drew attention, and if Falstaff had hunters after him, drawing attention was the dumb move.

He needed to move like a traveler, slow and smooth. Just another rider following the road through town to the capitol. Maybe with hopes of making it there before full dark.

Even so, even with so much on his mind, Cavan could not stop himself from seeing the streets around him with the eyes of childhood.

So much still looked the same, even though that could not have been true. He knew from long experience that the hills he, Ehren and Amra had arrived on should have been a good hour south of town. But the ride here had not taken nearly that long.

Tradeton had expanded. But the builders still followed the same familiar patterns Cavan knew so well.

All the buildings were stone and wood, and most of them painted in browns and reds. Most of the shops and smaller homes had stone foundations and cellars, but the rest was all wood. Maple, oak or beech for those who could afford it, pine or spruce for those who couldn't. The bigger buildings, the inns, guildhalls and larger houses, they all had stonework first floors before the wood began. Some few, like the masons' hall in the town square, were all stone.

The masons' hall was a grand thing. Four stories tall, fashioned from red, white, and black stones, with veins of blue in swirling decorations. All handcrafted from stone, without so much as a drop of paint or a single spell, they say.

The wealthy of Tradeton had glass windows. The poor had wooden shutters. And between the two were houses and shops with one or two glass windows mixed in among the shutters. As much a mark of progress and standing as to provide a flyless view.

And the flies were bad this time of year, just as he remembered. Not the full heat of summer yet, but the tiny buzzing things pestered the horses. Not that they left the riders alone. Well, they left Ehren alone. Amra grunted irritation each time she slapped at one. Cavan didn't bother. He'd remembered them too well to make the effort.

The streets fell into two categories — a few were narrow and straight, to accommodate scouts and messengers. The rest were broader, but tightly curved as they wove through town. Cavan was riding on a narrow, straight street now, surrounded by single story houses and shops. No makers here. No smiths or wheelwrights or masons or such. They weren't allowed on straight streets. Only cheaper housing, rooms to let, and at every corner, a two-story building that looked like an inn but doubled as a barracks.

King Draven did not believe in letting enemies ride any straight streets.

Made sense though. From where he rode, Cavan could see all the way to the town square. The great masons' hall. The three-branched temple of Ulsina, the Lady of Ways. Even a hint of the mayor's grand mansion, which served as both his home and his place of business. He could see all the way through, even hints of the capitol in the distance.

But that was down the street. Here on this block were some of the poorer townsfolk, going about their days. Carrying sacks or crates to or from the market square or any of the shops on other streets. No carts here. Too narrow. Not even any other horses. The denizens of the narrow streets probably couldn't afford horses, and couldn't have stabled them nearby if they could.

No vendor working this street except Old Jan, as much a fixture of Tradeton as the masons' hall. Wrapped, as always, in faded green linens over her ageless frame. Yes, she was withered with wisps of white hair, but no more than she'd been when Cavan was a boy. Or so it seemed to him now.

"How much farther?" Amra said. Apparently she was far less interested in Old Jan, or the apples she sold from her cart, than Cavan was.

But then, Amra didn't know that this woman had been selling apples since Kent was a child. That, at the start of the season, she had golden apples that rivaled anything Ehren could pull from that strange brown backpack of his.

Too late in the season for those apples now. All she had were her reds, which were as ordinary as her hump.

"Want to try again?" Cavan said to Amra. "I doubt they heard you in the capitol."

Amra gave him a look that clearly said, "Answer my question or you'll hear how loud I can ask."

"Not far," he said quickly. "We'll just need to hang a left at the third barracks. Which isn't actually a barracks these days. Or maybe it never was one. Last I heard it was a brothel, and—"

"Cavan," Ehren said, showing at least enough sense to keep his voice down, "we don't know which is the first barracks, much less—"

"The taller buildings at the corners," Amra said. "Not all of them though. Maybe every other. So the third barracks would be about six streets from here."

"Four," Cavan said, impressed.

"Then you're counting a barracks that isn't one," Amra said with a shrug.

Cavan started to object, but Ehren cut in ahead of him. "Don't bet on it, or you'll lose money to her."

Cavan closed his mouth. Amra smiled and fluttered her eyelashes.

"Bigger question," she said, "what are we going to do about the ambush?"

Cavan stopped riding.

"Get that horse moving," she said, "you want the whole town to notice us?"

As if to make her point, she waved at three children running playful circles around their harried-looking mother. The children didn't notice, too swept up in their game. Apparently travelers riding on this street weren't all that uncommon. Even three riding abreast, which meant the locals had to press against the buildings to let them pass. But apparently that wasn't uncommon either.

Ambushes, though, were another story.

"What do you mean ambush?" hissed Cavan as he started Dzint forward.

"You think the duke only sent four hunters?" Amra raised her eyebrows. "You think there aren't armed men watching Kent's shop right now? Waiting for us?"

Cavan blinked. Between the worries that pushed him to get here, and the unexpected overwhelming memories, he hadn't thought about that at all.

"What do we do?" he asked.

"You're adorable," Amra said with a chuckle. "Listen up. This is how it's going to go."

———

CAVAN HAD TO ADMIT HE WAS IMPRESSED. FOR A WOMAN WHO HAD never been to Tradeton before, Amra had quickly grasped the flow and feel of the streets. The anti-ambush plan she'd sketched out would have had a reasonable chance of letting the three of them fight off a force of four or five times as many armed warriors.

It only had one problem: Ehren.

The moment Amra had finished describing her plan, Ehren turned his horse onto a side street. This turn was two blocks early, onto a curving affair that would take them away from the center of town before it joined up with a wide, snaking street that would lead the way they needed to go.

He made the move without warning, so that Cavan and Amra had to follow before they could even ask why. Ehren reined to a halt two buildings in, in front of a tavern, the Empty Chest. A brown-and-copper two-story affair with shuttered windows. Two stories was odd for a tavern without an inn, meaning the owners either slept upstairs, or they rented private rooms for one reason or another.

Cavan reined up next to Ehren. Amra joined a moment later. Her mouth was set in a line, nostrils flaring in irritation. But she did not look to be in a hurry to ask the question on Cavan's mind, so he asked it himself.

"Care to tell us why you've—"

"This is not some wilderness," Ehren said, before Cavan could even finish the question. "We are not facing bandits who would kill us for our horses and everything we carry, and we're not fighting some kind of war. This is a *town*. And I will not have us fighting in the streets like brigands."

"Men are waiting to kill us," Amra said. "I doubt stern conversation will dissuade them."

"And those are the only two solutions you see?" he said. "Stern conversation or spilled blood?"

"Most conflicts come down to one or the other," Amra said with a shrug. "And time could be a factor."

"If we knew the angle of their attack," Cavan said, thinking through the spells he knew, "I might be able to cast something."

"All right," Amra said, one hand raised against the rising anger in Ehren's clear blue eyes. "Why don't you tell us what *you* would have us do before it explodes out of you in some kind of sunburst."

"There is no warrant for Cavan's arrest, yes? No formal writ to have him detained, much less killed on sight?"

"Couldn't be," Cavan said. "If Falstaff issued anything formal, word would spread and the king would want to know why."

"Exactly," Ehren said. "Instead he sent his own hunters after you. Men loyal to him, who won't talk about why they're doing what they're doing. And they have the crest of the king's own brother on their shoulders, so no one is likely to interfere if they see them in action. Most people will just accept any explanation they give."

"Which is why," Amra said, with as much patience in her voice as Cavan had ever heard — which, admittedly, wasn't much — "we must kill them before they kill us."

"Wrong," Ehren said, and now he was smiling. He looked back and forth, but Amra didn't seem to see his logic any clearer than Cavan did. Ehren sighed and said, "If they kill us and people ask questions, they can say they were on the duke's own business, and no one will likely interfere. Right?"

Cavan nodded.

"But they haven't killed us yet."

"Yes," Amra said. "That's the part we're trying to avoid. Keep up, Ehren."

"You keep up," he said, but he was still smiling. "Explaining dead bodies is one thing, but explaining murders they haven't committed? That's something else entirely."

Cavan felt his eyebrows raise and a smile light his face. But Amra didn't seem to get it yet, so Cavan said, "You want to go to the town guards now."

"Exactly." Ehren's smile got even broader. "You're known here, and everyone knows that Kent the Jeweler raised you."

"Oh," Amra said. "So you want us to go to the town guards and tell them we think something's happened to Kent. They'll escort us. The hunters won't be able to attack us with the guardsmen right there."

"Better than killing people we don't have to."

"Maybe," Amra said, but she didn't look convinced. "No guarantee we'd be able to leave safely. Plus, they'll probably figure out our next move and get to set up for another ambush. And maybe that one won't have a predictable kill zone. The safer way is to kill these hunters now."

"Suppose we do," Cavan said. "Suppose there's a dozen of them and we kill them all here and now. More will come, and next time there won't be a dozen. There'll be two dozen. Or three."

"He has a point," Ehren said.

"This way," continued Cavan, "at least we aren't guaranteeing ourselves a bigger fight next time. And if we're lucky, we'll catch sight of them while we're with the guards. Maybe get a look at what we'll be in for."

Amra opened her mouth to speak, but hesitated, and closed her mouth. Then she smiled a wicked smile, and said, "Make you a deal. How about you two go to the guards and get an escort, while I do a little reconnaissance?"

"Just reconnaissance?" Ehren said, one golden eyebrow suspiciously low.

"That's all I plan on," Amra said. "I'll swear to Zatafa if you like. Mind you, I'll defend myself if I have to..."

"Save your swearing," Ehren said. "Zatafa wouldn't be fooled by it."

"Come on," Cavan said. "She won't want to fight on a reconnaissance mission. That would mean she wasn't sneaky enough to avoid detection."

Cavan winked at Amra, who started chuckling.

"Fine," she said. "No fighting. Just a look around."

And with that she turned Caramel off in a different direction, while Cavan and Ehren rode for the nearest guard outpost.

11

TOHEN AWOKE TO THE SOUND OF HARSHLY WHISPERED ARGUING.

He'd been dreaming something about orcs and great goldenrod stalks, but now he was awake, and his head hurt, and his mouth was dry. And his men were arguing.

One hour. All he'd wanted was one hour before the moon rose high again, and his men couldn't even give him that.

He sat up on the lumpy straw mattress. His eyes fixed on Qalas, first thing, but the dark-skinned blue-eyed southerner stood to one side, his great, double-curved bow in hand, but down. An arrow ready, but not nocked.

And he wasn't involved in the argument.

Over beside the small window, Rudyar had an arrow nocked and was trying to take aim. Lutik wouldn't let him. And the two of them were practically hissing at each other.

"Stand aside."

"Don't shoot."

There were other words thrown in — with a generous helping of curses for good measure — but that was the gist of it, as far as Tohen's aching head could puzzle out.

"What?" Not a mere question. He made it a command. And his men knew it.

Lutik stepped aside, hands raised to show no threat, and turned to face his commander. Rudyar lowered his bow, relaxed his grip on the arrow and string, and turned to face Tohen as well.

Qalas only watched.

"It's Cavan," Rudyar said, sounding for all the world like a child having a toy stripped away from him. "He's in view right now!"

"He's not alone," Lutik said. "Town guards are with him."

"This is what we've been waiting for." Rudyar's shooting hand started twitching with the need to turn and loose before his quarry fled.

Tohen got to his feet, rubbing his temples, and stepped to the window.

Cavan all right, on that blue roan of his. That white-clad priest beside him on the blond chestnut. Ehren. And surrounding them, four town guards. All four with crossbows raised and looking around for trouble.

Tohen stepped back from the window.

"Put that thing away," he said to Rudyar. To Lutik he said, "Thank you for preventing a disaster."

"We're the duke's hunters," Rudyar started, but Tohen cut in over him.

"And this is *the king's* land." He let those words sink in a moment before adding, "What did I tell you? *No important witnesses.*"

"That usually means nobles," Qalas said, and from the look in his eye Tohen was damned sure Qalas knew better.

"Well, then I'll say this real slow so I can be sure you understand. We have an *order* to kill Cavan. Not a writ. Not a license. Nothing formal at all. We get caught *doing this* by anybody with the power to object, and the duke will probably let them hang us."

"But—" Rudyar started.

"But we've killed men in front of witnesses before," Tohen finished for him. "What's the missing link, Rud?"

"Never town guards," Qalas said, apparently eager to remind

Tohen that he did, in fact, understand. "Never soldiers. Never nobles. Never rich merchants."

"Right," Tohen said. "Never in front of anyone who matters. But if you'd been paying attention, you'd have noticed two things that are very important to us right now."

"Those guards have crossbows," Lutik said, "and they're looking for us."

"They're looking for *someone*," corrected Qalas. "Cavan couldn't know we got a teleport, but he'd know the duke has more than four men."

"Important," Tohen said, "but secondary to the other point."

"Where's that warrior woman?" Lutik said, realization spreading across his face and leaving a sickly pallor in its wake. Not that Tohen could blame him. Tohen still wasn't sure how Lutik survived those cuts.

"Amra," Qalas said.

"Maybe she died," Rudyar said. "Dangerous between the worlds, you said."

Lutik scoffed, and Tohen smirked.

"No way we got that lucky. If she's not with them..."

"...she's looking for us," finished Qalas.

"Right."

"So we find her first?" Qalas said. "We take her out, the other two will go down easy."

"Not a bad plan," Tohen said, wishing his head would stop aching. He hated changing plans on less than two hours sleep. He'd done it time and time again over the course of his career, but he still hated doing it. "But not good enough. No way we can take her out without it getting noisy and messy. That'll draw attention we don't want. Plus, she may have some means of contacting the other two."

Tohen shook his head.

"What then?" Qalas said with the impatience that Tohen was coming to know so well.

"We filter out one at a time. Hoods up and weapons concealed.

Ride out to the rendezvous spot by different routes, and wait until we're all together."

"And then?" Lutik said.

"He came here first," Tohen said, pointing toward the window and Cavan beyond it. "That's good. That means I'm getting a feel for the way he thinks. Wasn't expecting him to bring guards, but that's fine. More information."

"But what good does it do us?" Qalas said.

"It means I know where he's going next." Tohen smiled. "And this time, I'll have a pretty good idea of the route he'll take. We can hit him before he knows to look for us."

Even Qalas nodded at that.

"Rudyar," Tohen said, "you're first."

As he watched the big man try to hide that bushy blond hair and beard under a green hood, Tohen cursed that orc shaman again. Cavan and his cronies should have at least had to abandon their horses. Fresh horses, ones not yet trained to their system of battle commands, would have given Tohen a significant advantage.

Well, he thought as he rubbed his temples, *I'll just have to make due.*

12

Cavan always figured that if he returned home under armed guard, he had to be in some sort of trouble.

Then again, he never expected Jamse to be leading those guards. For that matter, he never expected to see Jamse in a guard uniform, much less with a diagonal sergeant's stripe across the left breast of his chainmail. Jamse had been just as much a troublemaker of a kid as Cavan had been. Maybe more. Certainly the last person Cavan would have guessed would...

Then again, Jamse had none of his father's talent for cobbling. Had to make his living some way...

Almost as odd to Cavan was that the town guards wore chainmail now. Cavan wondered when that had changed. When he was a kid, they'd worn leather that always looked well broken-in. Sometimes even in need of repairs. The guards had tended toward blunt weapons in those days, the kind that didn't need much training. Maces, clubs, that sort of thing.

These days the town guard looked like soldiers. Chain mail from the neck down. Steel caps with nose guards. Tabards over the chainmail, the royal sigil on the right shoulder — twin rivers crossing at a heart, on a pale blue background — town's seal on the left shoulder — three gold coins against a green background.

They all wore swords now, in addition to their clubs. Short swords, but still. And they had small, round shields on their backs, the kind with a jut in the middle that could pack a punch, if swung right.

Their armament didn't stop there. Crossbows weren't only for special units of the town guard anymore. Apparently every guard was expected to carry and use one, when the need arose.

Cavan wanted to ask about these things. Wanted to ask how Jamse ended up a guardsman, too. But this was not the time. And he knew, as he looked around, watching the rooftops for archers, that this was not the place either.

"I don't see anyone," Jamse said. He had even more freckles now than he did as a child. And though his red hair was trimmed short under that steel cap, he still apparently had just as much trouble keeping his face free of dirt. "You're sure they're there?"

"Positive," Cavan said. "They hit us once on the road coming here. And they knew this was our destination."

"Get inside then," Jamse said, eyes still scanning for trouble. "We'll take a look around." He glanced at Cavan, and just for a moment Cavan saw the friend he remembered so well, underneath the sergeant. "If you need long in there, I can't guarantee we'll be here when you come out."

"Of course," Cavan said. "Thanks, Jamse. Believe me when I tell you you saved lives today. Maybe even ours."

Jamse smiled, and Cavan would have sworn a quip made it as far as his old friend's lips before fading out. Not the time or place. But reassuring.

With town guards watching their backs, Cavan looked over the back of the house where he grew up. Three stories, the first two of stone. Glass windows on the second and third floors, no windows at all on the first. Kent preferred to work by torchlight, and he refused to tempt thieves by allowing breakable glass windows in his shop.

The shop was the front part of the first floor, plus the basement for storage, gem cutting and jewelry making. But here at the back, the green wood door set into large, mortared blocks of stone. The latch had a lock, and if the family had followed Kent's rules, a steel bar reinforced the door.

Kent *hated* thieves.

"Have you been carrying a key all this time?" Ehren said.

"After a fashion," Cavan said.

He raised his hand to his mouth and breathed power across it while whispering a certain word. He pressed his hand against the top right corner of the door, where he had inscribed a certain symbol before painting over it with green paint. The green paint didn't matter. The symbol was still there, and still carried the power Cavan had breathed over it that day, so many years ago.

On the other side of the door, the bar thunked out of place.

Cavan wiggled his eyebrows at Ehren and opened the latch.

Blood and raw meat. The first smells assailing his nose. Not fresh meat either. Rank, like whatever it was had been left to rot where it fell.

Cavan's heart began pounding. He started forward, hand reaching for his absent sword, but Ehren stilled him with a hand on the shoulder.

"Slow," he said. "Careful. If they can set an ambush outside, they can set one inside."

"The bar was in place," he said.

"And who set it?" Ehren said.

Cavan shook his head. Ran through calming exercises. Got his breathing and heart rate under control. Only then did he push the door all the way open.

Small stone entryway. A door into the shop, open. Next to it, stone stairs going up.

"Is that door usually open?" Ehren whispered.

Cavan shook his head.

They stepped inside the green door and closed it behind them. The raw meat smell clung to the air, coming from somewhere up the stairs.

The blood-covered stairs.

Well, not quite blood-*covered*, but there was a definite trail of blood leading up — or down — those stairs.

If this was a trap, that was the way Cavan was supposed to go. No doubt whoever did this expected him to rush straight up the stairs.

"Down first," Cavan said, following the blood trail into the main room of Kent's shop.

Cavan remembered this room so well. The way it was supposed to look. Large mirrors along the walls, of brass, copper and silver, all hammered and smoothed not for vanity, but to reflect a different quality of light. Kent always said that gems and jewels had to be seen in three different lights to be truly understood.

Kent didn't count sunlight among those lights. He called sunlight a cheat. Said it made everything beautiful, so nothing could be judged fairly.

The mirrors were still in place. That was something.

Kent always kept one large, smooth oak table in the center of the room, where he would meet with customers and show them wares he thought they would appreciate. Not like, or love. Those were never the words Kent used. "Appreciation is what matters," he always said. Customers who appreciated a piece would take care of it and display it well.

The tables were overturned now. Kent's stool was broken.

Cavan knelt by the stool. Picked up the pieces. The seat was still intact, but the legs were shattered. Ehren stood over him, saying nothing.

"Kent made this stool," Cavan said. "When he was young. Before he found his flair for gems and jewels. Tried to be a carpenter." Cavan looked up at Ehren. "He could never get the legs even. It always teetered. But he didn't mind. He said the best gems were the ones with a slight flaw."

Ehren gave Cavan a moment to set down the pieces of the stool before saying, "There's more blood over here."

He was right. Had been a puddle. Wide across as Cavan's hands laid side-by-side. That was the start of the trail that led to the stairs up.

"What's behind that door?" Ehren said.

By reflex Cavan looked up at the front door. But it was locked and barred as it was supposed to be. He shook his head and looked at the other door. At the back of the room, where it would lead under the stairs to the second floor.

"That's the cellar door," Cavan said, relaxing his mind and stretching out with his feelings. "Still locked."

"We should check it."

"No," Cavan said, shaking his head. "You misunderstand me. That's spell-locked. Did it myself. No one could open it but Kent. Or me." Then another possibility occurred to Cavan. "Or one of his sons. If Kent's dead."

"They could have made him open it," Ehren said, soft, like if he'd said the words too loudly they would have become true.

"Not Kent." Cavan shook his head. "He'd die before he'd bring anyone down there. He really hates thieves."

"Maybe," Ehren said. "We should check it anyway. They might have threatened his wife."

"Maybe," Cavan said, rising to his feet and dropping the seat of the broken stool. "But first, we need to check upstairs."

* * *

CAVAN PICKED UP ONE OF THE BROKEN STOOL LEGS TO USE AS A CLUB. Not as good as a sword, but better than nothing. He kept a dagger in his other hand, just in case. A thin one, edged on both sides, with a wooden handle molded to his grip. And along the blade, certain symbols Cavan had engraved himself.

Ehren wanted to lead the way up the stairs, but Cavan wouldn't let him. Stepped in front and took the stairs one at a time for probably the first time in his life. Or at least, the first time since his legs had grown long enough to make more than one stair per stride an option.

He went slowly now.

Light filtered in through a glass window at the top of the stairs. Couldn't see the upstairs landing yet, much less the door to the household, but he could see the gray stones of the stairs and walls.

And he could certainly see the blood. A thinning trail. Like the bleeder was running dry. Dragged up the stairs, dying. Cavan had to fight not to picture it. To keep himself from guessing if this was Kent's blood. Or Reed's or Alec's. One of their wives'. Maybe even one of their children's.

Anger burned through Cavan. Sped his heart and forced his breaths out through clenched teeth. He could feel the grip on his weapons growing white-knuckled.

He had to pause halfway up the stairs to get hold of himself. To run through a quick calming exercise and bring his focus back to the world around him. Shut out the fantasies that did not serve him.

He still felt the tightness in his gut. That he held onto. Anger had power of its own, and Cavan would not surrender it entirely.

Through calmer eyes, the blood didn't look so fresh. Cavan could see that it was dry, as the puddle had been downstairs. Old blood. But the smell of blood in the air was still strong. The smell of rotted meat too.

Cavan started up the stairs again. He could feel Ehren behind him, more than hear him. Ehren was like a warm, silent, comforting presence at his back.

Small landing at the top of the stairs. And it was the top. These stairs went no higher. Cavan knew a separate wooden flight of stairs would lead to the top floor, the apartments Kent shared with his wife.

The landing was more gray stone, a red-and-gold striped rug running down the center. Wide enough to walk on. Or drag a body. Cavan could see spots of blood on the carpet, brown against the red and gold.

The landing was wide. Growing up it had felt big as a castle. Later he realized it was wide enough to bring in furniture.

Now the landing's width only told Cavan that Ehren had room to swing his staff.

More important, the double doors at the end of the short hall stood open. Not a crack. Not halfway. All the way open, as though to receive guests. Straight ahead Cavan could see the hat rack and cloak rack. Still at least a dozen men's and women's hats on the rack, but the cloak rack looked like a barren tree of blond, oiled wood.

Cavan could hear something now. A fluttering sound. Wings?

He glanced back at Ehren. Ehren nodded. He heard it too.

Cavan waited for Ehren to join him on the landing. Not wide enough to fight side-by-side. Not really. But it would do in a pinch.

"What are we in for?" Ehren whispered.

"It sounded like..." Cavan started, but stopped as soon as he realized what Ehren meant.

"Sitting area ahead and left. Dining table farther left past that. Far left corner, a door leading upstairs." He pointed to the wall to their left, with the chair leg. "Four rooms there. Used to be the order was Reed, me, Alec. No idea what those rooms are used for now. Last room is the kitchen."

Ehren nodded.

Another flutter.

Cavan drew a deep breath and jumped into the room.

It looked disturbingly pristine, despite the rank smell, even stronger here.

The big, comfy blue couches Cavan remembered in the sitting area. Three of them, set up around the triangular coffee table. Big window on the wall to his right, unbroken. Big window on the far wall, unbroken. All the doors closed. The tapestry next to the sitting area window, done in red and gold like the carpet around the couches, showing the path of a gemstone from mine to necklace.

The dining table yet stood. Seven of its eight high-backed chairs empty.

In the eighth chair was a corpse, bloody and picked at by the room's other occupant.

A hellcrow.

Big as a small dog. Eyes that blazed yellow flame. A sharp black beak that could cut through the stone walls of this house. Black wings, but the feathers of its body were white tinged with red. Like blood on snow. Black talons big enough to grab Cavan's shoulder. If it got close enough.

The hellcrow perched atop the high back of the corpse's chair, busily finishing off what looked like a bite of cheek when Cavan jumped into the room.

The hellcrow looked up, coughed almost like a normal bird, and cawed.

The caw was nothing like any normal crow could produce. Loud as the screams of the damned, and piercing as its beak. Every window in the room shattered, scattering glass to the streets below.

Cavan nearly dropped his weapons, reeling from the pain. He slammed his wrists against the sides of his head to try to shut off that hellish racket, but too late. His ears must have burst. He was sure he could feel blood trickling down his jaw.

And the world went silent as the grave.

Ehren sped past Cavan into the room. A golden glow surrounded both him and his staff, but Cavan could see blood trickling from his ears as well.

Cavan ran forward to join him.

The hellcrow took to the air. Closed the distance between to Cavan with a single flap.

Cavan's chair leg and dagger came up by reflex, between himself and the flying creature. Sparks flew where a talon ground across the dagger blade, and Cavan could feel the heat even through the grip. His chair leg thumped against the hellcrow's body, but if he hurt it he couldn't tell.

But he kept that beak from his throat for at least a first pass.

Cavan whirled, trying to keep the hellcrow in sight while it circled them for its next attack.

Golden sunlight flared out of Ehren. A dome? No. An attack. Like a wave of power in all directions at once, but only striking the hellcrow.

Cavan imagined a splatting sound he couldn't hear, like swatting a fly.

If only.

The hellcrow was knocked back against the wall.

Cavan threw his dagger. Caught the hellcrow in the chest. Black blood trickled out, and the rotted meat smell grew stronger.

The hellcrow leapt back into the air with a mighty flap.

Cavan screamed words he couldn't hear. Words keyed to the symbols he'd carved into that thin dagger. Words to trigger the spell those symbols represented.

Green fire burst out from the blade.

The hellcrow flew into the ceiling. Green flames spreading through its body, burning the thing away from the inside. The hellcrow's beak snapped nonstop, as though cawing or crying in pain. But Cavan could hear nothing.

The hellcrow fell to the floor, and the fiery yellow light in its eyes went out.

Cavan struck the body once with his chair leg, just to be sure, but it looked dead.

He pulled back out his dagger.

A hand on his shoulder. Cavan whirled, weapons high.

Only Ehren, who pulled his hand back tapped his ear while his other hand held his goldenwood staff at the ready.

Cavan shook his head and shrugged. He pointed his dagger at his ear, then made a cutting motion. He turned to see about that corpse at the dinner table.

Ehren sighed, and Cavan thought he saw exasperation. The priest held up one hand to keep Cavan from turning away.

Ehren's lips moved as if in prayer, then he kissed his fingers and touched each of Cavan's ears.

Sound rushed back into the world. Shouting from outside. Sounded like orders. Wind whistling through the broken windows. Boots on the stairs behind him.

Cavan whirled in time to see Jamse lead his guardsmen into the room, crossbows pointing.

Jamse looked at the dead hellcrow, then up at Cavan.

"Guess you didn't need the help," Jamse said.

"We're not done here yet," Cavan said.

***

CAVAN HAD NEVER FELT SO GUILTY TO BE GRATEFUL SOMEONE WAS ALIVE.

The corpse hadn't been Kent, or either of his sons. And the corpse had been male, so it couldn't have been any of their wives. An *adult* male, which meant it couldn't have been any of Alec's or Reed's children. If they had children.

And the moment Cavan realized that, relief washed over him. But guilt followed hot on its trail, because a man was dead. To lay a trap for Cavan.

The dead man had to have been Kent's assistant. Either someone to help out while Alec and Reed were traveling, or perhaps to do their work, if they'd opened up shops of their own.

So long. Cavan had been away so very long. Didn't know Kent had hired an assistant, much less the man's name. He didn't even know if Alec and Reed were married — much less had children — or if they'd founded shops of their own. Or moved. Or if they were still living in their old rooms.

Their rooms had looked much the way Cavan had remembered them, but that told him nothing. Cavan's own room sat waiting for his return.

And Jamse had never gotten along with Alec and Reed. Once Cavan left, Jamse had scarcely even kept an eye on Kent.

But that body, the one the hellcrow had been dining on, that wasn't Kent. And it wasn't Reed or Alec. And Cavan couldn't help the swell of hope that all three were still alive, even if they were probably being held somewhere, as bait for him.

If they were still alive, Cavan could try to keep them that way. But if they were dead, then the gods themselves would not keep Cavan from Duke Falstaff's throat.

Nothing else in the place had been touched. The fresh blood and rotted meat smell had come from the hellcrow, and with the windows broken, the afternoon breeze cleared the smell away soon enough.

Kent's rooms upstairs were just the way Cavan remembered them, down to the way he arranged his pillows — four feather pillows forming a rectangle at one end of the large, wide mattress. Oh, a few things were different, but nothing that couldn't be explained by his marriage to Rena. Nothing that looked out-of-place, or like a signal to Cavan.

Even Kent's family sword was still there. Well, Kent called it his family sword. His father had served in the king's army for a time, during the Winter War. Came home with a longsword and hung it on the wall. Kent, his father's only son, inherited it, but neither Alec nor Reed wanted it. So it had stayed on the wall above Kent's bed.

It needed oil and a whetstone, but Cavan took that longsword and its scabbard, and hung them from his belt. He'd need a new one of his own soon enough, but the image of swinging Kent's father's sword while fighting to rescue Kent and his sons appealed to Cavan.

Ehren agreed with him.

Nothing odd down in the basement either. Except for the dust. Kent always dusted that room himself, in part because he wasn't willing to let anyone else do it, but mostly because he insisted that his work area be dust free.

Dust in the basement meant that even Kent's abductors hadn't been able to get past Cavan's wards. Good.

Now Cavan stood with Ehren just inside the half-open green back door. Jamse and his men were gone. They'd stayed long enough to inspect the scene, then Jamse had sent two of his men for boards to cover the broken windows. They'd helped nail the boards in place — while Ehren cleaned up the blood — before Cavan warded the windows as well.

Amra was not back yet. With the rest of the house locked up, that was the only reason to stay and wait.

"Why kill an innocent?" Cavan said. "The assistant. What did it serve? A warning? I already know they're after me."

"Food for the hellcrow," Ehren said. "They couldn't know how long it would take you to arrive. Needed the hellcrow satiated enough to wait."

"Yeah, I imagine it would have attracted attention if it started killing locals at random."

"What's this about killing locals?" Amra said, stepping up to the doorway. Her eyes immediately spotted Cavan's new sword, but she said nothing.

Cavan blinked at her sudden arrival, wondering why he hadn't heard her horse approach on the cobblestone streets. He shook his head and brought her up to speed.

"You killed a hellcrow without me?" she said.

"Might not be the last we see," Ehren said. "Someone summoned it. They could summon another."

"And that's all there was to learn here?"

"Not quite," Cavan said. "Someone locked the place up with the hellcrow inside it."

"So how'd they get out?" finished Amra, voice full of thought. "Magic, I assume."

"Teleportation isn't easy," Cavan said. "Gods know *I* can't do it. And it isn't quick, even for a master. A lot to risk around a hellcrow. They aren't known for their patience or loyalty."

"Whatever they did," Ehren said, "it does suggest a wizard. Even the Lady of Ways doesn't transport people outside from inside something."

"True," muttered Cavan, "and the Hawkspeaker's style of magic couldn't have done it either."

"So we'll face a wizard before all this is over," Amra said with a shrug. "Die the same as anyone else, if you cut their head off."

"Speaking of dying," Ehren said, "how was your reconnaissance?"

"Nobody on any of the roofs. I did find a room with a window that would have given archers a shot at us whether we came in the front or the back. Odds are, that's where the ambushers were."

"What makes you say so?" Cavan said.

"Small room. Four men. Smelled like they'd been there a few days. Cleared out only minutes before I got there, which means after you two showed up with guardsmen and crossbows. Set of stairs that would dump them out in an alley where most people wouldn't notice."

"Anything from the innkeep?" Ehren said.

"Denied anyone'd been there at all."

"Paid him off," Cavan said.

Ehren gave Amra a look. He had this way of raising one eyebrow that was both asking a question without asking, and rendering judgment without judging. Cavan would have loved to be able to do what Ehren could do with a raised eyebrow.

Unfortunately, Amra had had years to build up an immunity to its effects. She only fluttered her eyelashes at him and smiled with more innocence than she had any right or claim to.

"Amra?" Ehren made her name a question.

"Yes?"

"Are you going to make me ask?"

"Fine," she said with a sigh. "I didn't hurt the innkeep. I didn't even threaten him, or anyone in his employ. Wouldn't have done much good anyway. Odds are, he wouldn't have told me anything I hadn't figured out already."

"Which is?" Ehren said.

"Most of it I told you," she said. "Four men, in a good vantage point for archers. Obviously they had to be the duke's men, and just as obviously his hunters, not his soldiers."

Cavan nodded.

"Here's the thing," she said, holding up her hands as though she could illustrate her point, but not doing any more with them than moving them a little, for emphasis. "See enough campsites, and you start noticing little details. How they look when the food's bad. How they look when the campers don't know how to take care of their horses."

Amra smiled. "How they look when the warriors hate each other. And in that room, two of the men hated each other. Wouldn't come near each other."

"How could you—" Ehren started, but Cavan cut him off.

"The chief huntsman and the southerner," Cavan said. "The one who spoke Ruktuk, said he wasn't a dog."

When Amra nodded confirmation, her gave her a grim smile.

"You think these were the *same* hunters?" Ehren said, eyes widening.

"Persistent bastards," Cavan said. "Must have found someone in Riverbend, could teleport them after they got healed. But I didn't even know Riverbend *had* a wizard."

"She keeps a low profile," Amra said. "Probably already moved."

"You know her?" Ehren said.

"Used to. Long story."

"Doesn't matter right now," Cavan said. "We need to get moving. Which way did they go?"

"Wish I knew." Amra shook her head. "They were careful when they left. No way to tell. Not on cobblestones."

"We have to assume they're ahead of us," Cavan said. "Probably already heading for that piece of land I'm supposed to inherit. There's a manor house there, the baronial seat. Kent uses it when he checks on the place. That's our next—"

"No," Ehren said, thumping his staff on the stone floor. "This is stupid. Why chase the threat? We need to go to the king."

THE KING. EHREN WANTED TO GO TO THE KING. CAVAN ALMOST couldn't believe his ears. The thought of it was enough to turn his stomach. Not that it needed much persuasion, after the horrid smell of the hellcrow. Drove away any thoughts of hunger, though their lunch of jerked beef, boiled eggs, cherries and apples had been long hours ago.

Bringing problems to the king, that was for nobles to do. Not for bastards like Cavan. Bastards made their own way through life. Even bastards lucky enough to grow up in a fine home, where they were well-treated. Even bastards lucky enough to have land and a title in their future.

Once Cavan had land, and a title, then he would be someone to bring matters before a king. But now? Today?

"No," Cavan said, finally getting the word out when he, Ehren and Amra were back on the streets of Tradeton, preparing to mount their horses.

"No, what?" Amra said, swinging into the saddle while scanning the streets. "Do you see a foe?"

"No, we're not going to the king."

"Cavan," Ehren said in the same patient tone he used with children. He mounted his blond chestnut before continuing. "The duke of Nolarr — the king's own brother — is trying to steal land. This is a matter for the crown. Not for us."

"We don't have proof," Cavan said, thinking quickly. He kept his calf-high leather boots firmly planted on the red-and-brown cobblestones beside his horse. "All we have is the word of a free sword back in Riverbend."

"Well," Amra said, "that and the duke's sigil on the four men who tried to kill us on the road *from* Riverbend."

"A bit of cloth. Easily forged. Especially away from Nolarr." Cavan shook his head. "That far from Oltoss, might even have been some other noble's sigil. Or it might have been close, but not the same. Perhaps crossed black *greatswords* instead of spears, on a field the wrong shade of yellow. It's not like we cut one off and brought it back to show the crown."

"Cavan," Ehren started again, but Cavan wouldn't let him finish.

"No! Listen to me for once, will you? Have you ever been to the court of Oltoss?"

Cavan stared at Amra and Ehren in turn. Amra only stared back, mild interest in her green-and-gold eyes. Ehren had an objection on his lips, but let it die. He shook his head.

"I have. Five times. Let me tell you exactly what will happen if we try to take this to court." Cavan sighed and patted the neck of Dzint, who shifted uncomfortably beside him, reacting to Cavan's discomfort. "Not one of us has a title, nor a royal summons. Which means we won't make it into the court proper. We'll get fobbed off on the second or third assistant to the Royal Seneschal."

Cavan shook his head. "We'll tell him our story. He'll cluck his tongue, and it will sound like sympathy. Probably offers us food and drink. But he won't believe us. He'll ask for proof. And when we don't have any, he'll tell us to come back when we have some."

"What about—" Ehren started, raising his hand to point at Kent's house.

"Not proof," Cavan said, shaking his head slowly. "Not even close. Nothing about that leads back to the duke."

"He has a point," Amra said. "We don't have anything solid, and we won't until it's too late."

"If it were just the two of *us*," Ehren said, pointing back and forth between himself and Amra, "then that may be. But Cavan, you're the king's *son*."

"*Bastard* son," corrected Cavan.

"You're still the king's blood. That has to mean something."

"I have seen King Draven exactly three times in my memory." Cavan calmed Dzint by mounting up before he continued. "The first time is the first thing I can remember. I remember the glint of his gold crown, the sparkle of the diamonds set into its peaks. His strong jaw, and his brown eyes. I remember him saying, 'Yes, he has my eyes, and there's no disputing the mark.'"

"Mark?" Amra said, eyes full of humor now. "Where exactly is this *mark*, Cavan? And how have we not seen it before?"

Cavan blew out a sigh. "He didn't sound happy. Looking back, I'm pretty sure that was resignation in his voice."

"You were a baby, you couldn't possibly know that," Ehren said. "And even if you're right, I'm sure it wasn't about you. He probably just wasn't looking forward to telling the queen about his bastard."

"Kent always said my mom was a noble, not a serving maid. No way the queen didn't already know."

"What were the other two times?" Amra said, voice pushing for them to get back on topic, while her eyes scanned for threats.

"Kent presented me to the king before I went off for warrior training, and again before I went off to study with Master Powys." Cavan frowned. "In fact, I think the king may have arranged for Master Powys to take me on as an apprentice."

"That's a good sign," Ehren said.

Cavan gave Ehren a droll look. Amra cleared her throat.

Ehren looked chagrined, as though he only now remembered that neither of those trainings had ended well for Cavan.

"Anyway," Cavan said, "point is I never saw the king at *court*. Never in any official setting. The first time, I don't even know where we were, but the king wasn't wearing anything especially regal. In fact, maybe my memory is off here, but I think he was dressed in regular wools and a roughspun cloak."

"And a huge freaking crown," Amra said.

"Might not have arrived with it on," Ehren said, eyes thoughtful. "He wasn't going to acknowledge you, which probably upset your mother's family. Might be why your mother hasn't been in touch with you. Wearing the crown when he admitted you were his, even if he wasn't going to formally claim you and make you part of the royal family, that may have mattered."

"That's one possibility," Cavan said. " I think it's more likely he had some official business there that required him to wear the crown. Compensation, maybe, if the pregnancy harmed any marriage plans."

Ehren and Amra looked at each other. This was one of those moments when Cavan would have sworn those two could talk mind-to-mind. Usually Ehren was the first to speak afterward, but this time it was Amra.

"Cavan, if the king had to offer something to your mother's family, they were more than minor nobles..."

"Don't care," Cavan lied. "The other two times I saw the king were at the royal castle all right — in tiny little rooms near the sally port, where I never even saw a servant, much less any other nobility. One old guard escorted us in, and the same old guard escorted us out. Otherwise it was always just Kent and me, waiting for the king, who came in alone, said a few words, gave Kent something for me, and left."

"He gave you something," Amra said, "but he didn't give it *to* you?"

"Wasn't anything I got to keep. Letter and a pouch, each time. Wouldn't have known they had anything to do with me, if Kent hadn't called them my gifts from the king. Never even found out what they were."

"He didn't speak to you," Ehren said, certainty in his voice now. "Or look at you, even. Not directly. Did he?"

Cavan only shook his head.

"Placating the queen, I expect," Amra said. "Not acknowledging you officially, that probably helped soothe her a bit. But if he'd shown you any kind of attention or affection? That might have crossed the line for her."

"Would you have objected?" Ehren asked Amra. "If you were queen?"

"I'd've killed you," Amra said to Cavan, then frowned. "Well, effectively, anyway. I'd've killed your mother before she bore you. Probably would have killed the king too. Cheat on *me*, would he?"

Ehren gave Amra the kind of look Cavan only saw on his face once in a great while. Like he was looking at Amra and seeing a different person than the one he was used to riding beside. But that didn't make sense to Cavan, because everything Amra had just said was, in Cavan's estimation, entirely to be expected from her.

Whatever Ehren was thinking, he shook it off a moment later. He turned back to Cavan.

"So," he said, "not the king then?"

"No."

"Pity," he said. "Would've been nice to let someone else solve the problem for a change."

And with that, they trio began to ride.

13

———

THE LATE AFTERNOON SUN HUNG LOW OVER THE DWARFMARCHES
behind them, to the west. It would set before long. The east road out
of Tradeton had meandered through a few dozen farms before
bending north enough to join the main road east. The Royal Road,
which ran all the way to the huge city of Interr, at the eastern edge of
duchy of Nolarr, which formed the eastern boundary of the kingdom
of Oltoss.

Cavan had seen countless maps of Oltoss in his youth, and he
always felt it was shaped like the head of a hound, looking to the
northeast. Nolarr started at the blue mountains, and formed the
hound's snout.

The Royal Road started at Interr, ran the width of the country,
and continued west beyond the borders where it gained other names.
Might even have been the same road that led to Riverbend. Either
way, made traveling easier and faster. The road itself was ancient,
from back before the War of Three Kings, with that dust-free hard-
packed dirt that somehow seemed easier underfoot — or underhoof
— than even good, springy grass.

And the road was popular. Two caravans, going toward the capitol, had passed Cavan and his friends that late afternoon. And Cavan

had seen dozens of farmers and tradesmen on the road, going about their business on foot. Sometimes leading mules, sometimes pulling carts. The odd thing about them was that they seemed unaccountably ... pleasant. The first to offer greetings, or even just smile and wave.

Most such travelers on the road tended toward somewhat ... grim dispositions. Or at least standoffishness. At least, when Cavan had noted them. As though travel were a trial to be suffered for the prize of arriving at their destination.

These farmers and tradesmen that afternoon, though, seemed almost happy to be on their way. Perhaps they'd merely all enjoyed good fortune, but Cavan suspected something deeper there. Something about the roadway itself.

These ancient roads were more than mere spellwork, he was sure of it. And Cavan wondered briefly if even Master Powys had unlocked any of the secrets in their design.

On either side of the road around Cavan, the grass grew green and thick, tangled in places by weeds and blackberry brambles. He found his eyes drawn to every sight, still drinking in the color after that trek between the worlds. He reveled in the deepening blue of the afternoon sky. The white of the puffy clouds. The greens and browns of the elms, ashes, and madrones that grew in copses and small woods along the way.

Sometimes those trees grew between the road and the twin rivers to the north and south. Other times, farther off in the background, letting Cavan see the deep, wide rivers that rushed their way through the kingdom, occasionally allowing a branch or fork to diminish them by no more than a sliver.

And Cavan's ears thrilled to the songs of birds he'd remembered from childhood. Jays, like the ones he'd hunted with a sling when one dared swoop down at Fiddlestaff, the neighborhood cat. Larks and swallows too, singing joyously as they had when Cavan was ten and Kent brought him out this road for the first time, to see the land he would one day call his own.

Cavan had picked his fill of blackberries that day, nearly ruined his supper at the inn that night.

"Should be an inn before the sun sets," Cavan said. "The Bear Trap. Good stew, at least the last time I rode through."

"No inns," Amra said.

"We should stop then," Ehren said, "if we're going to set up camp."

"No camp," Amra said. "Nothing more than bedrolls, anyway. Certainly no fires."

"You want to just keep riding then?" Cavan said. "The road's wide, and easy enough. We'll—"

"We need to be ready for a fight," Ehren said. "We need rest, and we need food. An inn should—"

"Let everyone know exactly where we are?" Amra said. "Yes, I think it would do that splendidly. Shall we save ourselves some time and send the duke a formal announcement of our movements?"

"They know where we're going," Cavan said.

"*I* don't know where we're going," Ehren said. "Cavan, does this barony of yours at least have a name?"

Cavan blinked. Of course it had a name. Everyplace had a name...

Suddenly Cavan remembered. Maybe it was the road, or the memory of blackberries, or maybe just the tone of Ehren's voice. But for the first time in years, the name of Cavan's future barony leapt back to mind.

"Juno," he said.

"Please tell me you're joking," Ehren said, more urgency in his voice than Cavan liked.

"What's wrong with—" Amra started, but Ehren cut her off.

"*Cavan*. Tell me you're joking."

Cavan shook his head. "That's the name. The Barony of Juno. Why?"

Ehren looked back and forth between them. "No. Not here. If we're not stopping at an inn, we're stopping now."

"We're not stopping near the road," Amra said. "Follow me."

Amra glanced up and down the road to make sure no one was

watching, then led Cavan and Ehren off to the north side. Through the nearby grass and trees they went, making small turns here and there that looked random to Cavan. By the time the dark was rising around them, the three of them sat among a copse of alders atop a small hill. Barely enough room for their horses and bedrolls.

The river rushed nearby, and its fresh smell lifted Cavan's spirits in the face of whatever doom Ehren saw in the name of his future barony. Assuming Cavan ever did inherit it.

After he'd performed his sunset prayers, Ehren had broken out cold roasted chicken that tasted and felt entirely too fresh to have ridden around for days or weeks in that marvelous brown leather backpack of his. The chicken went well with fresh blackberries that Cavan picked, and a loaf of good Oltoss rye bread that Amra had picked up somewhere on her reconnaissance.

They washed it all down with horns of river water that tasted as good as it smelled.

Finally, in the dim twilight, Cavan asked, "So why does the Barony of Juno concern you?"

"You don't..." Ehren drew a deep, slow breath and sat back against the rough gray bark of an alder. "Obviously you don't. Obviously no one around here does, or the name would have been changed before you were born. Unless there's a *reason* they kept the name. As a warning to—"

"Ehren," Amra said in a sweet voice, "will you tell us what you're talking about? Or would you prefer I water that tree with your blood?"

"Sorry," Ehren said, and this was now officially the longest Cavan could remember Ehren going without a smile. In and of itself, that was enough to start a gnawing worry deep in Cavan's guts.

Ehren untied the leather thong from his hair, and ran his fingers through his blond locks as he talked. Cavan wondered if this was a calming routine of Ehren's. If so, he didn't use it often.

"This was said to happen ... maybe three centuries ago? I was studying with the elves when I ran across the story, and they don't measure time quite the same way we do. They couldn't, long as they live."

"Focus," Cavan said.

"Right." Ehren shook his head. Tough to tell in the twilight, but Cavan thought he looked pale. More so than usual. "Back then, the area south of the Wailing Woods and east of the Dwarfmarches was entirely controlled by the Dunaian."

"The Dunaian are extinct," Cavan said. "After the War of Blood."

"Not entirely." Ehren's fingers were tapping on the pristine white linen of his breeches. "They interbred with humans. Their blood lives on in some of us, especially here in Oltoss."

Ehren glanced at Cavan. "Nobles and royal lines, especially. You probably have some Dunaian blood."

"*Anyway*," Amra said.

"Right. The Dunaian had fewer gods than the rest of the races. They had a Creator ... Nuwin, I think ... and a Destroyer, Yeenach. The Destroyer was said to live in the Underworld, while the Creator lived in the seas."

"And Juno?" Amra said, apparently in no mood for a lecture.

"Juno was a mortal who fell in love with the Destroyer when he spent the dark part of a year walking the world. She traveled with him. Loved him. And when he left her before the turn of the seasons, she followed."

"To a mountain range?" Cavan said.

"A range of mountains that 'glittered like sapphires by the light of the high sun.'"

"The Blue Mountains," Cavan said. The name of the range between Nolarr and the rest of the kingdom of Oltoss. When Cavan thought back, he could imagine someone describing them as glittering like sapphires, at least during the high summer. They had ridges of crystalline deposits that ranged from pale blue to almost indigo.

"It was there she found a cave that lead to the Underworld."

"And lived unhappily ever after, I'm sure," Amra said. "As though there's another option with a god called 'the Destroyer.'"

"That wasn't how the Dunaian viewed—"

"*Ehren*," Amra said, cutting off the lecture at the source.

"The point is," Cavan said, "you think maybe there's a cave or cavern somewhere in the barony that goes a little deeper than we'd like?"

"I'd assumed some mine had been discovered. Gold maybe, or gemstones."

"Couldn't have been gemstones," Cavan said. "No way the duke could have found out in time to keep *Kent* from spreading word of that."

"You think they've found a god?" Amra said.

"I'm not sure about *that*," Ehren said. "Kind of hard to keep the discovery of a god quiet."

"Power," Cavan said. "You think they've found power."

"People have certainly killed for less," Amra said.

"I think they found something powerful enough to spark a legend. And I think we're going to have to worry about more than rescuing Kent."

Amra burst out with a sudden bark of laughter, and looked a bit embarrassed when Cavan and Ehren stared at her in the dim moonlight.

"Sorry," she said. "It's just ... Cavan, I think this barony just got too valuable to be the inheritance of a bastard."

Cavan shook his head. Another time, he might have laughed. Surely it was funny — on some level — that he and Kent were under threat because he stood to inherit something so valuable that, if anyone else knew about it, he would not have been allowed to inherit it.

But right now, Cavan couldn't laugh. Couldn't even smile as he lay down to get such sleep as he would that night. Guilt weighed heavily on him. Kent and his family were suffering — possibly even being tortured or murdered even now — and Cavan had been wasting his thoughts on smiling farmers and easy roadways and bright, shiny colors. Like some spoiled child, with barely a thought spent on their mission. Their goal.

Goals now. Plural. Ehren was likely right. Chances were they'd have to do more than save Kent and his family.

But Kent and his family came first. And Ehren would just have to accept that.

CAVAN AWOKE FIRST THE NEXT MORNING, SHORTLY BEFORE SUNRISE. BY his own planning, of course. Even a failed wizard could feel the approach of sunrise, sunset, midday and midnight. The easiest thing in the world to waken himself when he chose. And in this case, he wanted to be awake before even Ehren arose to offer his morning prayers to the rising sun.

Cavan threw off his undyed roughspun cloak, which had done double-duty as a blanket because he had not bothered with his bedroll.

His friends still slept, and Cavan slipped away from them, down toward the river's edge. What he had to do, he had to do alone.

Cavan's guilt last night had been a weighty thing, sitting on his chest and making all his worries worse. That was no good. That was no way to ride into danger.

But drifting away into memory with every wisp of cloud or hint of birdsong, that was no good either. Cavan hadn't even realized he was doing that, not until Ehren's story. Not until the guilt hit.

Then it became clear. Cavan had lost his focus. Left some of it in the place between, when he'd thrown all of his being into that memory to escape the giant spider and its kin.

Ever since then, every little thing seemed to demand Cavan's attention.

Even now, the predawn gray had tinges of red and purple, more color than that place between and drawing Cavan's eyes. His ears ate up the gentle breeze through the alders and ashes, the rushing of the river, the chittering and rustling of squirrels, the first songs of the morning birds. The smell of the blackberries made his stomach rumble and his mouth water and he could already feel a part of his mind casting back to the place between, trying to remember if the underbrush in the gray forest had included any berry bushes.

Cavan sat down cross-legged near the river's edge, on soft green blades of grass, moistened by dew and spray.

And there he ran through every focusing exercise he could think of. First, those taught by Master Powys. Clearing his mind by following his breath in and out, over and over until there was only his breathing, and the clean air and the rising and falling chest were incidental to the process.

Then he shifted his focus, carried his attention from his lungs and into his veins, following his lifeblood as it pumped through his body. Three cycles through his system, he followed, then back to his breaths.

Cavan began to breathe in the quiet power of this place. The gentle insistence of the breeze. The unstoppable rushing of the wide river. The deep permanence of the earth beneath him. These things and more he breathed in until their power filled him up like a well in a storm.

Once full, Cavan sprang to his feet and whipped his longsword from its scabbard in a single movement. Cavan went through the eight basic strikes first with his blade in one hand, then the other, then with a two-hand grip that did not quite suit the shorter pommel of this sword.

He followed the eight basic strikes with the four basic blocks, the twelve counterstrikes. And then on to the advanced attacks and defenses. Every single move he'd been taught and a few he'd developed on his own.

And with each movement Cavan was deep inside his muscles. Ensuring not only were his feet placed properly, but his weight distributed correctly on the soft grass, his legs tensing when they needed to, loosening when they could. His back, his shoulders, his arms, his wrists — every movement, every muscle, proper tension, proper placement, proper timing.

When Cavan finished, his breaths weren't shallow and quick like a novice. They were full and deep as they were supposed to be. A light sheen of sweat coated him in the first rays of dawn.

Soft applause came from nearby. Cavan looked to his right to see Amra, leaning against an ash tree. She'd already donned her black leather armor, which meant Cavan had not slipped away so unnoticed as he'd hoped. Back near the horses, Cavan could hear Ehren chanting his morning prayers.

"How long have you been watching?" he said.

"Very well done," she said, and there was nothing teasing in her voice, for once. "Not that I'm surprised. I've fought beside you. Still." She cocked her head to one side, her short black curls almost dancing as she did. "Much as I tease you about tactics, I'm not sure how you failed warrior training. Your entire self was in every one of those movements."

"I didn't have that much focus when I studied with Ser Dreng. Not until—"

"You're kidding." Amra blinked. "You're telling me training to be a wizard made you a better warrior?"

Cavan shrugged. Sheathed his sword.

"Now I've heard everything." Amra chuckled, then turned and started back toward camp.

Cavan took the moment alone to wash in the river, before returning with blackberries to add to their breakfast of sharp, hard cheese and good Oltoss rye bread.

Most important, Cavan felt like himself again. Not like some child, traveling as much through memory as across the land. Not like the half-man who'd left a piece of himself in another world.

He was Cavan Oltblood. And he had work to do.

CAVAN BARELY NOTICED THE LAND AROUND THEM AS THEY RODE THAT day. A few hills. A small valley. Trees came and went. The rivers were closer at times, farther away at other times. He knew them well enough, and they didn't need his attention.

Clouds smeared and passed quickly through the pale sky over-head. Clearly they were traveling faster than he was. The road was wide and easier than it should have been — thanks to ancient magics — and still Ehren and Amra held the hobbies to a moderate traveling pace.

They were right. Cavan knew they were right. Knew they had to take breaks to rest and water the horses. Knew they couldn't simply gallop all the way to the baronial manor house in Juno.

But he didn't have to like it.

Amra tried distracting him with tactical questions. What was the layout of the manor? Of the surroundings? What land features could we expect before we get there? Pinch points? Likely ambushes? Where would we be crossing the river?

Answering only did so much good. No more than a few hundred yards later she'd ask the same question again. Or for clarification of some detail. Tell me more about this bridge. Do the foothills around the Blue Mountains get those crystalline deposits? And so on.

Cavan answered every question as best he could, but so much had happened since he left home. His recollections were never clear enough to satisfy her.

And Ehren, he asked questions Cavan had never known the answer to. How many herds of goats? How many farms? How far up the mountains do they go during each season?

Cavan knew they had reasons for each question. But that didn't help Cavan gain knowledge Kent had thought him too young to learn.

On and on through the day they rode, while the Blue Mountains in the distance grew slowly larger. Somewhere past midday, Cavan first noticed an azure glint among the snow near the peak of the tallest mountain, the Ice Dagger.

Cavan, Ehren and Amra were just remounting their horses to continue on after a supper of cold chicken, roasted with herbs — and not the same taste as last night's fare — with apples and a bread so light it was almost cake, when Amra stood tall in her saddle and stared into the distance.

"Cavan," she said, "how broad is the pass to Nolarr?"

"Broad enough that no one calls it a pass. It's like there's a tiny break in the mountains for the Royal Road. Some folks call it—"

"The Street of Death," she said, sitting down in her saddle now.

"Yes, how did you know?"

"It's used in tactical studies. Twelve leagues long, and wide enough to march an army down. Except that the sides have small, hidden nooks and passes where soldiers can hide and rain down death. Arrows, rocks, hot oil, that sort of thing."

"Not to mention the scorpions the duke had built at key points."

"Why does the king allow it?" Ehren asked.

"Because the only way to invade Oltoss from the east is to cross Nolarr, which means that army will be stopped dead at the Blue Mountains. Every one of those defenses can be aimed at an army approaching from the east as easily as one from the west."

"Good thing we're not bringing an army," Ehren said. "And that we're not going to Nolarr."

Amra and Cavan exchanged looks. She looked as certain as he felt that they would have to go to Nolarr before all this was over.

"Do you know a way *around* that pass?" she asked.

Cavan wanted to smile and give a mysterious answer. Master Powys would have approved of that. Or even just a confident assurance. Ser Dreng would have commended him for that. But as it was, Cavan could only say one thing honestly.

"Sort of."

Amra sighed and nodded. Apparently she understood exactly what he meant — he knew the routes the soldiers used, but not well.

They turned back to riding, and Ehren began to sing one of his paeans to Zatafa.

Cavan hung his head as his blond friend began to sing. As though the day's ride weren't long enough...

14

No more than an hour before sunset, Cavan, Ehren and Amra finally crossed the border from the County of Twall into the Barony of Juno. They'd been off the Royal Road to the south for hours now, and Cavan could feel the difference. He tasted dust from the roads now. Their horses had to watch out for wagon ruts.

And the ride itself was more jarring. Not uncomfortable for a man who spent so many days of his life in the saddle — and certainly better than riding cross-country — but noticeable after the Royal Road.

Thicker, taller trees through here. Pines and redwoods, mostly, though even those didn't look so large as Cavan remembered them. But then, he'd spent a fair bit of time among the giant trees of the Wailing Woods since then. Compared to those trees, these were fresh-sprung saplings. As though a stiff wind could blow one down.

Not much chance of that today though. The winds were still mild things, easing their way up from the south. Cavan resolved to enjoy that while it lasted. Those winds would get stronger all too soon.

The closeness of the Blue Mountains did nothing to help the trees look tall. The peaks towered now, taking up nearly half the sky. Impressive. Especially since Cavan knew that between the mountain range and the place he sat ahorse rose a series of hills even before the first gentle slopes of the mountains themselves.

It was ever the trick of mountains to look closer than they were.

"I expect we'll reach an inn before sunset," Ehren said, and Cavan could hear the hope underlying his attempt at a neutral tone. "The road's too well-used for us not to. We could learn much at an inn."

"So could the duke," Amra said. "No inns."

She looked around as though her eyes would pick out something in the late afternoon sunlight that she had somehow missed until now. But the rocks near the road yielded little, and the grass beyond them even less. And whatever secrets lay tucked behind the tree lines on either side of the road did not leap to offer themselves up. She even looked over her shoulder at the road behind, almost as though she expected riders.

She shook her head as she turned back.

"I'm surprised we haven't seen those hunters by now. And I still can't believe we got past that bridge without an ambush. We *had* to cross it, and visibility was so low—"

"Perhaps we got ahead of them," Ehren said. "Or perhaps they went the wrong direction. Perhaps they thought we'd go to the king."

"Falstaff knows I wouldn't go to the king," Cavan said. "Not without—"

"Proof," Amra said. "Yes, we know. How well do you know this area, Cavan? Any idea where we'd find a good place to camp?"

Cavan shook his head.

"Farms!" Ehren said, with real joy in his voice. "We passed the last of Twall's farms hours ago, but we can't be too far from the farmsteads here in..."

He trailed off because Cavan was shaking his head.

"Nothing we'd reach before dark."

"Besides," Amra said, "if we're being watched, the last thing we'd want to do is lead hunters to a farm. They wouldn't blink at killing the farmers."

"Wait..." Cavan said, staring into the trees east of the road as memories surfaced. "The manor's huntsman, Gregor. He took us hunting in those woods…"

"How long?" Amra said, excitement in her voice.

"Just a couple of days at a time, but…"

"Come on," she said, spurring Caramel off the road to the east, forcing the others to follow. "Let's find the game trails while the light's still good. Then I'm sure we can reach one of the clearings where Gregor had you camp."

Cavan wondered briefly, and not for the first time, if Amra could read his mind.

They'd barely reached the tree line before she spotted a game trail, and it was one Cavan remembered when he recognized the old bear scars across the trunk of a nearby pine tree. The trail was used mainly by deer. Wide enough for a hunting party, so long as they were careful.

Cavan started toward the trail, but Amra whistled the horses to a halt.

"Nope," she said, smiling. "We tie the horses just inside the tree line, where they won't be seen. We go in on foot, weapons ready."

"I'm not sure how far it is," Cavan said. "We might not make it before dark."

"Oh, we *must*," Amra said, pulling her sword. "We simply must. Otherwise those hunters will have lain their ambush for nothing."

"No," Ehren said. "Ridiculous. There's no way they could—"

"Bet me," Amra said, taking one hand off her sword and offering it to Ehren. "Ten crowns says the duke's hunters are waiting to ambush us at the clearing. Twenty more says they're the same ones we fought near the Firespears."

Cavan shook his head. He knew that gleam in her eye. And Ehren knew it too. Amra never offered a bet unless she was certain she was right.

Ehren sighed and shook his head.

"Come on then."

"No," Cavan said.

Amra didn't say anything this time. She just turned and looked at him. She did flutter her eyelashes, which Cavan knew was a warning sign. He had wondered on occasion if she ever fluttered her eyelashes to flirt with lovers, but he doubted it.

He didn't waste time wondering now, though. He just answered her unspoken question.

"We have the tactical edge," he said. "We know they're there. But strategically, this is a mistake."

"No," she said. "It isn't. I know you two aren't fond of killing, but we *will* face these four again. This may be our only chance to take them when we have the advantage."

"We have the advantage right now. But we have a chance to compound it. They're sleeping outside, in shifts. Waiting on alert. Eating trail rations. Certain we're coming." Cavan smiled. "But we're going to bypass them and sleep in an inn tonight. A good night's sleep in real beds. Hot meals."

Amra started to shake her head. Ehren chimed in.

"Plus gossip. A chance to get the lay of the—"

"No," Cavan said. "We draw as little attention as possible. Talk as little as possible. Eat, sleep, and ride before dawn."

"Fine," Amra said, sheathing her sword. "But you may be recognized."

"Doesn't matter," Cavan said. "The men who are hunting us won't hear about it until we're gone."

Amra sighed, but clapped Cavan on the shoulder. "Every time I start thinking of you as a warrior, you remind me you're half a wizard."

Cavan wasn't sure what to say to that, but the three of them mounted and rode hard for the inn.

By the time the sun finally rose over the Blue Mountains the next morning, Cavan, Ehren and Amra had been riding for hours. Fortified by a good night's sleep, and not one but two hot meals. This morning had been carrot porridge with beef in a beer broth. More than thick enough to stick to their ribs as they rode in a pre-dawn gloom that lasted for hours.

But then, so close to the mighty Blue Mountains, the sun wouldn't clear the peaks and shine its light down on the Barony of Juno until close to midday.

By then, the trio had cleared the forest, ridden past a number of creeks and small rivers, farms and mills, and were closing in on the baronial manor itself. The road grew smoother, though more from care than magic, and farms around them now grew beets, lettuce and spinach, mainly, but a scattered few grew corn and carrots.

Cavan had kept an eye on Ehren through the morning ride. The priest never seemed fully awake when he rose before the sun, even when that sun rose hours later than they were accustomed to. He seemed almost to be sleep-riding, relying as much on the training of his blond chestnut, Highsun, as on his own attention.

All that changed when the first rays of sunlight struck him. The little, sleepy half-smile he'd had stretched to its normal width. He inhaled deeply through his nose, eyes closed as though savoring the warmth of the day's first sunshine.

And aloud he began to pray to Zatafa.

Pray, not sing, which was the way Cavan preferred it. The rhythm of the ancient Penthix verses went well with their ride.

Ehren kept up those prayers as they rode. Occasional farmers or other travelers doffed hats or raised their left hands high in praise of Zatafa, but most ignored Cavan and his friends. Either wary of their weapons, or concerned with their own business.

So far, there'd been no sign of the huntsmen. Cavan could tell that bothered Amra, but she didn't say anything.

Soon the baronial estate was in sight, scant minutes ahead of them, and they slowed their approach. Just west of the manor spread a town. Small wooden houses and larger wooden buildings, with only a few using the Blue Mountain rock at all in their construction.

The trio wouldn't have to ride through town to reach the manor though. Just pass the last of the corn farms that surrounded them now, where the corn grew tall and reached almost to the road itself.

Then ride past some of the outlying buildings, that looked like housing for the rich, primarily. As though proximity to the manor was status to be sought in this area. Cavan thought he remembered Kent mentioning that to him, years ago, but in the moment Cavan was too busy looking at the manor itself.

It stood on a high hill, and he knew that any watchers from the walls were probably already watching them come. Solid stone foundation — quarried from the Blue Mountains, like the twelve-foot wall rimming the top of the hill, just before the downward slope — and the rest of redwood and pine.

Seeing the wall again after so many years, Cavan realized that the blue glitter of the crystals embedded in the rocks might blind enemies, from certain angles. An interesting tactical advantage, and one he knew Amra was already assessing.

Inside the walls grew a grove of fruit trees. And behind the manor itself, a series of pools that had some local spiritual significance that Kent had never shared with Cavan.

"Archers," Amra said, calling Cavan and Ehren's attention to the guards on the walls, who were keeping an eye on the trio. "You're certain we'll be welcome? I'd hate to try to assault that place with just the three of us."

"I don't know *what* to expect," Cavan said. "But unless they have a royal decree, they should still treat me as their future lord."

Amra snickered at that, but Cavan ignored her.

"Why do we think Kent's here?" Ehren said, speaking his first words of Rentissi in hours.

"Where's a better place to hold him?"

"Interr," Amra said, as though expecting the question. "In the duke's dungeon."

"We're on the safe side of the mountains from the duke. The locals won't fear invasion, so if the duke's men tried to capture the steward, they'd—"

"Do nothing if he was taken in the night," Amra said. "If evidence was planted to make it look as though he rode home."

"He'd be reported missing by now," Cavan said, "and the king would investigate. No. The quietest way to hold Kent would be to keep him at the manor, incommunicado."

Cavan clucked Dzint forward, but Amra whistled the halt.

"If I'm the duke and I'm holding a steward at his seat, I put *my* men on the walls, not his."

Cavan shook his head. "Why risk it? People around the manor will recognize me. Why risk being seen killing me? Better to let me in and kill me quietly."

"I wasn't talking about archers. I was saying the duke now knows we're here."

As if to prove her point — or perhaps to acknowledge the return of his future lord — one of the archers raised an arm in salute.

A hunting horn blew, and six men came running out of the corn. All with weapons drawn.

And all bearing the duke's sigil at their left shoulder.

THREE OF THE ATTACKERS HAD LONGSWORDS, ONE WITH DAGGER IN HIS off-hand. Two of the others bore two-handed maces, and the last had a spear. All looked like Nolarr men — tanned and rugged from life in the field, wearing the studded leather armor of huntsmen.

Cavan, Ehren and Amra slid off their mounts in the same moment, weapons in hand by reflex. Ehren whistled a command to the horses, who ran quickly away from the fight while the huntsmen vaulted the low wooden fence that was all that separated the cornfields from the road.

Cavan leapt forward. Caught a mace-wielder coming down over the fence, weapon out of line. Gutted him and spun away while the man gurgled to the ground. Two swordsmen facing him now, one with a dagger in his off-hand. Behind him he heard a man's scream.

They had plenty of room to fight. A road wide enough for four carts, smooth after a fashion, but ruts that could break an ankle.

Cavan danced toward the ruts. The swordsmen spread out, trying to flank him. From the corner of his eye he saw Ehren thrust his goldenwood staff past the spearman's guard. Cavan heard the snap of at least one rib.

He couldn't see Amra, but he could hear her taunts as she fought. Had to be someone good. Amra didn't taunt the "useless."

Cavan continued backing away. Shoved his free hand into his pouch of spells.

One swordsman threw his dagger.

Cavan batted the dagger away with his blade, but his weapon was out of line when the other swordsman charged.

Cavan threw himself backwards. Felt the tug as the blade slashed through part of his roughspun cloak.

Cavan rolled to his feet, spell in hand.

He flung forward a scattering of mustard seeds and shouted power across them. *"Neelin akah!"*

The seeds swarmed like hornets, stinging the dagger-thrower from a dozen angles at once. Forcing him back as he waved and slapped at them.

The other swordsman came at Cavan. Their blades clashed together in a rapid series of strikes and parries.

Cavan heard a cry and a thump, but had no attention for it. This swordsman was good. Maybe better than Cavan. Fast attacks, pressing Cavan back and back. Steering him toward the fence.

So much for tripping one in the wagon ruts.

Cavan could barely squeeze in a counterattack. The swordsman pressed him hard. Cavan's arms and back complained at each parry. The man didn't look big enough to be so strong. Not as tall as Cavan, and only a little broader. But his attacks were powerful, as though he had orc or ogre blood.

Cavan panted for breath by the time his back reached the fence. Orc blood. Had to be. Now that they were so close, Cavan could see a greenish tint under the tanned skin. The hints of teeth that wanted to be tusks but didn't know how.

Amra yelled something then, but Cavan didn't catch what. Didn't have time. All he could do was keep his sword dancing. Hold back those mighty blows just a little longer while each parry grew more jarring. Find the way to…

Of course.

The swordsman was almost orc-strong, but not orc-broad.

Cavan waited for the next high strike. When it came, Cavan didn't parry. He ducked. Dropped straight down.

The sword changed direction. Cavan didn't need to see it to know. He only had a moment. Not even enough time to turn his sword. To stab. Only a moment. Had to be enough.

Cavan slammed the pommel of his sword into his opponent's kneecap.

It popped like a tree branch snapping.

The swordsman's slash came off-line, accuracy lost as the man screamed and fell.

Cavan slammed the flat of his blade across the swordsman's hand, and kicked the weapon away when it fell.

The swordsman rolled on the ground, screaming. Clutching his knee.

Ehren and Amra stood watching. Ehren as pristine as ever, but Amra with a sheen of sweat as though someone had made her put in at least a *little* effort. Her sword was clean, but blood never seemed to cling to that odd dark blade.

The other huntsmen lay dead in the road. The one Cavan had distracted with mustard seeds died of sword-through-the-neck.

"Next time," panted Cavan, "Ehren helps *me*."

"We should do something for him," Ehren said, pointing at the man who continued to scream.

"If you mean kill him, fine," Amra said. "But we're not healing someone who will try to kill us again."

Ehren hesitated, then nodded. Though he didn't look happy about it.

"These aren't the same hunters," he said.

"No." Amra whistled back the horses. "Which means those four are still coming."

Cavan took the pommel of his sword and knocked the screaming swordsman unconscious.

"Neat trick with the knees," Amra said as she mounted up. "But the groin would have worked as well. Or a tackle—"

"He has ... orc blood," Cavan said, still hunting for breath as he mounted Dzint. "Almost orc strong. Figured ... his joints..."

Amra nodded and said, "Maybe we'll make a warrior of you after all."

And the trio set a brisk pace as they rode for the baronial manor house.

15

———

When the first rays of sunlight finally broke through the canopy, Tohen finally called a halt. He and his men stopped there in the middle of the game trail, surrounded by tall, broad redwoods. Good, solid kinds of trees. The kind that grew plentiful in Nolarr.

This was as good a place to stop as any. No clearing, as such, but the trail was wide enough for caribou, so more than wide enough for the four of them and their horses.

Rudyar started rubbing down the horses, while Lutik broke out hard, mild cheese and some of that too-thick Oltoss rye bread. Little better than rocks, that stuff, but it did fill the belly.

Qalas was glaring at Tohen again, and Tohen had to remind himself for the fifth time today — he's lost count of how many times total — that when the fight came, he'd want Qalas and his halberd fighting beside him.

Tohen made the southerner wait through a long sip of from his water skin before he finally said, "What?"

"We should be at the manor. They're going to the manor. You know it. I know it. Everyone knows it."

Tohen shook his head.

"You were wrong about that campsite," Qalas said, showing more courage — or maybe just more frustration — than he had so far. "How much time did we waste there? And they never showed up."

"That Amra," Lutik said, paling as he said her name. Tohen reminded himself to make sure Lutik fought Ehren or Cavan when the battle was joined at last. Lutik continued, "It's her. Got to be. Outthinking us, she is."

"No," Tohen said. "She's a warrior, and a good one. If she knew we were waiting in ambush, she'd've flipped it on us. Had to be Cavan. Knew some local trick we didn't. Or maybe just afraid to face us."

"Doesn't matter who made the call or why it happened," Qalas said. "They still slipped past us. Again."

Qalas had that look in his blue eyes again. Like he was thinking of making the challenge.

Tohen laughed.

"Funny thing about hunting," he said. "The best prey slip away from you two or three times. Lead you on a jolly chase. Makes the kill all the sweeter at the end."

"Or they get away, and you end up making excuses."

"Happened to you a lot, has it?" Tohen closed the gap between them in two quick steps. Stood nose-to-nose with Qalas. "My prey never escapes me. Nothing ever has."

"And if some other hunters get your prey around the manor? What then?"

"Won't happen," Rudyar said, still rubbing down the horses, and the interruption was so unexpected that both Tohen and Qalas turned to look at him. The big man shrugged. "These guys, they're too good. We're the best the duke has, and they almost killed us. You think any of the other hunters have a serious shot at them?"

"Depends," Tohen said, turning back to look Qalas in the eye. "How good are they with their bows?"

"I missed one shot," growled Qalas.

"One shot was all you had. You missed." Tohen smiled, and there wasn't an ounce of humor in it. "You berate me for my choices. My tactics. Question me at every turn. But hunting is as much execution as planning. And when we had them dead to rights, you missed. When it mattered most, you missed."

Tohen raised a single pointing finger. "You. Missed."

"I won't miss again," Qalas said, and Tohen was sure it was meant as a warning.

Tohen turned away and took his meal from Lutik. He found a rock to sit on while he ate. Qalas did the same. Before long, the horses were as rested as they were going to get, and all four hunters had refreshed themselves as well as they could, given their lack of sleep and long hours in the saddle on these rough trails.

"Master Huntsman," Qalas said, and Tohen was impressed that the title didn't sound sarcastic. "Will you be letting us in our next destination? Our next plan?"

"Why?" Tohen said, standing and stretching. "You'll just question it. And frankly, I'm only going to take so many more questions from you before I decide you're too much trouble and kill you."

Rudyar laughed like it had been a joke, but no one joined him.

No anger from Qalas this time. Only distant awareness. Like a predator watching his dinner. Waiting for the right moment.

"Yes!" Tohen said, pumping his fist. His smile was sincere when he stepped up and clapped Qalas on the shoulder. "That's the look I've been waiting for."

Qalas blinked confusion, and the look was gone. But that didn't matter. It had been there.

"You've been angry. You've been impatient. Those qualities will ruin a hunter faster than anything else. You need to get distant. Inevitable. Yes, little irritations will come and go, but you hold your focus. Keep your perspective. *That's* how you get the kill."

Qalas drew breath to speak, but Tohen wasn't going to let him. Not now. He needed to hear this.

"That's why you missed, back by the orcs. Impatience. Hunger for glory. You wanted to be the one who killed Amra. Who opened the attack. You wanted it too much. Made you tighten up in the wrong moment."

Qalas was listening now, and Tohen stepped in close. Put his hands on the southerner's shoulders.

"Yes, you're good in a fight. But when you fight angry like that, even your talent and training won't save you. You'll miss, or you'll get parried or countered, and your emotions will throw you off. You need to get distant. One swing, one arrow, one ambush — they don't matter. The result is inevitable. Distance is the key. Detachment. When you study your prey. When you make your plans. When you fight."

Tohen could see the wheels turning behind those blue eyes. Qalas was listening now. Considering. Tohen let go of his shoulders and stepped back, smiling a sincere smile.

"I was starting to despair of you. Thought we might really fight. That I might really have to kill you. And believe it or not, I don't want that. You're one of my hunters. Worse, you're talented enough to become my right hand. Maybe chief huntsman yourself one day. But you were always so angry. Like with the orcs. Who cares if they call you a dog?"

Qalas opened his mouth to retort, but words didn't come. His nostrils flared in a deep breath, and he closed his mouth.

"Exactly. Get that anger under control and keep it there. Release it when and where *you* choose. Not just when it boils out of you."

Qalas nodded. Suspicious, but not angry. Better and better.

"So what does this mean?" Qalas said. "Here and now."

"It means I can now let you know that I got more than a teleport from that wizard."

Rudyar started to make a rude comment, but Tohen cut it off with a look. As though he'd sleep with a wizard. Or, for that matter, as though she would have slept with a man like him.

"What?" Qalas asked, still cautious.

"In a minute. First it's time to share my plans with you. Gather 'round." Tohen brushed away twigs and needle leaves as he smoothed some of the dirt of the trail. He picked up a stick to draw a map. "This is what we're going to do."

16

———

Under the warm noontime sun, the gates of the baronial manor stood wide open. Two pikemen in chainmail stood guard, but offered no challenge as Cavan led Amra and Ehren riding past. In fact, one of the guards hailed him by name.

That was good. Cavan hadn't wanted to admit it, but he'd been a little concerned that he'd changed too much since he was last here. Wouldn't have been so easily recognized.

Whatever was going on between Duke Falstaff and Kent, the manor's majordomo was keeping the lands in good shape. Even now there were gardeners tending the dozens of fruit trees off to Cavan's right, and others weeding the roses and chrysanthemums that grew on either side of the road and led to a small flower garden in front of the manor itself.

Already servants were coming out of the great, green double-door to greet Cavan. Though not the majordomo himself. Where was ... Olivart? Yes, that was his name. Bent back old graybeard, with sparkling hazel eyes and an easy smile. Where was he?

"Archers still watching us," Amra said. "Smart enough not to raise their bows, at least."

"We're riding into a trap," Ehren said, for the fourth time since Cavan started counting. "Why am I the only one who sees it?"

"Best way to handle an ambush is to charge it," Amra said.

"I told you," Cavan said, "Falstaff can't kill me here. Not in front of witnesses."

"So there won't be witnesses," Ehren said.

"Lord Cavan," a man no older than Cavan called out. The apparent leader of the servants. Slender, in deep green livery featuring the blue mountain baronial sigil at the left shoulder, with blond hair just touching his shoulder. He stood before a line of three others, two women and a man, all of about his age but all with their hair cropped short, and all in matching livery. One of the women had the dark skin of a southerner. "Forgive us for not being prepared. We were not informed of your coming. Your chambers are being prepared as we speak."

"I wasn't expecting to be here," Cavan said, reining in a comfortable distance from the servants, "and I don't know that I'm staying yet. And it's not 'Lord' Cavan while His Majesty yet lives, may he live a thousand years."

As one, the servants bowed their heads and echoed, "May he live a thousand years."

Ehren and Amra glanced at each other, but said nothing.

"Where is Olivart?" Cavan said, before the servant could say anything else. "He should have been the one to greet me."

"The majordomo is" — the servant glanced at Ehren and Amra — "occupied with official matters that are best not discussed in front of—"

"Bring him to me immediately." Cavan dismounted, but held onto his reins when one of the servants tried to take them. "Right here."

"But—"

"Now."

"Of course, my lord," the servant said. "May we at least bring you refreshment?"

"Just the majordomo."

As the long-haired servant led the others away, Amra said, "Such a commanding presence. So lordly."

"Truly," Ehren said, "he was born to rule."

"May he live a thousand years."

"May he live a thousand years."

"Anytime you two are finished," Cavan said, turning back to them.

"You haven't asked about Kent," Ehren said. Like Amra, he remained in the saddle.

"I don't know any of those servants. I know Olivart. If he lies to me, I'll know it."

"Meanwhile, no one has the chance to poison us," Amra said, "and you've made sure there are plenty of witnesses."

They stopped talking as a pair of angry farmers marched past, apparently ready with a grievance. One of them stopped no more than a half-dozen paces past Cavan. He turned.

"You. You stand to be lord here one day, yes?"

"That's right," Cavan said, as the other farmer turned back to see what the holdup was. Both men were old and weathered, but strong, and plainly dressed in undyed cotton. And they both looked certain they were right. One had a deeper tan, but the other had more wrinkles.

"Let's have his judgment then," the one farmer said.

"He ain't lord here yet," the other said. "It's that Olivart who knows us and knows our land. I'll have his judgment."

"Perhaps," Ehren said, "I can be of service?"

The two farmers looked up and down the pristine white clothes of the blond man on the blond hobby.

"Don't look like no priest of the Green Lord to me."

"I worship Zatafa, Who—"

"Right," the one farmer said. "Olivart it is."

"Right," the other said. And together they turned and set an angry pace toward the front doors.

Where even now, Olivart was hurrying up the wide, smooth road. Just as bent and old as Cavan remembered, but surprisingly quick of stride. He had a dark brown cane with a gold handle and gold tip, but he carried it like a scepter of office, rather than using it to help him walk.

"Olivart!" the one farmer said.

"We need judgment," the other said.

"And I'm afraid you'll both have to join the queue inside," Olivart said. That quaver in his voice did nothing to diminish the smooth ease of his words. "I've a great deal of business to tend to before the sun sets."

The farmers gnashed their teeth, but swallowed their objections and set an even angrier pace toward the manor.

"My future lord," Olivart said, greeting Cavan as he always did, with a smile and a kiss on both cheeks. "You grow taller and stronger every time I see you. You'll be grander than the Ice Dagger at this rate."

"Always good to see you, Olivart." Cavan clasped the old man on both shoulders and leaned in to touch foreheads as though Olivart were his grandfather. The old man beamed at the gesture. Cavan continued, voice pitched low, "If you are not free to speak, remark on the weather."

"What?" Olivart said, matching Cavan's low volume. "Why would I not be free to speak?"

"Is Kent in residence?"

"He was scant weeks ago. But he's gone to Interr. Took his wife, and his boys with him. What's wrong?"

"Why would he go to Interr?"

"He didn't tell me, but I had the impression it had something to do with you." Olivart shook his head. "Whatever it was, it was secret, and urgent. He left in a hurry. Didn't take more than a half-dozen guards for the trip."

"Which guards? Did you know them?"

"Of course. Picked them out myself. Cavan, what's going on?"

"Has anything ... odd happened lately? Any discoveries?"

"Odd sightings up the mountain?" added Ehren.

"Now that you mention it..." Olivart tugged at his beard. "Just before the steward left, there was a rider with news. The rider looked

... excited ... in a way most messengers don't. Didn't get to hear the message myself. The steward took the news in private."

"And this was just before the duke summoned Kent?" Cavan said.

Olivart nodded. "Didn't see any reason to connect the two. You're saying there's a connection?"

"Definitely. And don't trust your guards. The duke has—"

"He knows," Amra said. "Look at the grounds. Look at the way those farmers deferred to him. Olivart knows everything that goes on around here. Don't you?"

"That is rather my job," Olivart said, trying to draw himself erect and not quite managing it.

"So you know the duke has spies among the guards?" Cavan said.

"Of course," Olivart said, as if this were the most obvious thing in the world. "So does Twall. I could tell you which ones, if you like."

"But—"

"If I fired their spies, they'd send more. Better to know who the spies are, and not let them learn anything they shouldn't."

"Then you lapsed there," Cavan said. "Whatever that message was, the duke knows about it. He's making a play for this barony, and he intends to kill me to get it."

"Do you have proof?"

"No."

"Then leave Oltoss." Urgency in the old man's voice now. "Cross the Dwarfmarches, where the duke's power shrinks away to nothing. Or go visit the elves. Falstaff wouldn't dare come after you there."

"I can't. He's holding Kent. He'll kill him if I don't save him."

"Then he's good as dead," Olivart said, shaking his head slowly to emphasize his point. "He's at Interr. The seat of Falstaff's power. You'd be a fool to..."

Olivart must have seen the look in Cavan's eye.

"I'm going," Cavan said.

"They found something in the mountains," Olivart whispered, so quietly that even Amra might not have heard him. "I don't know what, but it's major. I don't know why Kent went to the duke instead of the king, but—"

"Do you have the message?" Cavan said, suddenly realizing he was shaking the dear old man by the shoulders. He let go before continuing, "Any evidence?"

Olivart shook his head.

"Then I have to go to Interr." Cavan turned and mounted up. He looked back to say goodbye.

"Cavan," Olivart interrupted him. "At least let me replace that slashed cloak of yours first. Hardly befitting our future lord."

CAVAN'S NEW CLOAK WAS LOOSE-WOVEN GRAY WOOL, WITH A GOLD CLASP featuring a blue mountain carved from local crystal. It would serve him well in many of the temperate and warm places he, Ehren and Amra rode.

Right now, though, Cavan wouldn't have minded something tighter-knit. Perhaps fur-lined.

The wind had picked up closer to the mountains, and now here, on the narrow trail used by soldiers to defend the Royal Road between peaks of the Blue Mountains, it was downright chilly as it tossed Cavan's brown hair about. The air even smelled cold. Fresh, yes, clean, yes, but cold, even in the afternoon sun.

Fortunately, Olivart had fortified the trio before sending them off. Had the horses fed, watered and rested while pointing out that they themselves needed a little rest and hot food in their bellies before riding through the mountains. He sealed the deal by pointing out that both could be accomplished — in private — while reviewing maps of those mountain passes.

Cavan had hated the wait, but he was grateful for those maps, and for the roast venison with beets, spinach and carrots. Especially now that he, Ehren and Amra rode through those passes.

Amra and Olivart had worked together to choose the route. He knew which of the three or four on each side of the Royal Road were in use this month, and she knew which ones she liked for speed and cover.

Cavan had to admit that the choices seemed good. They had a clear view of the Royal Road beneath them, where caravans hurried both directions, intent on one destination or another before nightfall.

They were sheltered from the view above them by overhanging rocks, and though the trail was too narrow for them to ride abreast, that also meant it was too narrow to set up a good ambush. Not so far, anyway.

Cavan wasn't in a hurry to fight on the pass anyway. Solid mountain on one side, and upjutting stone of various heights on the other. Yes, there were strong points every hundred yards or so, with barrels of pitch, caches of arrows, or piles of stone, but those were less useful as weapons for a skirmish on the pass than against those on the Royal Road below.

Then there were the oddities of the mountain itself.

Most of the stone that made up the passes wasn't blue. Much of it was pale gray, with bluish highlights. But the crystal formations that crusted here and there, seemingly at random, all glinted from deep indigo to the palest sky blue. Those crystals, Cavan would have to make a study of them someday. They seemed to eat sound, and they carried a magical resonance like a background hum as he rode among them.

Not something he'd noticed before, and he'd never heard of anyone studying it, which was even odder. He was reluctant to say anything, though, lest Ehren take it as a sign that he was right about his cavern to the Underworld, and try to steer them off-course.

Juno could wait. Kent, his wife, and his sons came next. Then they could worry about the mountain and the discovery.

The path wound back and forth as it rose. According to the map, it would never get more than a few hundred feet up, but the back-and-forth weave followed the natural formation and impeded visibility to those watching for guards up high.

He could hear the caravans down below. The background blend of voices raised in conversation or to give orders, but the details were difficult to pick out. And not just because of the number of people in those long caravans. The echoes were wrong when they reached

Cavan's ears — half bounced by normal reflections, while some half the sounds were eaten by the crystals along the way.

Made for an ominous background noise that wedged against the low hum of the crystals and set Cavan's teeth on edge. Tightened his shoulders. He began to expect an attack.

What if he were riding into an ambush? What if Olivart was in on it? If bought by the duke, he'd be able to hand the barony over on a platter. And the locals might support it. They knew Olivart. Why should they care if he reports to the duke, or to some little bastard they hadn't seen in half a dozen years or more?

Olivart might be betraying them. Might be sending them into a trap.

Cavan reined to a halt.

He looked back to see Ehren's puzzled expression and Amra's long-suffering-patience look.

"What if Olivart's betraying us?"

"He's not," Amra said, before Ehren could wedge in a word. "That man's loyal to the bone."

"What if you're wrong? What if he's sending us into an ambush?"

"Well," Amra said with a sweet smile, "then I suggest you be ready to fight. Just in case."

Cavan couldn't think of anything clever to say to that, so he loosened his sword in its scabbard, and went back to riding.

Only about another hour passed before the ambush came.

WHEN THE AMBUSH CAME, CAVAN, EHREN AND AMRA WERE RESTING their horses. They'd stopped near the apex of the trail, where they found about as large a resting place as they could expect to see before they reached the ground again. A round area, maybe fifteen feet across, sheltered from the wind, but with no stone ledge to protect anyone from a long, long drop.

The horses were hobbled safely against the mountainside, while Cavan, Ehren and Amra sat on the cold blue-gray stone beside them, snacking on cold roasted chicken and golden cherries, while Amra speculated about the tactical uses for a place like this. Her leading theory was that this was where soldiers slept in shifts during battles.

The sun was midway toward the horizon.

All three of them had their weapons nearby, but not in hand.

Cavan turned to spit out a cherry pit, which was the only thing that kept him alive.

An arrow whistled through the air and slammed into his left shoulder. It hit hard as an orc punch, and he grunted in pain.

Amra was on her feet in an instant, sword in hand.

Hunters melted out of the stone. One moment nothing but mountain and empty air. The next moment, bits of mountain shifted into the duke's hunters.

Cavan recognized them. The ones from the Firespear territory. The left-handed leader with the longsword, the forest elf-dark tan, and the graying curls. The skinny one-eyed man with the two-handed sword. The huge axeman with the bushy blond beard and the scar down his left cheek.

And behind them, the archer. The dark-skinned southerner. Already dropping his bow and taking up his halberd.

They came without war-cries. No shouts. No threats. Silent as mountain cats.

Cavan rolled to grab his sword. Shunted the shoulder pain away. Hid it in his mind. But his left arm hung useless.

The axe kicked up shards of stone when it hit where Cavan had been.

Suddenly Amra was there, kicking the axeman's belly and parrying the two-handed sword of the one-eyed man. Saving Cavan's life. Again.

The southerner cut the air between Ehren and his staff. Forced the unarmed priest away from his weapon.

And their leader was coming quickly. While Cavan was still on his back.

Not good.

Cavan found his sword and his feet just in time to stop a cut inches from his neck. His left arm dangled. Cavan could move it just enough to keep his balance as he leapt clear of the next sword cut.

The leader smiled. Drew a dagger in his right hand.

"I should kill your horses," he said, "just for spite."

"Do it and I swear I'll find a way to raise you from the dead so I can kill you twice."

The leader closed. Swinging attacks that Cavan had to parry, but those blows were meant to corral him, not cut him. Force him back. Cut him off from help.

Empty air to his left now. The mountain only a step or two behind him. A little room to his right, to maneuver, but that would bring him back toward the horses.

Just past the leader, Amra slashed the axeman from belly to throat. He went down in a screaming, bloody mess while she squared off with One Eye. Ehren was pressed hard by the halberd-man, ducking and dodging and keeping himself clear, but only just. Blood dripped from his arm and his right cheek.

But Cavan had to stay alive before he could help anyone else.

"You've give us a jolly hunt," the leader said, cutting again for Cavan's neck. Cavan parried, but it jarred him. Pain tried to creep in from his shoulder, and Cavan had to work to shunt it away.

The leader, damn him, was smiling. "But the best part of a good hunt is the kill."

Pain under control now, Cavan picked up the rhythm of the lead huntsman's attacks. Gut and throat, he never cut for anything else. He had that dagger in his right hand, but he kept that hand back like it was empty.

"No fancy words, bastard?"

Cavan's only answer was a thrust for the throat. Parried by the leader's dagger. Cavan's sword out of line now. The leader cut for Cavan's belly.

Cavan threw himself backward against the mountainside. Bumped his head, but spared his gut. His heart raced and all he could taste was gritty air from the mountain dust. It gave him an idea, if he ever got the chance to use it.

Another cry. Out of the corner of his eye, Cavan could see One Eye go down. Slashed through the middle, spilling all the things that kept him alive.

Cavan rolled back toward the horses, trying to open and close his left hand. He could do it, but the ghost of pain threatened to spike into something numbing. The worst part about shunting pain away was that when that pain came back, it would hit all the harder.

More clanging in the background. Amra fighting with the halberd-man, no doubt. Was Ehren down?

Cavan came to a crouch just in time to parry three rapid strikes from the leader. He wasn't laughing now. His black eyes had gone flat. Cold. Lethal.

"Your men are dying all around you," Cavan said through gritted teeth. He kept his blade moving fast, but he could do nothing more than keep that huntsman's longsword at bay. "Any moment it won't just be me. You'll be fighting all three of us."

"You'll be dead by then."

Cavan missed a parry. Or maybe the leader feinted too well. Either way, the leader's longsword cut along Cavan's right forearm. Deep.

Cavan dropped his sword. His mind rallied fast, whirling to keep the screaming pain from reaching him. He ducked under the follow-up. Dove and rolled again, closer and closer to the ledge.

"Cavan!" Amra yelled. Too far away to help.

The leader threw his dagger as he closed. The handle thumped off Cavan's wounded shoulder.

The pain broke free.

Agony washed over Cavan. Radiated out from his shoulder and forearm, fever hot and wrenching.

Cavan grabbed that pain. Embraced it. Forced himself into it, until the pain came from everywhere at once. Blacking out the edges of his vision.

The leader was almost on him now. Sword high and swinging.

Voices called his name. Ehren? Amra? No way to know. No attention to spend on them.

Cavan forced his wounded arms to scoop up blood and dust and he spat power born of pain across them. So much focus, the spell was taking his consciousness with it.

He muttered the words, *"Usu isath."*

And then the blackness overwhelmed him.

17

Cavan did awaken later, but he wasn't sure he wanted to. His left shoulder and right forearm spiked pain with every heartbeat, and his heart was beating rapidly.

Hardest bed he could ever remember. Dark room, but a fire crackled in the hearth. He could smell ... was that tea? Soup? Something strong and herbal anyway. Didn't smell great, but parched as his mouth was, he'd choke it down if someone offered it. He could smell horses too, not just their hides but their leavings.

That was when Cavan realized he was alive. Maybe prisoner.

He sat up ... and fell back just as fast. Thumped his head on something hard until the thin excuse for a...

No. That wasn't a pillow. Cavan had used his cloak as a pillow too many times over the years to not recognize the feeling. Even if this new woolen cloak was softer than his old roughspun.

His eyes blinked, adjusting to the gloom. He could see the stars above now. Blue-gray mountain floor, dancing with shadows in the firelight. The crackling fire wasn't in a hearth. It was ... a campfire?

Ehren stretched out next to it. Salve on his cheek, and his left forearm wrapped. Amra ... where was Amra?

Cavan tried to speak, but all that came out was a dry, almost choked sound.

"Hush," Amra said, from the shadows. "There's a waterskin next to you, if you can manage it."

Cavan's left shoulder was wrapped tight, and he could feel the poultice underneath the bandages. That arm was going nowhere. Someone had bound it to his chest to keep Cavan from moving it.

His right arm was mobile, but his fingers were twitchy. The forearm was bandaged, and stained a dark brown. He could feel the poultice under the bandages there as well. But his fingers still obeyed his commands, even without resorting to wizard tricks he'd regret later.

Cavan picked up the waterskin, pulled the cork with his teeth, and rinsed out his mouth twice before swallowing a grateful mouthful. He wanted more, but stopped there. Had a feeling he needed to ease into drinking or risk puking it all back out.

Moving slower, he could sit now, back against the mountainside. He was glad that the gloom meant no one could see the sheen of sweat on his forehead from just getting to a sitting position.

He could see the horses now, and they looked unharmed, at least. He still wasn't sure where Amra was, but he could see a couple of shadowy lumps over near the ledge.

Cavan cleared his throat a couple of times, and managed a word.

"Amra?"

"I'm here," she said, from somewhere over by the lumps. "Need something?"

"So ... we won?"

Amra laughed, rich and full. Ehren chuckled and sat up. The salve on his face made his smile look ghastly and a sickly kind of pale.

"Doesn't feel like winning right now," Ehren said, "does it?"

"Please," Amra said, "if we lost, you wouldn't have breath to complain with. You're both alive, and neither one of you is going to die from those wounds."

Amra stepped back into the firelight, and Cavan saw no bandages on her. Her step light and even, until she crouched between Cavan and Ehren.

"How are they?" Ehren said.

"They?" Cavan said.

Amra glared at Ehren. "We have two prisoners."

"Someone want to catch me up?"

"Well," Amra said, "while you two were fooling around, I killed two of them."

"I wasn't—"

"You had a weapon and Ehren didn't, so I stepped in and saved his ass. The guy with the halberd was pretty good. Been a while since I'd fought one of those, and he knew how to use it."

"Doesn't look like he got you."

Amra scoffed. "Didn't say he was *that* good. Anyway, while I had him engaged, our ray of sunshine here—"

"I took up my staff," Ehren said, "and caught him at the small of the skull while he was busy with short-but-deadly. Knocked him out."

"I expected him to finish Mr. Halberd off," Amra said, shaking her head. "Don't know *what* I was thinking."

"I don't kill the helpless," Ehren said, "and neither should you."

"*Anyway*," Amra said, turning back to Cavan, "you were disarmed, bleeding from two nasty-looking wounds, and on your knees while the lead huntsman was swinging his sword."

"We were both too far away to help you," Ehren said. "Even Amra couldn't have gotten there in time to stop his killing blow."

"But you managed some kind of whirlwind spell."

"Never seen anything like that before," Ehren said, sounding impressed. "Like a tiny tornado made of dust and blood. Yanked his sword away."

"Hope it didn't hit anyone down below," Amra said, shaking her head.

"And then it spun him around and around and slammed him into the side of the mountain."

"And Mr. Sunshine here wouldn't let me do the smart thing," Amra said. "So both our 'prisoners' are unconscious over there." She pointed to the two shadowy lumps. "Assuming they don't do anything stupid, like roll themselves over."

"Amra," Ehren said, and if Amra were capable of shame, that tone would have brought it out in her.

Amra fluttered her eyelashes at Ehren.

"It's good that they're alive," Cavan said.

"Not you too," Amra moaned.

"They have information we need. If the duke is holding Kent and his family, these two'll help us figure out where and how to free them."

"I think we can find the dungeon without them."

"And if they're not in the dungeon?" Ehren said, smiling at Cavan.

"Of course," Amra said. "Whenever I build something big and defensible, something built to keep people from escaping it, the first thing I do is use it as a distraction so I can keep my actual *important* prisoners someplace ill-defended and easily taken."

"You don't believe in hiding in plain sight?" Ehren said.

"*We're not talking about hiding!*" Amra looked back and forth between Cavan and Ehren as though she couldn't believe they were being this stupid. "The duke doesn't have to hide them. Not in Interr. All he has to do is stash them someplace safe until he kills you, Cavan."

Amra turned and put her hands on the cold stone so she could lean in nose-to-nose with Cavan.

"Now you tell me, here and now, that you think there's anywhere smarter or safer to keep Kent than the duke's own keep. And you tell me how there's anywhere — *anywhere* — that makes more sense for that than the dungeons."

"I can't," he said, tone level despite the demand for agreement in Amra's eyes. "For the same reason you can't — because if there *is* anywhere smarter, the duke keeps it a secret. Which means people like you, me, and Ehren have never heard of it."

"He's right," Ehren said, apparently untroubled that Amra was still locking eyes with Cavan. "But if anyone *does* know such a secret, it's the chief of the duke's own huntsmen."

"This is a waste of time," she said.

"We're here 'til morning anyway," Ehren said. "I can only heal these wounds by the first rays of the sun. We might as well ask some questions."

Amra sighed.

TOHEN AWOKE, WHICH WAS THE LAST THING HE EXPECTED. THEN AGAIN, what woke him was a sharp slap across the face, and that had happened so many times in his life it was almost like greeting the day with a gentle caress.

A gentle caress would have been nice. He'd taken one hell of a shot to the skull, and his head was throbbing like that time he'd tried drinking with dwarves and woken up three days later in a goblin cell.

His mouth was almost that dry too, but it tasted better. Gritty, with a hint of blood, but anything tasted better than the aftermath of dwarven ale.

This time he was lying down. Arms behind his back. Tied at the ankles, wrists, and elbows, and the knots felt solid. Sword was missing, but they'd probably disarmed him.

Tohen knew he was still in the mountains. He could smell the clean air, blowing on the wind over the ledge beside him.

Ledge?

Tohen tried to shift his body away from the drop, but a boot stopped him.

"That's far enough. We're more than happy to throw you over if you don't cooperate."

Cavan's voice. Talking tough. If it were just him, probably an empty threat. That Amra though...

Wait. Cavan still lived? Tohen tried to remember what happened before that blow to the head. He remembered the ambush. The skirmish. He'd wounded Cavan. Had him on his knees. Sword coming down for the killing blow...

Then nothing. Just waking up here. Bound and hurting.

Well, they knew he was awake anyway...

Tohen opened his eyes. Still on that mountain ledge. And all three of them still lived, and all three were still mobile. Damn. Cavan was bandaged in two places at least, and so was his priest, but Amra didn't look like Qalas had scored so much as a light cut.

Maybe Tohen overestimated him.

"Wh..." it came out a croak, and Tohen had to hock and spit before he could grind out any words. "What happened ... to my men?"

"Did you catch that?" Cavan said.

"Give him some water," the priest said.

"He asked about his men," Amra said, but she didn't stop the priest from squeezing a stream of water into Tohen's mouth from a waterskin.

While Tohen swallowed, he took in more of the scene. Campfire with good dry wood. That explained the smell. They'd added water to the dry soup stock. Smelled ... well, it smelled like camps and safety, but Tohen knew better than to let the familiar smell set him at ease.

"Two of your men are dead," Cavan said. "The one-eyed man and the one with the bushy beard."

"Guess Lutik's luck finally ran out then." When that didn't get a response, Tohen said, "The one-eyed man. Lutik. Used to call him Lutik the Lucky."

"You're beaten," the priest said, with the same quiet certainty that Tohen had heard from everyone who thought they spoke for the gods. "Your hunt is over and the prize has slipped away. Now you—"

"Prize is right there," Tohen interrupted, nodding at Cavan. "And I'm still breathing, so the hunt goes on."

"Now can we kill him?" Amra said.

"Qalas surrendered, did he?" Tohen said, grimacing. "Told you where to find the stash of firewood and supplies?"

Cavan started to say something, and Tohen read the hesitation and spoke first.

"No. He'd have made you believe you didn't need me. Given you reason to kill me."

"The supplies were easy," Amra said. "I just looked where I would have hidden them."

"And Qalas," the priest said, "is unconscious."

"Waiting his turn for the question?" Tohen shook his head. "Might as well kill him. Too much pride to talk. Even if he did, he doesn't know anything. He never did learn to listen."

"Where's Kent?" Cavan said.

"With the duke. Where do you think?"

"Where's he being held?" Amra said, following that with all the typical warrior strategy questions — guards and armament and the like — but Tohen was too amused to pay attention to the details.

He just let her finish, then smiled.

"What do I look like to you? A counselor? Someone the duke invites to his private meetings and consults about all his plans?" He shook his head. "I'm a huntsman. I find people the duke wants dead, and fulfill the duke's wishes."

"You're the *chief* huntsman," the priest said. "That merits some respect. Don't tell me—"

"That just means I get my orders from the duke's seneschal instead of from the chief huntsman. His grace never wastes time on the likes of me."

"Can I kill him now?" Amra said, with the same matter-of-fact tone Tohen would have expected from someone with her reputation.

"We don't murder prisoners," the priest said.

"You'll just come after us again," Cavan said, voice thoughtful. "Won't you?"

Tohen nodded.

"*Cavan*," the priest said, "tell me you're not—"

"We have to do *something*."

Tohen shut his mouth, quickly. Tried to look unobtrusive. Maybe if he gave the priest enough time, the sunny boy could get Cavan to let him go. Unarmed or something.

But Amra spat. She pulled her sword and struck faster than

Tohen would have believed possible. On his best day, he was never that fast.

She severed his left leg just below the knee. So quick and clean Tohen watched it happen without feeling more than a tug on his skin.

The bottom part of his leg, boot and all, just ... fell. Blood spurting everywhere. Someone was yelling, but sounds became gray haze. So much blood. How could there—

Then the pain hit. Excruciating. Beyond anything he'd ever experienced.

Tohen screamed like he'd never screamed before. Like his soul was ripping free of his body. As though screaming might take the pain away, if it came out loud and harsh enough.

Then it got worse.

Amra had a flaming log from the fire by its unburnt end. Held it against his leg. Burning the wound shut.

Tohen's own screams were the last thing he heard before he passed out. Wishing he were dead.

CAVAN STOOD BETWEEN EHREN AND AMRA, ONE HAND ON A SHOULDER of each of the two as they glared at each other. The trio stood over the unconscious body of the chief huntsman. He smelled of burnt pork, and he'd soiled himself.

"He's alive," Cavan said, trying for soothing but even he could hear the tension in his voice.

Amra threw the burning log back into the fire. Clapped her hands free of dust with a sense of finality.

"You had no right," Ehren said. "Not without consulting us."

"You want him alive, yes?" Amra said, but she didn't wait for an answer. "He'll live. And when the sun rises, you can pray his wound clean and mended."

"Zatafa can't give him back his leg."

"So much the better. I won't have to do it again."

"Sit down, both of you." Cavan shook his head. "My shoulder hurts. My arm hurts. And I don't want to ruin these bandages by beating you both into submission."

That got them to look at him. Ehren with a puzzled expression. Amra's was amused.

"Happily," she said. "The soup's ready anyway. Won't be great, but it'll keep us from overtaxing that pack of yours, Ehren."

"This matter isn't settled," Ehren said sitting down cross-legged near the fire.

"No," Amra said with a sigh, "I could never be that lucky."

Cavan didn't shunt away the throbbing pain from his left shoulder and right forearm, but he did use a few tricks to soothe them into calming down as he sat on the cold stone.

"Look," Amra said, dishing soup into clay mugs she'd found in a hidden cache, along with the firewood, tinder and flint, soup stock, water, and scores of arrows. "You don't want him dead. I get that. It's bad tactics, but I get it."

"A life is worth more than a tactical advantage," Ehren said.

"Sometimes," she conceded, "but in this case I'm inclined to disagree." Ehren started to speak, but she got louder. *"Hear me out."*

She shoved a mug of soup into his hand, and passed another to Cavan.

"Since the Firespears, we've had three encounters with these guys."

Cavan wondered what two he missed, but before he could ask she continued.

"First, in Tradeton. They knew where we were going and got there ahead of us. We only avoided an ambush because the guards knew Cavan well enough to follow him at his word."

She took a sip from her own mug, and Cavan found it encouraging that Ehren didn't leap into the moment of silence. When these two started fighting...

"Second," she continued, "in the woods back there. I'm positive they were waiting for us in that clearing. If you doubt me, wake up the southerner and ask him."

She hesitated, but neither Cavan nor Ehren moved to awaken the southerner. Cavan sipped some of his soup — a little sour, but the dried pork held up well.

"Right," she said. "We evaded them and sped past. Twice they had a tactical edge, and twice we slipped them." Ehren started to say something, but she got loud again. *"Let me finish."*

Ehren settled back in, and she continued while Cavan drank his soup in silence. The more he drank the better it tasted. Or maybe he was just that hungry.

"Everyone knew we were heading for the baronial manor. But they knew they couldn't catch us there. So they skipped that over, and *guessed our next destination*. They not only knew we'd have to cross the mountains, but that man" — she pointed at the unconscious chief huntsman — "figured out which route we'd take. Knew where we'd take a rest. And in case you didn't notice, he managed to catch all of us completely off-guard."

"Yes," Ehren said, "we should have asked how they managed it."

"Magic," Cavan said, and his casual tone brought curious looks. "It wasn't quite invisibility. More like a chameleon effect. Nothing I know how to do, but I've read about it. And the wizards who know the technique can prepare it for another to use. They say the Order of the False Dawn uses the same approach."

Ehren bristled at the mention of the order of assassins.

"My point is," Amra said, "each time they've come closer and closer to killing Cavan. Maybe killing all of us. He's too good to leave alive and functional at our backs." She shrugged. "You insisted on alive, so I did something about the functional part."

"You should have discussed it with us," Ehren said.

"Why?" Nothing mocking in her voice. Just honest curiosity. "Taking a limb was the simplest answer. By the time he learns to adjust to this, we'll have either saved Kent and his family, or gotten ourselves killed trying. Did you think it kinder to discuss which limb to take? Right in front of him?"

Ehren opened his mouth to speak, but nothing came out, so Amra continued.

"Ever try to cut the limb off a struggling man?" She shook her head. "Even when they know it needs to happen. When they've got a corrupted wound. They still fight like hell." She shook her head again. "My way was quicker. Cleaner. Made sure I didn't cut too high and get an artery."

"We could have discussed it privately."

"No," said a rough, groggy voice off to one side. "Her way was better." The southerner sat up. "If you're going to take one of my limbs too, I'd request the left leg, also below the knee."

Cavan downed the rest of his soup and stood. Ehren did the same and Amra was on her feet so fast her empty mug clattered on the blue stone floor.

The trio moved over to stand between the southerner and their campfire. He was closer to the ledge than the lead huntsman had been, but he looked comfortable enough with his position. And Cavan was amazed to see his blue eyes, a rare trait in a southerner. And they weren't any of the paler blues found here in the north. They were a dark, almost royal blue.

"I am Qalas, son of Mitala, daughter of Mitaka, so you may count me properly among your defeated enemies."

"Well, Qalas, son of Mitala, daughter of Mitaka," Cavan said, "do we *need* to take one of your limbs?"

"I can tell you, you won't," Qalas said, shrugging against his bonds. He didn't move or sound like a man in pain, but the tension in his face and around his eyes suggested he still felt the effects of Ehren's blow to his head. "But you have no reason to believe me."

"Convince us," Amra said.

Another attempt at a shrug. "Tohen failed as chief huntsman. Failure means death. For him, and those who were part of his failure. That includes me, in case you doubted it."

"Couldn't you redeem yourself by finishing the job?" Ehren said.

"How?" Qalas said, simple bitterness in his voice. "The four of us, with surprise on our side and a magical edge couldn't kill you. I'm supposed to do it on my own?"

"You're an archer?" Amra said. "One good arrow—"

"Might kill Cavan, yes, but I'd be just as dead when you two caught me." He looked at Ehren, eyes full of respect. "You were unarmed, and I still couldn't do more than scratch you."

"Felt like more than scratches," Ehren said, but he was smiling. "Still, no one who walks under Zatafa's beneficence can easily strike her priests. You were fighting yourself as much as me."

Comprehension spread across Qalas' face, respect following in its wake.

"Swear you will not come after us," Cavan said.

Qalas gave Cavan a grateful look, and spoke slowly and carefully while Amra stared into his eyes.

"I swear in the name of my mother and my mother's mother to leave you and yours in peace unless the day comes when you bring a fight to me."

"Well spoken," Amra said, with a nod. "We can trust that."

"All right," Cavan said. He pulled a dagger from his boot, but thought twice about cutting bonds with his hurt muscles. He handed it to Amra, who cut Qalas loose.

The first thing Qalas did was tear the duke's sigil from the leather of his left shoulder. He tossed it over the ledge, and watched it fall.

Ehren handed the former hunter a mug of soup, which he drank greedily.

"There's more," Ehren said with a smile.

"Your leader," Cavan said, "Tohen you said?" When Qalas nodded, Cavan continued, "he said you wouldn't know anything that could help us. Was he right?"

Qalas looked from one to the other of the trio, then back at Cavan. "What if I do?"

"We beat you," Amra started, but Cavan cut her off.

"We could hire you as a guide."

Qalas looked Cavan up and down, as though seeing him for the first time.

"Are you really going to be a baron?"

"If I live." Cavan shrugged then regretted it through a throb of pain. "And if the land isn't too valuable to pass to a bastard."

"But you'll still inherit something. Some land. A title."

Cavan nodded.

Qalas looked at Ehren the same way, then Amra. Maybe his gaze lingered a little on Amra.

"Just what exactly do you three do, anyway?"

All three of them laughed.

"We're problem solvers," Ehren said.

"I like 'adventurers,'" Amra said.

"If you ask most people, we're troublemakers," Cavan said.

Ehren and Amra started to object, but Qalas spoke loudly.

"Keep your money then. I help you three with this, you owe me a favor." He looked over the three of them again. "I get the feeling that's better than gold."

Qalas nodded. "All right, the first thing you need to know is where we stashed our horses."

18

CAVAN WOKE HIMSELF BEFORE SUNRISE AGAIN, AND FOUND THAT EHREN was already passing hardboiled eggs and hunks of good, strong cheese to Amra, Qalas and ... Tohen was it?

Cavan couldn't get away from this blue mountainside soon enough. Now that the battle was over, every moment's delay felt like a great glacier between himself and Kent.

But he knew the wait was necessary. There were other hunters on the watch for him, and this resting area along the paths through the mountain was as secure a location as could be arranged.

Besides, he'd stiffened up. Not just his wounded and painful left shoulder and right forearm, but his back and legs as well, after a whole night on the cold stone.

On the whole, he felt as though he'd been on the road for weeks. Even though only the night before he'd slept on a comfortable bed in an inn. Eaten hot food, freshly cooked.

Seemed an eternity ago.

Ehren handed Cavan his share of the eggs and cheese, along with a mug of warmed soup. And once their fast was broken, Cavan joined Ehren and the chief huntsman over near the ledge. This Tohen was sullen and quiet this morning. Eyes full of resentment, and not only when he glared at the unbound, unmaimed Qalas.

Cavan couldn't blame him though. The chief huntsman had gambled and lost everything. And if Qalas told it true, Tohen'd lose his life soon unless he got well away from Nolarr. In a hurry.

Not to mention that Qalas was matching him glare for glare. Cavan got the feeling that those two never got along.

But the chief huntsman held still where Ehren seated him, and he didn't object to armed and ready Amra standing behind him. Then Ehren stripped their bandages away, from first his own wounds, then Cavan's, then finally Tohen's shortened leg.

Ehren turned to face east, raised his goldenwood staff above his head, and began to chant in ancient Penthix. From the corner of his eye, Cavan noticed that Qalas bowed his head. Was that a gesture of respect, or did he worship Zatafa?

When the first rays of dawn broke through the sky, Ehren looked like part of the sunrise himself, with his golden hair, his pale skin and his white, white clothes. A golden halo surrounded him, closing the cuts on his face and forearm while Cavan watched. Leaving his skin as unblemished as his clothing.

Ehren brought the tip of his staff down to touch Cavan on the wounded shoulder.

Warm, blissful relief eased through Cavan as though he'd slipped his sore muscles into a hot bath. The image made him think wistfully for a moment of the inn back in Riverbend, the pretty serving girl, and the assignation that was not to be.

But under the touch of such soothing warmth, Cavan could not even regret the lost night of pleasure. He could only smile and hope that serving girl found love and a long, happy life.

Cavan's forearm was next, and when the tip of the staff touched it, it was as though this spot of perfect warmth and comfort connected to the spot at his shoulder, and the blissful, healing relaxation of both spread through the whole of his body. Unkinking and unknotting his muscles until Cavan felt good as new.

As though he'd been born again with the new day.

While Cavan reveled in the lack of pain and stiffness, Ehren tapped his staff to Qalas' head.

Finally, Ehren touched the stump of Tohen's leg, and the man passed right out. Overwhelmed by the relaxation and bliss? Must have hurt even worse than Cavan had thought. It was a wonder the man hadn't moaned and groaned all night.

Fed, healed and rested, the trio and their guide were ready to ride. They had three extra horses — even Ehren hadn't wanted to leave the chief huntsman with a mount — but Cavan felt certain they'd find a home for those steeds soon enough.

They moved faster now. Apparently Tohen had been receiving reports of the movements of his other hunters, so Qalas led Cavan, Amra, and Ehren along paths and routes where the hunters weren't.

For two days they rode swiftly across the Nolarr countryside. Avoiding the towns, and riding mostly through rolling farmland. Trading horses for food and information that seemed to help Qalas understand how the duke's troops were moving, where they were situated.

Whenever Qalas interpreted what rumors they'd heard into solid troop movements, Amra seemed to nod along in agreement, so Cavan assumed they were right.

Funny thing about the farmers. They knew they were getting too good a deal for the horses. Cavan could see that in their eyes. But they didn't question it, and if anything the knowledge seemed to make them more eager to pass along gossip. As though they suspected Cavan and his comrades were trouble, but didn't seem to mind because they were trouble for someone else.

Cavan was getting the impression that the duke was not well-loved by his own people.

By the end of the second day, they could see the duke's keep, sitting high atop a hill with a great lake at its back.

Keep wasn't really a good enough word though. Not in Cavan's mind. This was a castle. Cavan had only seen a few — and he'd only ever been inside the royal castle at Oltoss — but he knew the difference between a castle and a keep.

Castles were bigger, for one thing. The duke's castle jutted high into the sky, hundreds of feet up. Seven towers that Cavan could count from where he and his group hid among a grove a yew trees. It had a gatehouse the size of the baronial manor of Juno, an inner wall just as tall, and an outer wall that looked to stand twice as tall as the guards.

The castle itself looked three or four times the size of its gatehouse. The original color of the stone was difficult to determine, because it had been enameled a dark blue.

The whole castle. Roofs and all. Every inch of it a dark blue. No simple craftsmen could have accomplished that. Not without mindboggling time, effort and expense. No. Cavan had no doubt this was the work of magic, but why would anyone...

"Wards," he muttered.

"Of course there are wards," Amra said.

"You can detect them from *here*?" Qalas said.

"What kind?" Ehren said.

"No," Cavan knelt in the thick, green grass, then flopped onto his back and stared up at the white, puffy clouds in the late afternoon sky. A deep sigh brought him the smell of trees and grass, but he didn't find it cheery.

The other three continued to stand, looking down at him while their hobbled horses grazed nearby, but that didn't matter.

"I mean the whole castle is warded," he said. "Carved into the stones themselves. That's got to be it."

"That's why the enameling?" Ehren said.

Cavan nodded.

"The roofs too, then?" Amra said. "The parapets?"

"Maybe." Cavan shook his head. "You understand, I can't be sure. And if I'm right, it still might not even be the whole castle. But my gut tells me the enameling does double-duty, protecting the spells and hiding how many there are."

"The duke doesn't keep a wizard," Qalas said. "Tohen said not in a score of years, at least."

"Doesn't mean the wards are bad." Cavan puffed out a breath and ran his fingers through his short brown hair. "If I were doing it, I'd ward against deception at the entrances, keep guards on the walls alert, and, of course, protect the castle itself from infiltration and siege."

"So they slam the front door in our face," Amra said, "What, we can't break it down?"

"Probably not."

"Those wards," Qalas said. "How far do they reach?"

"I'd need to be close to know for sure," Cavan said. "Get a chance to study the spells, but if I got that close—"

"They'd know we're here," Amra said.

"Best guess," Qalas said.

Cavan dragged himself to a sitting position. Looked back at the dark blue castle in the late afternoon sun.

"Even the duke could only spend so much on his wards." Cavan tilted his head in thought. "Smart way to go would be to let each engraved ward protect its stone. *Maybe* the surrounding stones, but not much farther out than that, unless he wanted to accept weak spots."

"So the spells don't go far beyond the engravings?"

Cavan shook his head. "Probably not. If they did, they'd need to be refreshed, which would be difficult because—"

"Then they don't matter." Qalas smiled for the first time Cavan could recall. "The entrance we're using isn't enameled."

ANOTHER HALF-HOUR ON THEIR HORSES, AND QALAS LED THEM TO A ruined farm.

The whole place looked like a dead farm. Dry dirt fields, not recovered from someone sowing them with salt. Burnt out, dead fruit trees. The remnants of an old rail fence. And in the center, a burnt-out farm.

The barn might once have been tall and full of hay, but now it was a collapsed ruin. Half-burnt away and the rest ruined by rain. And near the barn, the vague structure of what Cavan thought might have been a two-story farmhouse.

Unfortunately for whoever lived there, only three of the walls remained, and a few of the crossbeams. The roof was gone, the second floor had collapsed. It was all such a mess, that Cavan was half-surprised it wasn't still smoldering.

"Bandits?" Ehren asked.

"The duke," Amra said, with quiet certainty. "This looks like a lesson to those who anger their liege lord."

"Neither," Qalas said, dismounting. "This was never a farm. Soon as it was built, the duke put it to the torch. Has the land re-sown with salt annually, to make sure no down-on-their-luck peasants think of settling nearby."

"How do you know?" Cavan said.

"Tohen was the sort to look down on anyone he considered his lesser. Man would have killed for a title. Me, I like getting to know everyone. Never know when you'll luck into a couple of dungeon guards who like to drink and gamble, but aren't all that great at either."

Qalas smiled.

"You're telling us this is an entrance that isn't guarded?" Cavan didn't try to keep the disbelief out of his voice.

"Guards draw attention," Amra said. "People see soldiers, they wonder what's going on. So I'm betting we've talking about a tunnel that can be collapsed in at least three places."

"Five," Qalas said, sounding impressed. "And there will be tunnel patrols to worry about."

"We're not tying the horses here," Ehren said.

"There's a perfect spot just inside the wall of the house," Qalas said.

"There's nothing to eat. They'll die if we don't make it back."

"If we're escaping with prisoners, we'll need them as close as possible."

"If we're escaping with prisoners," Amra said, "they'll collapse the tunnel on top of us."

"Only if they sound the alarm."

"There," Cavan said, pointing to a grove of oak trees that looked to have decent grass growing around them, and bushes with berries as well.

Not too close, but better than nothing.

"That'll be a long distance," Qalas said, "if we're running."

"If we're running, that means they sounded the alarm," Amra said. She imitated the sound of a collapsing tunnel.

"We leave the horses at that grove," Cavan said. "And if we have to run, we steal horses from the duke to get us back to our own."

"Why not just ride away on the stolen horses?" Qalas said, and something sharp in his tone made the question sound important.

"A horse isn't a sword," Cavan said, reaching down to pat Dzint's neck. "These horses are our friends. We don't abandon our friends."

Qalas nodded, slow and respectful, and for once Ehren chose not to elaborate. So the four of them rode their horses to the grove, and tied them in among the trees, where they would have grass and berries to eat, at least. And they rubbed down their horses, and fed and watered them to make sure they had a good meal before being left to their own devices.

Then, back at the burnt out pretense of a farm, Qalas led them inside the standing walls of what was supposed to have been a house. Rubble everywhere, right down to details that made Cavan wonder if Qalas had the truth of this place. Who would think to include a half-burnt child's doll for such a pretense?

Cavan's stomach sank. He tried not to think about it. Tried not to imagine a happy family being slaughtered and having their farm pillaged for the duke's convenience.

Qalas took some time looking around. Stomping with his feet on the desiccated wood and ash. Long enough that Amra got restless and Ehren checked on the sun, which was getting closer to setting than Cavan liked. Hunting around for a tunnel entrance in the dark didn't sound like a good time, but he was too close to wait for morning.

"Here!" Qalas called. He'd shifted some of the rubble in front of a stone hearth, and revealed an iron door set into a stone foundation. "If you ever need to find this without me, stomp until you feel stone, then more until you hear iron."

Cavan stomped around a few paces while the others watched him, curious. The stone spread well beyond the iron door, but not throughout the first floor. This was never a house with a stone foundation. This was a house that was built partly on a slab of stone, and not in a way that would have strengthened the design.

Cavan sighed relief.

"You saw the doll," Ehren said.

Cavan nodded.

"No other farms are nearby." Ehren put his hand on Cavan's shoulder. "I don't think anyone lived here. The duke is a man who pays enough attention to detail to enamel his whole castle to conceal facts about his wards. He probably had the closets stocked with clothes and the larder with food before he set fire to the place."

"That does sound like him," Qalas said. "At least, from what the guards say. They say he knows who gets drunk on their shifts and who doesn't. And that those who do always get the worst assignments."

"Well, if we're all satisfied that we don't need a round of blessings for the restless dead," Amra said, "can we see about getting into the tunnels before the sun sets?"

Qalas took hold of the door's handle and yanked.

It didn't budge.

Amra looked at Qalas, one raised eyebrow saying more than words ever could have. Enough that a bead of sweat broke out on Qalas' brow.

"No one ever said anything about it being locked," he said defensively.

"You mean the guards didn't give you all the details you'd need to break in?" Amra fluttered her eyelashes. "I'm shocked. Shocked, I say."

"There must be a trigger," Ehren said.

But Cavan had already figured that much out. The door had been concealed under rubble, but it was built into a stone foundation. A stone foundation near a stone hearth.

Focused attention, first skill of a wizard, and useful for so many things.

Cavan didn't interrupt the argument brewing behind him. He just stepped around it to the hearth. Large stones, all mortared together. All browns and grays, originally, but mostly soot-blackened now. But the mortar, that hadn't burnt away...

There. Down near the bottom, on the right hand side. One stone, in place but not held there by mortar.

Cavan kicked it gently. It popped in and out with a *click*, and the argument behind him stopped when a grinding sound came from under the door.

"Try it again," Cavan said, smiling.

Qalas pulled.

The door came right open.

CAVAN HAD NEVER BEEN IN A MINE, BUT THE TUNNEL WAS WHAT HE imagined one might look like. Hewn into dirt and rock, reinforced with wooden beams. Barely enough room for a tall man like him to stand and narrow enough that he could touch the sides. If they had to fight in here, daggers would be their best weapons.

He still hadn't spotted any torches when Ehren closed the door behind them. That grinding sound came again, blessedly quiet — considering the circumstances — but it added a sense of finality to the pitch darkness.

Qalas started to say something, a tight sound in his voice, but he didn't get a syllable out before Amra hushed him.

Mines were unknown to Cavan, but dark tunnels under castles and keeps? Cavan, Ehren and Amra had seen their share, and Ehren had long ago proven that Zatafa offered a better solution to the darkness than any spell Cavan could have managed.

Ehren whispered sibilant syllables in Penthix, and the sound slithered around Cavan as the words drifted away.

A moment later, the tip of Ehren's staff gently touched Cavan on the forehead, and it was as though dawn had broken here in the tunnel. Warm, gentle light seemed to surround him, easing into every crack and crevice and chasing away the shadows.

Cavan could watch Ehren work now, as he tapped Amra's forehead next.

"I love this trick," she whispered with a smile, but Ehren scowled at hearing his prayer called a trick.

He ignored her and tapped Qalas on the forehead last.

"Wha—" was as much question as he got out before Amra reached up and clapped a hand over his mouth.

Qalas' eyebrows came down and his halberd hand twitched, but held still. He raised his free hand in surrender. Amra took her hand away.

"There's no light to give us away," she whispered. "Zatafa's blessing" — Cavan noticed that Ehren looked mollified by her words — "just lets us see as though the sun was shining down here."

Qalas' eyes widened, the pupils so huge on a thin band of blue iris was visible. He started to say something, then clamped his lips closed and nodded.

The four of them followed the tunnel. Qalas in front, in theory because he might have known any of the guards they encountered. In truth, Cavan suspected, Amra wanted him in front in case this was all a trick to get Cavan where the duke wanted him.

Cavan didn't want to believe that.

Side tunnels began branching out every few hundred feet, leading one direction or another. Down a few, Cavan could even see intersections with other tunnels.

"This place is a warren," Ehren said softly. "Are you sure we're going the right way?"

"*I'm* sure," Cavan said, just as quietly. "I'm betting we'll take no turns, and that when we get to the end there'll be dozens of possible tunnel entrances to choose from."

Qalas gave Cavan a look, as though Cavan knew something he wasn't supposed to.

"Old wizard trick," Cavan said. "If you know the secret, the path is easy. If not, you get lost and never find your way out."

Qalas looked from Cavan to Amra to Ehren and back, then shook his head. "You guys are scary."

Amra fluttered her eyelashes and gave him a smile. Qalas hesitated, as though he wasn't sure if she was flirting or menacing, which, in Cavan's opinion, proved he was paying attention.

Patrols came in groups of three. All short men, in chainmail, and all armed with short swords and small, round shields. Each trio was accompanied by an unarmed torchbearer, who wore simple linens, decent boots, and a backpack.

The patrols were easy to avoid. Cavan and his companions could see them well before they could be seen, so they only needed to find the nearest juncture and hide around a corner until the patrol passed.

Amra grimaced each time, no doubt irritated about hiding from a fight, but she never objected.

After the fourth such patrol, and well over two leagues of tunnels, Cavan finally whispered, "Where are the cells?"

Qalas stopped, and knelt in the dirt. He sketched a square and called it the castle. He reached a ways, drew an X and called it the tunnel entrance. Finally he drew a circle on the other side of the castle.

"That's about where the cells are, I think. That way even if an escaped prisoner knows about the exit, they have a long run before they can escape. Plenty of time for the guards to release their dogs and ... well, you get the point."

"What else is down here?" Amra said.

"Not sure." Qalas brushed away his sketch then tromped over it a few times to obliterate any sign of it. "Storage. And I think he's got an alchemist who works down here somewhere. Inquisitor too, from what the guards said. I got the impression there was more that they wouldn't talk about."

"Torture, they'd talk about," Ehren said, "but—"

"Let it go," Amra said.

"Doesn't matter," Cavan said. "They could have a dragon's treasure hoard down here for all I care. Let's go."

"Wait," Qalas said, before Cavan could take a step. "Are we avoiding patrols to be smart or to avoid killing?"

"Both," Ehren said.

"We reach those cells, there'll be guards. Are we killing them?"

"We'll make that call when we have to."

"I should have brought my bow," Qalas grumbled, but started to lead the way again.

The farther they went along, the more Cavan began to notice footprints along the side tunnels. Even occasional wagon ruts. They had to be getting close.

Another patrol passed. Or maybe it was a patrol they'd seen before, circling back through one of the side tunnels. Cavan wasn't sure. The torchbearer looked familiar though.

Finally the tunnel took a slight curve to the left. Qalas slowed. Took his halberd on both hands. When he did, Amra drew her sword. Only a moment later, Cavan drew his, and Ehren readied his staff.

Qalas pressed his back to the inside wall. Cavan and his friends followed suit.

Qalas inched along now. Closer and closer.

Then he paused. Pointed to his ear. Amra nodded immediately, but Cavan had to strain to hear what they heard: people. The muddied sound of distant conversation. Something dripping. Someone groaning, weak, like for old pain that wouldn't go away.

Qalas turned his head and whispered.

"We're here."

THE DIRT TUNNEL ENDED IN A BIG GRAY STONE ROOM. ROUND, MAYBE thirty paces across. Ceiling maybe three times Cavan's height. Torches in sconces along the wall, and a pair of guards playing cards at a small table beside two locked and barred doors.

Barred on this side, which meant cells on the other side, as far as Cavan was concerned.

The smell of greasy roast pork was in the air. After the cauterizing of Tohen's leg, Cavan found that the smell turned his stomach.

He focused his mind elsewhere. He'd been right about the doors. From where he stood with his friends and Qalas, just at the edge of the tunnel's curve, he could see three doors. The two beside the guard table. Another to his right from there — no lock or bar that Cavan could see. There was also an entrance without a door. Looked like stairs leading up. Good stone there too.

"Only two," Cavan whispered.

"Four," Amra corrected. "I hear two others. Probably out of sight to our right."

"Echoes?" Qalas asked, but Amra shook her head. He started to say something else, but Cavan said, "Trust her hearing," and he nodded.

Looking closer while Amra and Qalas muttered a quick exchange, Cavan noted that these guards had shields leaning against their table, but they weren't armed with short swords. Maces, instead. Ridged to better dent armor. But then, Cavan wasn't wearing armor.

He also noticed a hunting horn on the table next to the deck of cards.

"Can you put them to sleep?" Ehren whispered.

Cavan shook his head. "Not from here. And by the time I tried, they'd have too much fire in their veins." He tilted his head, looking at the horn. "I can stop them from sounding the alarm though."

"So we're agreed then?" Amra looked at Ehren. "There's no gentle path here?"

Ehren sighed and shook his head. "Try not to kill them. They aren't hunting us."

Amra only drew her sword and nodded at Qalas.

The two of them rushed in. Qalas turned swiftly to the right, halberd already in motion. Amra sped for the distant guards, only now looking up from their card game. Comprehension slow to dawn on their faces.

Cavan threw sand into the room and sucked in air as he mouthed, *"Ulta na-sach."*

Silence pressed down on the room. Amra's boots soundless as she ran. No clatter to the chairs as they fell backwards. Their guards scrambling for weapon and shield.

Not even a cry as Amra mashed her pommel against the chainmail coif protecting a guard's temple. He went down in a silent heap.

Ehren rushed about the room, checking for other guards. Witnesses or aid. Cavan got into the room in time to see Qalas take a guard's head with his halberd. Surreal in such silence. The momentary fountain of blood. The tumbling of the severed head. The way the body stayed standing. Didn't fall until Qalas brought the steel-wrapped handle end around to thump the other guard into unconsciousness.

Just that fast, the fight was over. Three guards unconscious. One very dead. Amra had one hunting horn in her hand. Qalas had the other, looking at Cavan as though wondering if he were responsible for the silence.

Cavan nodded.

Amra tapped her ear, and Cavan released the spell. Ehren muttered a prayer for the dead guard. Looking around by reflex, Cavan saw that this circular room had some two dozen exits. A few of them closed by doors, but most of them leading into wooden tunnels just like the one he and his companions had been following.

Similar enough that Cavan wasn't a hundred percent certain he could lead them back into the right tunnel, if he needed to right now.

But leaving wasn't what he needed anyway.

"We need to find the keys," Cavan said.

"Oh," came a voice from the staircase, "I don't see why you'd need those. I'm only holding a few merchants and a smattering of bandits, and I doubt you have business with any of them."

The duke stepped down the stairs and into the chamber.

The duke had the same height that the king and Cavan shared.

Same strong chin and nose, as well. But any resemblance to Cavan ended there. Duke Falstaff of Nolarr had short-cropped blond hair, and hazel eyes that looked almost golden in the torchlight. He was dressed for war. Full plates of armor from pauldrons to greaves, all of it enameled the same dark blue as his castle, save for the sigil on his right shoulder: crossed black spears on a field of yellow.

At his belt he had a great sword of war, with a long golden hilt.

And the duke was not alone.

A young serving boy — a squire perhaps — stood beside him, holding his helmet. Dark blue enameled, of course, with great bat wings coming off the back.

And behind them, soldiers. From the three double rows Cavan could see, he guessed at least a score of soldiers. All armed with spears and swords, and armored with chainmail.

But worse than all of that, Cavan could sense an aura of power about the duke. Not the awe-inspiring might of Master Powys, but there nonetheless, and probably more than Cavan possessed.

"How did you keep it a secret?" Cavan said.

"None of my prisoners are secret," the duke said with a smile. "Every one, tried formally and accounted for in the records. I promise you they're all quite guilty."

"No. Your training."

The duke's expression darkened. But before he could deny it, Cavan continued.

"You had an alert set up in the burnt out house, didn't you? I was too worried about that stupid doll to notice it. You knew we were coming. You—"

"You're veering away from the point, dear boy," the duke said. "Which is that I have you *here*. Very much in my power."

"Where's Kent? And his wife? And Reed? And Alec?"

"They're all very well taken care of, I assure you." The duke shook his head, full of disbelief. "No wonder you failed as a wizard. It seems you cannot grasp even the most obvious situations."

All humor dropped out of his expression. He snapped his fingers

— quite a trick in those gauntlets — and soldiers began filing into the room.

"Drop your weapons and surrender or die where you stand."

Amra held her sword higher, ready to fight. Qalas tightened, then loosened his grip on his halberd. Ehren looked at Cavan.

Cavan counted twenty armed soldiers then looked at the duke.

"So many men, when I'm the only one you need to kill." Anger burned through Cavan, and he used it. Let it make his voice taunting. "Not swordsman enough to best me? Not wizard enough?"

"A sword is all I'd need to beat you. Wouldn't even bother with my helm."

Anger in the duke's expression, and something almost petulant. As though he thought he was being so clever, hiding that he knew some magic, but never stopping to think that his secret would be out the first time he met another wizard.

Even half a wizard, like Cavan.

"Face me then. No need for anyone else to die."

The duke looked around at his gathered men, all of whom had their spears raised in a two-hand grip. He smiled.

"It's always the overwhelmed side that begs for single combat between champions. They cry honor. They cry tradition. But the truth is simple — they know it's the only way they have even a prayer of victory." He shook his head. "You're outmatched here. Surrender or die."

"If you think you brought enough men," Cavan said quietly, "you didn't. We've faced worse odds, and we're the ones still here to talk about it." Cavan pointed his sword at the duke. "And don't think that armor will save you. It won't."

"Surrender or I'll kill Kent and his family."

"Not if I kill you first. If I surrender, you'll kill them anyway, after I'm dead."

"Fine then," the duke said, shaking his head. Louder to his men, he said, "Kill them."

CAVAN HALF-EXPECTED THE DUKE TO WALK AWAY WHILE HIS SOLDIERS did his work for him. But he didn't. He stood there to watch the show. Probably was the sort of child who caught flies to put them in spider webs, then stayed to watch the spider eat.

The fly didn't have a priest of Zatafa on his side.

"Zatafa!" Ehren cried, thrusting his staff high while a dazzling sunburst of light exploded out from the end. Blinding all of their enemies at once.

Amra leapt on the attack, her unquenchable dark blade slicing through soldiers like so many well-cooked fish. Qalas followed her lead. Each of them starting from one end of the row of blinded soldiers, killing their way toward each other. The first few fell quickly, but then others gathered themselves enough to mount at least a token defense as they recovered.

Cavan ignored the soldiers. Barreled past them for the duke.

His squire had dropped that big blue helmet. Fallen back covering his eyes.

The duke had fallen back a step himself. One arm drew his sword of war while the other raised up to shield his face.

Cavan closed. Sword raised like a lance. Ready to slip past the duke's elbow and...

The duke may have been blinded, but his hearing was fine. He timed his kick perfectly. Caught Cavan in the chest. Shoved him back and bought time.

Sword of war raised in both hands now, weaving back and forth while the duke blinked against the aftereffects of Ehren's sunburst. No focus to his eyes though. Still unseeing.

Cavan tried to bat the huge sword aside, but the duke was strong and his sword was heavy. The duke turned the attempt into a cut for Cavan's head.

Cavan ducked the strike. The duke's blade nicked the stone wall of the stairwell. He immediately swung it back the other way. Low. Cavan had to jump back to avoid the blade.

Still the duke was blinking against the spell. He was doing all this blind.

Cavan pulled mustard seeds from his spell pouch. He flung them toward the duke and shouted power across them. *"Neelin akah!"*

The seeds swarmed like hornets, stinging at the duke from a dozen angles at once. The duke fell back another step to a small landing, where the stairwell turned up to his right. He almost stumbled, shaking his head against seeds that harried him high. But most of the seeds bounced harmlessly off his armor.

"Shyla sata," the duke said, spitting power into a ball of flame, but it was laboratory wizardry. Perfect in form and without any heart.

"Hass assan iikah," Cavan whispered, breathing power at the fireball.

The spell turned and leapt at the duke, twice as big and twice as strong.

It slammed into his breastplate. The duke roared in pain, blinking his watering eyes.

Eyes that now focused on Cavan.

The duke was panting as he stood and took a step closer to Cavan. Sword in a sure grip now.

"Make room," Amra called, over Cavan's shoulder. "I can take him."

"You wanted your challenge, boy," the duke said. "Still have the courage for it?"

"Don't!" Qalas called out. "There's no way he can get back to help before we can stop him."

"Move over, Cavan," Amra said. "Let me through."

"You don't need to do this, Cavan," Ehren said. "He's right. It's not about honor or tradition. It's desperation."

"Come back down here then," Cavan said. "You and me. Right now."

"To the death?" Amusement as much as curiosity in the duke's confident eyes.

"There's no need to be stupid about this. You're still my uncle and a duke. I'm still a royal bastard and your nephew. We fight until one of us yields."

"What happens then?"

"If I win, you release Kent and his family, and swear that you'll leave them alone. Also, you'll abandon any claim to my inheritance, whatever that turns out to be. Oh, and you'll put your seal on a letter of admission I write to the king, about what you've done."

"You, Kent and your inheritance are fine. I agree to those parts. Forget the letter."

"What do you guys think?" Cavan said, not taking his eyes off the duke.

"Good enough," Ehren said. "The king will listen when Kent tells the tale. That'll accomplish what you want."

"And if *I* win?" the duke asked.

"I will make a formal, written gift of my royal inheritance to you, whatever that inheritance turns out to be."

"Witnessed and sealed?"

Cavan nodded. "Officially you'll have won it from me in a game of cards."

"People would believe that of you," the duke said, thoughtfully. "I will also require your oath — and oaths from your compatriots — that you will be forever silent about any discoveries made in the land you stand to inherit."

"I can't promise for Kent."

"If you sign over your inheritance, I'll have no reason to harm him or his. I'll even keep him on as steward, or offer him something more lucrative. He's a gift for making money."

The duke smiled, and sounding almost avuncular as he continued.

"We can avoid the bother of a fight, you know. There's no real need for it. You could just agree to sign over your inheritance and swear the oaths. That will save Kent and his family, and isn't that the reason you're here? And, honestly, do you see yourself as a high lord? Handling the day-to-day tedium of running a barony? A man of action like yourself?"

Cavan smiled. "I'd do it just to keep the land out of your hands."

"Fine then," the duke said with a sigh. "Men like you always claim you don't want blood, but your hands are never clean, are they?"

Cavan started to retort, but the duke waved it off. "As soon as your compatriots agree that they will swear their oaths to silence when I beat you, we can get on with this."

"I'll swear," Qalas said.

"Of course I'll swear," Ehren said.

"If Cavan manages to lose to a pompous windbag like you," Amra said, "I'll swear your oath out of pure disgust. Just so I never have to talk about you, or such a pathetic loss, ever again."

"Good enough," the duke said. "I swear to uphold my end of this bargain if I lose."

"And I swear to uphold mine," Cavan said.

"Very well, then." The duke's eyes tracked the area behind Cavan. "Davan! My helm."

"What happened to 'I wouldn't even bother with my helm?'" Ehren asked.

"Easy to talk big behind a wall of spearmen," Amra said.

"Cavan's not wearing any armor at all," Qalas said.

"Fair points. I'll forgo the helm." The duke smiled at Cavan. "Shall we?"

Cavan didn't like the look in those nearly golden eyes.

"The fight is to begin once we're both back in the chamber behind me, standing six strides apart. Any strikes or spells before then shall be treated as cheating."

The duke smiled, lowered his sword, and gestured for Cavan to precede him.

Cavan backed down the steps anyway.

CAVAN HAD KNOWN THAT A BATTLE WAS GOING ON BEHIND HIM WHILE HE pursued the duke, but he hadn't quite been ready for the scene of carnage that awaited him when he returned to the round, stone room.

Blood everywhere. The room smelled of copper and death.

Worse, underneath it remained that greasy roast pork smell. It seemed somehow wrong now.

A score of dead guards, cut open in various ways. And not a mark on Amra or Qalas for their efforts. None of those dead men had recovered from Ehren's dazzling brilliance in time to mount a real defense.

Cavan might have felt sorry for them, if they hadn't been about to kill him and his friends. It wasn't as though there had been some quick and easy way to render them all unconscious. If there had been, Ehren would have found it.

"Efficient," the duke said, finding a clean spot on the floor and taking up a stance, his sword raised and on guard. "If either of you are ever looking for work…"

"I did work for you," Qalas said. "I was a huntsman."

The duke pursed his lips as he looked at the left shoulder of Qalas' leather armor, where the duke's sigil had been torn away, then shrugged. "Never mind you then." He looked at Amra. "You, though—"

"I'd sooner hang up my sword."

"What *is* that thing?" Now that the duke was paying more attention, he must have sensed something about the blade.

"None of your business, is what it is." She smiled. "Unless you'd rather fight me. I'll tell you *all* about it if you win."

The duke looked at his dead soldiers, especially the ones where cuts had shorn cleanly through their armor. "I think not."

Cavan took up his position, six strides from the duke. That left him standing in blood, which he had no doubt was deliberate on the duke's part. Wouldn't matter for long.

Amra stepped up, ostensibly to check Cavan's sword. "Blue enameling on his armor," she muttered while checking it over.

"Spells in it. I know. Already checked them. Nothing too impressive. Make him a little stronger. Harder to cut."

"Figures," she said with a smile, handing Cavan back Kent's sword. "So widen that sneering mouth for him."

Amra stepped aside, and Cavan took a stance, sword high and

free hand near his spell pouch. Rolled his shoulders and neck, relieving just a little of his tension.

Groaning. A voice … no … more than one groaning voice. Surely those guards were…

A guard sat up. Not one of the twenty with spears. One of the original four. And he wasn't alone. The other two who'd survived that initial furious attack were all coming around at the same time.

"Stand down," ordered the duke, without looking away from Cavan, as though those men had been about to grab weapons and leap to his defense. "This is between me and your king's bastard."

The dazed guards all sat there as though they couldn't understand anything that was happening around them. Then one of them turned and retched.

"Hardly a moment from the sonnets, eh?" the duke said with a smile. "Nevertheless, we've both agreed to the stakes, so let's get—"

"One moment," Ehren said stepping between them and raising his staff high.

"There's no need for—" tried the duke, but Ehren called in a loud voice, "Zatafa, witness this battle, and bind both men to its outcome, and the words of promise they've uttered."

Cavan felt a warm glow settle around him, then fade.

The duke grimaced. "I did not agree to that."

"But of course you're a man of your word anyway," Ehren said with a smile, "so what difference could it make?"

Ehren then stepped aside, whistling.

"Ready?" the duke asked. "Or would one of your other friends like to do a song and dance?"

Cavan couldn't help glancing over at Amra and Qalas. "I'd pay to see that."

"*Enough!*" One word, but Cavan heard regal command in the duke's voice. "You wanted this, boy. Let's get it over with."

Cavan leapt forward out of the blood, sliding his boots to try to scrape them clean.

The duke muttered something and his gauntlets glowed with a

dark blue light that spread up his sword of war as he continued to mutter.

Cavan threw a dagger. Clanged it off that dark blue breastplate.

The spell fizzled.

Cavan leapt forward, swinging through a series of rapid cuts while digging through his spell pouch with his free hand. The duke had his sword in place to block each, but only just. Powerful blade in powerful arms, but not so fast as Cavan.

"The problem with hiding your studies," Cavan said, pressing his flurry of attacks, each ringing out as it met the sword of war, "is that you get no real field practice, do you?"

The duke turned a parry into an elbow strike at Cavan's head.

Cavan had to duck, slip back a step. Lost his momentum.

The duke swung high. Cavan parried. A feint. The duke kicked at Cavan's gut. Forced him to jump back a step.

"I'll get it when I need it," the duke said, pushing Cavan on the defense now. Striking as often with the great pommel of that sword of war as with the blade. Made it seem like two faster weapons, instead of one slow weapon.

Cavan timed a long right-to-left swipe from the duke. Spun away from it toward the unguarded right side.

The duke's mighty wrists yanked his sword back to protect his neck...

But the attack wasn't there.

Cavan slapped a lodestone to the back of the duke's armor, breathing power across it as he whispered, *"Multa fasah."*

The duke turned his attempted parry into a stab. Cavan needed both hands to parry the strike and still took a cut across his shoulder.

"That's your sword arm," the duke said. "Surrender now before something ... unfortunate happens."

Cavan smiled through the pain and cut at the duke's head. Parried, but the duke had a puzzled expression now. Sweat broke out on his forehead.

"Getting hot in here?" Cavan said, launching a triple-cut at the duke's exposed head. The duke interposed his sword twice, but the last cut came too fast. Too fast the way the duke was sweating. The way building heat through his metal armor warned of incoming pain.

The duke parried that third cut, but with his right vambrace. Taking one hand off the grip of that sword for a key moment.

Cavan swung to disarm. Both hands gripping his sword. Everything into the strike. Blow aimed at the dark blue gauntlet holding the weapon.

The other dark blue gauntlet smashed Cavan in the face. Broke his nose.

Blood down his face now. Aim spoiled. His swing missed. He spun with the force of the blow. Such strength...

Sword coming at his head.

Cavan dove. Tried to roll. Slipped in blood. On his back now. His nose throbbed. His shoulder began burning from the effort of fighting through his pain. Cavan shunted both pains away in a corner of his mind.

The duke. Coming. Drenched in sweat. Teeth clenched against pain. Hacking for Cavan's gut.

Cavan rolled aside. The duke struck stone. Cavan managed to get his boots under him. Came up swinging. Blocked by that giant sword. Quick cut at Cavan's head. Missed, but still coming.

The duke grunted nonstop through gritted teeth now. Blinked against a downpour of sweat. Something frantic to his strikes. Fast cuts.

Cavan jumped back and back from the blade's tip. Studying his foe.

Too fast. Trying to press for victory. The duke overbalanced on each swing. Just a little.

Maybe enough.

Cavan waited for the next attack. Charged. Slammed his unwounded shoulder into the duke's breastplate. Hot pain in Cavan's shoulder, but the duke went down. One hand came away from his sword.

"Finally!" Amra called, the first sound out of any of Cavan's companions.

Cavan kicked the duke's sword away. Knelt on the hot breastplate and brought the edge of Kent's family sword to the duke's throat.

"Do you yield?"

"Yes!" the duke yelled. "Yes! I yield. Make it stop. It burns!"

Cavan flipped the duke over and knocked the lodestone away with the pommel of his sword. The duke shuddered in relief when the source of the heat vanished. He'd feel even better in a few moments, when his armor cooled down again.

Cavan stood and gave him that time. Panting for breath himself, and wiping away more than a little sweat and blood.

Amra stepped in front of him. Cavan was ready to smile and accept congratulations — or maybe an apology for the "Finally!" — but all she did was grab his nose and yank it into place.

"Ow!" Cavan cried, and the sudden, unexpected shock snapped the barrier that held back the rest of his pain. His hand dropped his sword, his right arm twitching from the cut shoulder on down. His nose throbbed and complained, dripping more blood toward his mouth.

"He should never have gotten that shot in," Amra said. "But we'll go over your mistakes later."

"No doubt," he said, while Ehren looked over his wounds and began pulling some healing herbs from his brown leather pack.

"Hey," Qalas said with a big smile. "You won. Any fight you win, is—"

"A fight you could lose next time," Amra said, "if you don't learn from your mistakes."

"If you're all quite finished," the duke said. He sat, then stood, with quiet dignity, despite the fact that Cavan was sure he'd suffered painful burns.

Apparently Ehren agreed.

"Don't move too much," Ehren said. "You have burns that will need salve, and—"

"I have healers of my own thank you."

"Please," Ehren said. "When the sun next rises, Zatafa can take those burns away. Don't suffer them out of spite."

The duke nodded, then said, "Thank you." He drew a deep breath, let it out. But if he was trying for ease, Cavan wasn't fooled. The duke's brow was still crinkled against the pain.

"That heat spell," he said. "Can you teach it to me?"

"Will you admit to your training?"

"Never mind then." The duke turned to his guards, the three who were still recovering from being knocked unconscious. "You three, I want a list of names of the fallen, and tell their sergeant I ordered their families be given twice the normal compensation for their loss. Then get the bodies cleaned up and prepared for their families."

He looked about for a moment, sighed, and called, "Devan!"

The squire poked his head out of one of the dirt tunnels.

"We'll have words later about the helmet, but for now fetch Uli and tell him to bring soap, water and a towel." The duke cast a sour eye over Cavan's bloody clothing. "Oh, and clothes for someone as tall as my brother."

He turned to Cavan. "We have some details to attend to, but you will *not* walk around my castle filthy and covered in blood."

"Don't worry," said Ehren with a smile. "I've got this."

19

THE DUKE'S WHOLE CASTLE APPEARED TO BE ORGANIZED IN SECTIONS. As though it were actually several smaller buildings that all just happened to share common walls. The cells were below the castle barracks, which were just about the most ascetic place Cavan had seen in a long time. Maybe ever.

Then again, maybe not. He'd been inside the temple of some very philosophical dwarves, who had shaved their heads and beards and committed to wearing only kilts of undyed roughspun as part of their dedication to a world without gold. Incredible stonemasons.

These barracks weren't much more comfortable than that dwarvish temple had been though. Gray walls, gray floors, straw-stuffed pallets, and that dirt and sweat smell that Cavan associated with men-at-arms.

From there they passed briefly through luxury. Rich, thick red-and-gold carpets. Tapestries covering whitewashed walls. Enchanted, smokeless torches for light. The smell of fresh melons in the air. Guards in crisp uniforms, carrying halberds that looked as though they'd never struck an enemy in anger.

Cavan noticed Qalas smirk at the guards. Or perhaps at their weapons.

That was only a single hall, though. Then it was through a secret door behind a tapestry, along narrow gray stone passages lit by more smokeless torches. Along the outside wall of the castle now. Cavan could tell by the arrow slits.

Up one set of stairs, then down two others, and finally into a room with no stone showing at all. Dark brown wood for the floors, walls, and ceiling. A chandelier with flameless candles. Tapestries of hunting scenes on three of the walls, while the fourth had large glass windows showing a peaceful view of an apple orchard beside the lake. One other door, on the opposite side of the room.

Animal furs served as rugs, wolf and bear and two others Cavan didn't recognize.

Large, overstuffed brown couches arranged around a large wooden hearth, where the illusion of flame gave off heat as well as light. A mahogany sideboard featured a variety of liquors in cut glass bottles.

"Whiskey," the duke said to his squire, who went to the sideboard and began to pour. To his older serving man, Uli, a pale, wrinkled man with kindly brown eyes and a small, apparently permanent smile, the duke said, "Fetch our guests, if you would."

Those last three words brought a surprised exchange of looks among Cavan, Ehren and Amra.

The squire returned with a silver tray, and five crystal tumblers, each featuring perhaps two inches of brown liquor. The duke accepted his first, then the squire offered glasses around. Qalas took his, but Ehren shook his head, and Amra said, "I don't drink with men who send killers after my friends."

"I never turn down a drink I'm not paying for," Qalas said.

The duke smiled and turned to Cavan. "The killers were politics. The drink is personal. Will you drink with your uncle?"

"If we meet at my father's court, I will drink with you. If you visit me at my holding one day, I will drink with you. If ever we come together as friends, I will drink with you."

Cavan shook his head. "But today you are the man who

kidnapped my foster family and tried to have me killed to steal my inheritance. Today even that drink is 'politics.'"

"You'll make a fine baron one day," the duke said, "but you must stop leaping to conclusions."

The duke sipped his whiskey then, and Cavan had the feeling that asking for clarification wouldn't help.

Cavan also noticed that Qalas quietly set his drink down, untasted.

"Ah," the duke said. "You're all missing an excellent whiskey. Brewed by the smallfolk in the Blue Mountains — north of the land you'll one day hold."

"I'm sure they'll brew another batch."

The duke was smiling, and about to say something when the door opened and Kent came through.

Cavan crossed the room in a flash and hefted his foster father in a hug. Pain shrilled out from Cavan's shoulder, but he ignored it. Kent looked just as Cavan remembered him. Silvery hair still short and silvery beard still long. His proud belly a little broader, and his laugh just as cheery as he hugged Cavan back.

"Put me down, lad," Kent said with a laugh. "I'm not a puppy."

"Sorry," Cavan said, setting his foster father quickly but gently and probing into those hazel eyes for signs of pain or stress. "You're all right? He's been treating you well?"

"Perfectly," Kent said, still laughing, "now stand aside so you can meet my wife and say hello to Reed and Alec." He held up an admonishing finger. "No picking up my wife now. Mind her dignity."

"Mind your own dignity," said a throaty woman's voice as the speaker pushed past Kent to size up Cavan. She could only have been Kent's new wife. A southerner, though her skin wasn't quite as dark as Qalas', she had long ropes of wooly hair, eyes so dark they were almost black, and a build much like her husband's. Where Kent wore fine wools for his brown and green garb, she wore silks or something like them, though of matching color.

She also matched her husband smile for smile, from her lips to her eyes.

"So you must be Cavan," she said, and her smile broadened. "They said you were tall, but no one said you were *handsome*." She spread her arms wide. "My name is Rena. Come, give me a hug as well. And if you want to pick me up, I assure you my dignity can take it."

The pain in his shoulder well behind a mental barrier now, Cavan did just that. She smelled like walnuts and cherries, and she hugged even tighter than Kent did.

Reed and Alec finally made their way into the room. Poor guys had never grown any taller than their father, and they both tended toward his build, but they were smiling, and their reddish blond hair told the history of their father's.

They greeted their foster brother as they always had, warm smiles and firm handshakes. Never quite brothers, but never quite just friends either.

"Satisfied that they've been unharmed?" the duke said, with so much humor in his voice Cavan was amazed the man didn't laugh.

"Unharmed?" Kent said, while his wife said, "Why would anyone hurt us?"

"You came here willingly?" Cavan said, amazement growing in his voice.

"Of course," Kent said. "I'm steward of lands belonging to the king, himself. No one would dare try to take me by force."

"But you left the manor in a hurry. Under guard."

"Yes," Kent said, looking a little guilty. "Well, about that."

"What's about that," Rena said, "is that Kent saw a business opportunity."

"Just what was discovered in those mountains?" Ehren said.

"You know about that?" Reed said, prompting Alec to retort, "Obviously not, or they'd know what was discovered." To which Reed replied, "Not true, we know about the discovery, but not what was found."

Kent cleared his throat loudly. His sons shut their mouths, and his wife gave him a look of dwindling patience.

The duke, for his part, looked amused.

"Wait," Cavan said. "Let me see if I have this much straight. Something was discovered in the Barony of Juno." He pointed at Kent. "You were in residence at the time. Got word about it. But Duke Falstaff had spies among the workers or the overseers—"

"I object to their characterization as 'spies,'" the duke said. "They were miners from Nolarr, who remained loyal to their liege. Nothing more."

"These ... workers ... got word to the duke, and the duke made you an offer before word of the discovery spread. Is that right?"

"Basically," Kent said, stroking his beard. "Though I'd love to know how word reached you so quickly, your grace. That offer came scant minutes after I got the news myself."

"I prize efficiency." The duke attempted a cryptic smile, but that might have been more effective if Cavan hadn't known the truth.

"It doesn't matter how," Cavan said with a meaningful look at the duke. "What matters is that I thought the duke had you taken, but instead it seems—"

"He invited us," Rena said, "and we've been his guest during negotiations."

"Negotiations for *what*?" Ehren asked.

The poor priest looked ready to burst if someone didn't tell him soon. Amra, for her part, appeared to have nigh infinite patience. Qalas looked like he was studying the dynamics of the room.

Kent pulled a green velvet pouch from his belt and handed it to Cavan. Even that simple motion made the duke lean forward, a hint of greed showing through those nearly golden eyes.

Cavan could feel power in the pouch even before he opened it. He loosened the string and dumped the contents into his hand.

They looked like crystals, the same as crusted the stones of the Blue Mountains. Some pale blue, some dark as indigo. But their resemblance ended there. These were clearer than their mountainside cousins. Purer. As though they were the true, refined versions of the pale imitations that gave the Blue Mountains their name.

And there was more.

Power.

Each of these crystals — these gemstones — carried power. Power that a wizard could tap into. Together the half-dozen gems in Cavan's hand might have granted enough power to break a siege or level a keep. In hands that knew what they were about.

These gems were worth more than sapphires.

"The mine is deep," Kent said. "And the vein doesn't look long. Not sure how many there are."

"What else was—" Ehren started, but Cavan cut him off. He was looking at the duke when he spoke.

"Kent, do you know what these are?"

"Rarer than sapphires is what they are," he said. "And once I cut them they'll be more beautiful than—"

"Magic," Cavan said. "These stones are like concentrated magic."

"They ... what?"

"They are?" the duke said with feigned surprise. "Then allow me to increase my offer."

"Your host," Cavan said, almost biting off the words, "wanted these gems so much he tried to kill me to improve his claim to that barony."

"He *what?*" Rena said.

"But killing you wouldn't be enough," Kent said, puzzlement through his features. "He'd need to ... oh."

Yes. With these gems to power his magic, the duke could have sped the king's death. Possibly without anyone growing the wiser.

"No deal," Rena said. "These gems aren't for sale."

"My wife is quite right," Kent said, anger blazing in his eyes as he looked at the duke. "These stones are a gift for my foster son, and the king himself will decide what to do about the mine."

Cavan almost shivered at what passed across the duke's face. Rage, bordering fury, followed by a peaceful quiet so deep it was as though the rage had never been there.

"Uli," the duke said, "see to rooms for our new guests, and dinner for them all. They're to eat here in this room, and depart in the morn-ing. *After* that priest keeps his sunrise promise to me."

"I don't break promises," Ehren said.

And with that the duke turned and left, his squire rushing to keep up with his pace.

"I'm glad you bound his oath," Amra said to Ehren, and Qalas nodded.

"*So*," Cavan said, "Kent, Rena, Reed, Alec, let me introduce you to my friends…"

———

THE NEXT MORNING, KENT AND HIS FAMILY DEPARTED SWIFTLY ALONG the Royal Road, bound for Oltoss and a meeting with the king.

Cavan hated saying goodbye to them so soon, but at least it was a goodbye filled with smiles and hugs and a promise to visit them in Tradeton — or Juno — sometime soon. Cavan had the feeling it would be Juno.

Cavan and his friends couldn't very well ride beside them, though, not with their own steeds a good several leagues away near a burned out farm that Cavan didn't want to draw attention to. And Kent's business couldn't wait.

So Cavan, Ehren, Amra and Qalas walked alone through the rolling green hills of the Nolarr countryside that morning. Waving to farmers and tradesmen as they passed. The early summer air smelled fresh, like farms and livestock and good wild grass. The sun shone bright in the clear sky above them, and Ehren sang, as he was wont to do.

The other three dropped back a few steps to talk.

"Didn't look happy, did he?" Qalas said, talking about the duke.

The duke had met them briefly at sunrise, wearing a white linen robe. Whether to hide his burns, or to honor Zatafa, Cavan wasn't sure. But his expression was a distant kind of sour, and it wasn't helped when Ehren healed Cavan's hurts before tending to the duke. A crisp, formal "thank you" was all he said before departing.

"Not in the least," Amra said, happily. "I'd say we just spoiled his next five years of plans."

"How can you sound so happy?" Qalas shook his head. "He

promised no harm to Kent and his family, but he didn't make that promise about us."

"Let him try." She shrugged. "Eventually we'll get bored of killing his agents and finish him off ourselves."

"He's the king's brother," Cavan said. "It's not that simple."

"Of course it is," Amra said. "There might be some fallout, but what of it?"

"What of it is that he has two sons and a daughter," Cavan said. "And killing him starts a cycle of revenge that won't end quickly."

"Finally," Ehren called back. "You're finally admitting that killing isn't always the answer."

"I never said it was," Cavan said.

"I'm not convinced it's not," Amra said. "It's done very well for us so far."

"How?" Qalas stopped walking and turned to face Cavan and Amra. Ehren stopped and turned back to see what was happening. Qalas looked from one to the other. "How can you do that? How can you support each other to the death one moment, then argue about something as basic and important as taking a life?"

"Ah ha!" Ehren said, raising a triumphant finger. "He admits taking a life is a big deal. I knew I'd like having him around."

"A fine meal is a big deal too," Amra said, "and there are times I enjoy the one as much as the other."

"This is what I'm talking about!" Qalas said.

Cavan blinked at him. Then shrugged.

"We're friends. Haven't you ever had a friend before?"

Qalas shook his head, and Cavan saw something sad in those dark blue eyes. Cavan smiled and clapped him on the shoulder. "Well, you have friends now."

"Come on," Ehren said, "our horses are probably thirsty by now."

Amra clasped Qalas by the shoulder and steered him to follow Ehren.

"Tell me why you choose the halberd over a good, honest sword."

"Will you tell me about that sword of yours?"

"Maybe later. You first."

Cavan watched the three of them walk down a hill together, and smiled. Kent, Reed and Alec were fine, even if Reed and Alec weren't married yet. And Rena, Cavan couldn't have picked a better wife for Kent.

And best of all, he, Amra and Ehren were all alive and intact. And Qalas was turning out to be a good guy, for someone who'd shot him with an arrow. But then, Cavan had taken quite a beating from Ehren on the day they met, too.

And then there were those gemstones Kent had given him…

"Come on!" Ehren shouted back at him. "We have a long ride ahead of us. And I still think we should check out those mines…"

Cavan hurried down the hill to join his friends.

SIGN UP FOR STEFON'S NEWSLETTER

Stefon loves to keep in touch with his readers, and loves to keep you reading. The best way for him to do both is for you to sign up for his newsletter.

Sign up at http://www.stefonmears.com/join

If you sign up for Stefon's newsletter, you get...

- Monthly updates about his publishing and travel schedules
- His latest news, in brief, and answers to reader questions
- A free short story for signing up
- List-only offers and occasional specials
- Plus a free short story every month!

ABOUT THE AUTHOR

Stefon Mears occasionally spots Iresk's hawks circling in the sky. Stefon has more than thirty books to his credit, and he never stops writing. He earned his M.F.A. in Creative Writing from N.I.L.A., and his B.A. in Religious Studies (double emphasis in Ritual and Mythology) from U.C. Berkeley. He's a lifelong gamer and fantasy fan. Stefon lives in Portland, Oregon, with his wife and three cats.

Look for Stefon online:
www.stefonmears.com
himself@stefonmears.com